Fritz Leiber, the son of a noted stage and screen performer, was born in the United States in 1910. A former actor, he has written many fantasy and science fiction stories, and contributed to *Weird Tales* before the Second World War. Leiber is well known and held in high regard by readers of both science fiction and fantasy: he has received several Hugo and Nebula awards for the former, and he is seen as the doyen of fantasy writers, as the man who practically invented the sword and sorcery genre as it is known today. Most of the leading writers in the field acknowledge their debt to him, but, as is often pointed out, what makes Leiber's fantasy adventures superior to those of the many writers who have followed in his footsteps is the strong vein of dry wit that permeates his work.

Also by Fritz Leiber

Novels
Gather Darkness
Conjure Wife
The Green Millennium
Two Sought Adventure
Destiny Times Three
The Big Time
The Silver Eggheads
The Wanderer
Tarzan and the Valley of Gold (based on the film)
A Spectre Is Haunting Texas
Our Lady of Darkness
Swords and Deviltry
Swords Against Death
Swords in the Mist
Swords Against Wizardry
The Swords of Lankhmar

Collections of stories
Night's Black Agents
The Mind Spider
Shadows with Eyes
Ships to the Stars
A Pail of Air
The Night of the Wolf
Secret Songs
Night Monsters
You're All Alone
The Best of Fritz Leiber
The Book of Fritz Leiber
The Second Book of Fritz Leiber
The Worlds of Fritz Leiber

Fritz Leiber

Swords and Ice Magic

Book 6 in the Swords series

MAYFLOWER
GRANADA PUBLISHING
London Toronto Sydney New York

Published by Granada Publishing Limited
in Mayflower Books 1979

ISBN 0 583 13113 1

A Mayflower UK Original
Copyright © Fritz Leiber 1977

Granada Publishing Limited
Frogmore, St Albans, Herts AL2 2NF
and
3 Upper James Street, London W1R 4BP
866 United Nations Plaza, New York, NY 10017, USA
117 York Street, Sydney, NSW 2000, Australia
100 Skyway Avenue, Rexdale, Ontario, M9W 3A6, Canada
PO Box 84165, Greenside, 2034 Johannesburg, South Africa
CML Centre, Queen & Wyndham, Auckland 1, New Zealand

Set, printed and bound in Great Britain by
Cox & Wyman Ltd, Reading
Set in Intertype Plantin

Acknowledgments

Contents

I: THE SADNESS
OF THE EXECUTIONER

There was a sky that was always gray.

There was a place that was always far away.

There was a being who was always sad.

Sitting on his dark-cushioned, modest throne in his low, rambling castle in the heart of the Shadowland, Death shook his pale head and pommeled a little his opalescent temples and slightly pursed his lips, which were the color of violet grapes with the silvery bloom still on, above his slender figure armored in chain mail and his black belt, studded with silver skulls tarnished almost as black, from which hung his naked, irresistible sword.

He was a relatively minor death, only the Death of the World of Nehwon, but he had his problems. Tenscore flickering or flaring human lives to have their wicks pinched in the next twenty heartbeats. And although the heartbeats of Death resound like a leaden bell far underground and each has a little of eternity in it, yet they do finally pass. Only nineteen left now. And the Lords of Necessity, who outrank Death, still to be satisfied.

Let's see, thought Death with a vast coolness that yet had a tiny seething in it, one hundred sixty peasants and savages, twenty nomads, ten warriors, two beggars, a whore, a merchant, a priest, an aristocrat, a craftsman, a king, and two heroes. That would keep his books straight.

Within three heartbeats he had chosen one hundred and ninety-six of the tenscore and unleased their banes upon them: chiefly invisible, poisonous creatures within their flesh which suddenly gan multiply into resistless hordes, here a dark and bulky bloodclot set loose with feather touch to glide through a vein and block a vital portal, there a long-eroded artery wall tunneled through at last; sometimes slippery slime oozing purposefully onto the next footrest of a climber, sometimes an adder told where to wriggle and when to strike, or a spider where to lurk.

Death, by his own strict code known only to himself, had cheated just a little on the king. For some time in one of the deepest and darkest corners of his mind he had been fashioning the doom of the current overlord of Lankhmar, chiefest city and land in the World of Nehwon. This overlord was a gentle and tenderhearted scholar, who truly loved only his seventeen cats, yet wished no other being in Nehwon ill, and who was forever making things difficult for Death by pardoning felons, reconciling battling brothers and feuding families, hurrying barges or wains of grain to regions of starvation, rescuing distressed small animals, feeding pigeons, fostering the study of medicine and kindred arts, and most simply of all by always having about him, like finest fountain spray on hottest day, an atmosphere of sweet and wise calm which kept swords in scabbards, brows unknotted, and teeth unclenched. But now, at this very instant, by Death's crooked, dark-alleyed plotting hidden almost but not quite from himself, the thin wrists of the benign monarch of Lankhmar were being pricked in innocent play by his favoritest cat's needle-sharp claws, which had by a jealous, thin-nosed nephew of the royal ailurophile been late last night envenomed with the wind-swift poison of the rare emperor snake of tropical Klesh.

Yet on the remaining four and especially the two heroes — Death assured himself a shade guiltily — he would work solely by improvisation. In no time at all he had a vision of Lithquil, the Mad Duke of Ool Hrusp, watching from high balcony by torchlight three northern berserks wielding saw-edged scimitars joined in mortal combat with four transparent-fleshed, pink-skeletoned ghouls armed with poniards and battle-axes. It was the sort of heavy experiment Lithquil never tired of setting up and witnessing to the slaughterhouse end, and incidentally it was getting rid of the majority of the ten warriors Death had ticketed for destruction.

Death felt a less than momentary qualm recalling how well Lithquil had served him for many years. Even the best of servants must some day be pensioned off and put to grass, and in none of the worlds Death had heard of, certainly not Nehwon, was there a dearth of willing executioners, including passionately devoted, incredibly untiring, and exquisitely fantastic-minded ones. So even as the vision came to Death, he sent his thought at it and the rearmost ghoul looked up with his invisible eyes, so that his pink-broidered black skull-sockets rested upon Lithquil, and before the two guards flanking the Mad Duke could quite swing in their ponderous shields to protect their master, the ghoul's short-handled ax, already poised overshoulder, had flown through the narrowing gap and buried itself in Lithquil's nose and forehead.

Before Lithquil could gin crumple, before any of the watchers around him could nock an arrow to dispatch or menace the assassin, before the naked slavegirl who was the promised but seldom-delivered prize for the surviving gladiator could start to draw breath for a squealing scream, Death's magic gaze was fixed on Horborixen, citadel-city of the King of Kings. But not on the interior of the Great Golden Palace, though Death got a fleeting glimpse of that, but on the inwardness of a dingy workshop where a very old man looked straight up from his rude pallet and truly wished that the cool dawn light, which was glimmering through window- and lower-crack, would never more trouble the cobwebs that made ghostly arches and buttresses overhead.

This ancient, who bore the name of Gorex, was Horborixen's and perhaps all Nehwon's skillfulest worker in precious and military metals and deviser of cunningest engines, but he had lost all zest in his work or any other aspect of life for the last weary twelve-month, in fact ever since his great granddaughter Eesafem, who was his last surviving kin and most gifted apprentice in his difficult craft, a slim, beauteous, and barely nubile girl with almond eyes sharp as needles, had been summarily abducted by the harem scouts of the King of Kings. His furnace was ice cold, his tools gathered dust, he had given himself up entirely to sorrow.

He was so sad in fact that Death had but to add a drop of his own melancholy humor to the black bile coursing slowly and miserably through the tired veins of Gorex, and the latter painlessly and instantly expired, becoming one with his cobwebs.

So! – the aristocrat and the craftsman were disposed of in no more than two snaps of Death's long, slender, pearly midfinger and thumb, leaving only the two heroes.

Twelve heartbeats to go.

Death most strongly felt that, if only for artistry's sake, heroes should be made to make their exits from the stage of life in the highest melodramatic style, with only one in fifty score let to die of old age and in the bed of sleep for the object of irony. This necessity was incidentally so great that it permitted, he believed as part of his self-set rules, the use of outwardly perceptible and testifiable magic and need not be puttied over with realism, as in the case of more humdrum beings. So now for two whole heartbeats he listened only to the faint simmer of his cool mind, while lightly massaging his temples again with nacreous knuckles. Then his thoughts shot toward one Fafhrd, a largely couth and most romantical barbarian, the soles of whose feet and mind were nonetheless firmly set in fact, particularly when he was either very sober, or very drunk, and toward this one's lifelong comrade, the Gray Mouser, perhaps the cleverest and wittiest thief in all Nehwon and certainly the one with either the bonniest or bitterest self-conceit.

The still less than momentary qualm which Death experienced at this point was far deeper and stronger than that which he had felt in the case of Lithquil. Fafhrd and the Mouser had served him well and in vastly more varied fashion than the Mad Duke, whose eyes had been fixed on death to the point of crossedness, making his particular form of ax-dispatch most appropriate. Yes, the large vagabond Northerner and the small, wry-smiling, eyebrow-arching cutpurse had been most useful pawns in some of Death's finest games.

Yet without exception every pawn must eventually be snapped up and tossed in box in the course of the greatest game, even if it have advanced to the ultimate rank and become king or queen. So Death reminded himself, who knew that even he himself must ultimately die, and so he set to his intuitively creative task relentlessly and swifter than ever arrow or rocket or falling star flew.

After the fleetingest glance southwest toward the vast, dawn-pink city of Lankhmar, to reassure himself that Fafhrd and the Mouser still occupied a rickety penthouse atop an inn which catered to the poorer sort of merchants and faced on Wall Street near the Marsh Gate, Death looked back at the late Lithquil's slaughter pen. In his improvisations he regularly made a practice of using materials closest at hand, as any good artist will.

Lithquil was in mid-crumple. The slavegirl was screaming. The mightiest of the berserks, his big face contorted by a fighting fury that would never fade till sheer exhaustion forced it, had just slashed off the bonily pink, invisibly fleshed head of Lithquil's assassin. And quite unjustly and even idiotically – but most of Death's lesser banes outwardly appear to work in such wise – a halfscore arrows were winging from the gallery toward Lithquil's avenger.

Death magicked and the berserk was no longer there. The ten arrows transfixed empty air, but by that time Death, again following the practice of economy in materials, was peering once more at Horborixen and into a rather large cell lit by high, barred windows in the midst of the harem of the King of Kings. Rather oddly, there was a small furnace in the cell, a quenching bath, two small anvils, several hammers, many other tools for working metals, as well as a small store of precious and workaday metals themselves.

In the center of the cell, examining herself in a burnished silver mirror with almond eyes sharp as needles and now also quite as mad as the berserk's, there stood a deliciously slender girl of no more than sixteen, unclad save for four ornaments of silver filigree. She was, in fact, unclad in extremest degree, since except for her eyelashes, her every last hair had been removed and wherever such hair had been she was now tattooed in fine patterns of green and blue.

For seven moons now Eesafem had suffered solitary confinement for mutilating in a harem fight the faces of the King of King's favoritest concubines, twin Ilthmarts. Secretly the King of Kings had not been at all displeased by this event. Truth to tell, the facial mutilations of his special darlings slightly increased their attractiveness to his jaded appetite. Still, harem discipline had to be kept, hence Eesafem's confinement, loss of all hairs – most carefully one at a time – and tattooing.

The King of Kings was a thrifty soul and unlike many monarchs expected all his wives and concubines to perform useful work rather than be forever lolling, bathing, gossiping and brawling. So, it being the work she was so uncontestably best trained for and the one most apt to bring profit, Eesafem had been permitted her forge and her metals.

But despite her regular working of these and her consequent production of numerous beauteous and ingenious objects, Eesafem's young mind had become viciously unhinged from her twelve harem moons, seven of those in lonely cell, and from the galling fact that the King of Kings had yet to visit her once for amorous or any other reason, even despite the charming metal gifts she had fashioned for him. Nor had any other man visited her, excepting eunuchs who lectured her on the erotic arts – while she was securely trussed up, else she would have flown at their pudgy faces like a wildcat, and even at that she spat at them whenever able – and gave her detailed and patronizing advice on her metalworking, which she ignored as haughtily as she did their other fluting words.

Instead, her creativity, now fired by insane jealousies as well as racklike aches for freedom, had taken a new and secret turn.

Scanning the silver mirror, she carefully inspected the four ornaments adorning her slender yet wirey-strong figure. They were two breast cups and two shin-greaves, all chiefly of a delicate silver filigree, which set off nicely her green and blue tattooing.

Once her gaze in the mirror wandered overshoulder, past her naked pate with its finely patterned, fantastical skullcap, to a silver cage in which perched a green and blue parrot with eye as icily malevolent as her own — perpetual reminder of her own imprisonment.

The only oddity about the filigree ornaments was that the breast cups, jutting outward over the nipples, ended in short spikes trained straight forward, while the greaves were topped, just at the knee, with vertical ebony lozenges about as big as a man's thumb.

These bits of decor were not very obtrusive, the spikes being stained a greenish blue, as though to match her tattooing.

So Eesafem gazed at herself with a crafty, approving smile. And so Death gazed at her with a more crafty one, and one far more coldly approving than any eunuch's. And so she vanished in a flash from her cell. And before the blue-green parrot could gin squawk his startlement, Death's eyes and ears were elsewhere also.

Only seven heartbeats left.

Now it may be that in the world of Nehwon there are gods of whom even Death does not know and who from time to time take pleasure in putting obstacles in his path. Or it may be that Chance is quite as great a power as Necessity. At any rate, on this particular morning Fafhrd the Northerner, who customarily snoozed till noon, waked with the first dull silvery shaft of dawn and took up his dear weapon Graywand, naked as he, and blearily made his way from his penthouse pallet out onto the roof, where he gan practice all manner of sword-strokes, stamping his feet in his advances and from time to time uttering battleshouts, unmindful of the weary merchants he waked below him into groaning, cursing, or fright-quivering life. He shivered at first from the chill, fishy dawnmist from the Great Salt Marsh, but soon was sweating from his exercise, while his thrusts and parries, perfunctory to begin with, grew lightning-swift and most authoritative.

Except for Fafhrd, it was a quiet morning in Lankhmar. The bells had not yet begun to toll, nor the deep-throated gongs resound for the passage of the city's gentle overlord, nor the news been bruited about of his seventeen cats netted and hustled to the Great Gaol, there in separate cages to await trial.

It also happened that on this same day the Gray Mouser had waked till dawn, which usually found him an hour or so asleep. He curled in penthouse corner on a pile of pillows behind a low table, chin in hand, a woolly gray robe huddled around him. From time to time he wryly sipped sour wine and thought even sourer thoughts, chiefly about the evil and untrustworthy folk he had known during his mazily crooked lifetime. He ignored Fafhrd's exit and shut his ears to his noisy prancings, but the more he wooed sleep, the further she drew away.

The foamy-mouthed, red-eyed berserk materialized in front of Fafhrd just as the latter assumed the guard of low tierce, swordhand thrust forward, down, and a little to the right, sword slanting upward. He was astounded by the apparition, who, untroubled by sanity's strictures, instantly aimed at the naked Northerner's neck a great swipe with his saw-edged scimitar, which looked rather like a row of short broad-bladed daggers forged side to side and freshly dipped in blood – so that it was pure automatism made Fafhrd shift his guard to a well-braced high carte which deflected the berserk's sword so that it whished over Fafhrd's head with something of the sound of a steel rod very swiftly dragged along a fence of steel pickets, as each razor-edged tooth in turn met the Northerner's blade.

Then reason took a hand in the game and before the berserk could begin a back-handed return swipe, Graywand's tip made a neat, swift counter-clockwise circle and flicked upward at the berserk's sword-wrist, so that his weapon and hand went flying harmlessly off. Far safer, Fafhrd knew, to disarm – or dis-hand? – such a frenziedly fell opponent before thrusting him through the heart, something Fafhrd now proceeded to do.

Meantime the Mouser was likewise astounded by the abrupt, entirely non sequitur appearance of Eesafem in the center of the penthouse. It was as if one of his more lurid erotic dreams had suddenly come to solid life. He could only goggle as she took a smiling step toward him, knelt a little, carefully faced her front at him, and then drew her upper arms close to her sides so that the filigree band which supported her breast cups was compressed. Her almond eyes flashed sinister green.

What saved the Mouser then was simply his lifelong anti-pathy to having anything sharp pointed at him, be it only the tiniest needle – or the playfully menacing spikes on exquisite silver breast cups doubtless enclosing exquisite breasts. He hurled himself to one side just as with simultaneous *zings* small but powerful springs loosed the envenomed spikes as though they were crossbow quarrels and buried them with twin *zaps* in the wall against which he had but now been resting.

He was scrambling to his feet in an instant and hurled him-self at the girl. Now reason, or perhaps intuition, told him the significance of her grasping toward the two black lozenges topping her silver greaves. Tackling her, he managed to get to them before her, withdraw the twin, black-handled stilettos, and toss them beyond Fafhrd's tousled pallet.

Thereafter, twining his legs about hers in such fashion that she could not knee him in the groin, and holding her snapping, spitting head in the crook of his left arm and by an ear – after futilely grasping for hair – and finally mastering with his right hand the wrists of her two sharp-nailed, flailing ones, he pro-ceeded by gradual and not unnecessarily brutal steps to ravage her. As she ran out of spit, she quieted. Her breasts proved to be very small, but doubly delicious.

Fafhrd, returning mightily puzzled from the roof, goggled in turn at what he saw. How the devil had the Mouser man-aged to smuggle in that winsome bit? Oh, well, no business of his. With a courteous 'Pardon me. Pray continue,' he shut the door behind him and tackled the problem of disposing of the berserk's corpse. This was readily achieved by heaving him up and dropping him four storeys onto the vast garbage heap that almost blocked Specter Alley. Next Fafhrd picked up the saw-edged scimitar, pried from it the still-clenched hand, and tossed that after. Then frowning down at the encrimsoned weapon, which he intended to keep as a souvenir, he futilely wondered, 'Whose blood?'

(Disposing of Eesafem was hardly a problem capable of any such instant, hand-brushing solution. Suffice it that she gradually lost much of her madness and a little of her hatred of humanity, learned to speak Lankhmarese fluently, and ended up quite happily running a tiny smithy of her own on Copper Court behind Silver Street, where she made beautiful jewelry and sold under the counter such oddments as the finest poison-fanged rings in all Nehwon.)

Meanwhile Death, for whom time moves in a somewhat different fashion than for men, recognized that there remained to him only two heartbeats in which to fill his quota. The extremely faint thrill of excitement he had felt at seeing his two chosen heroes foil his brilliant improvisations – and at the thought that there *might* be powers in the universe unknown to him and subtler even than his – was replaced by a wry disgust at the realization that there was no longer time enough left for artistry and for indirection and that he must personally take a hand in the business – something he thoroughly detested, since the deus ex machina had always struck him as fiction's – or life's – feeblest device.

Should he slay Fafhrd and the Mouser direct? No, they had somehow outwitted him, which ought in all justice (if there be any such thing) give them immunity for a space. Besides, it would smack now almost of anger, or even resentment. And after his fashion and despite his occasional and almost unavoidable cheating, Death was a sportsman.

With the faintest yet weariest of sighs, Death magicked himself into the royal guardroom in the Great Golden Palace in Horborixen, where with two almost sightlessly swift, mercifully near-instantaneous thrusts, he let the life out of two most noble and blameless heroes whom he had barely glimpsed there earlier, yet ticketed in his boundless and infallible memory, two brothers sworn to perpetual celibacy and also to the rescue of at least one damsel in distress per moon. And so now they were released from this difficult destiny and Death returned to brood sadly on his low throne in his modest castle in the Shadowland and to await his next mission.

The twentieth heartbeat knelled.

II: BEAUTY
AND THE BEASTS

She was undoubtedly the most beautiful girl in Lankhmar, or all Nehwon, or any other world. So Fafhrd, the red-haired Northerner, and the Gray Mouser, that swarthy, cat-faced Southerner, were naturally following her.

Her name, most strangely, was Slenya Akkiba Magus, the most witching brunette in all the worlds, and also, most oddly, the most sorcerous blonde. They knew Slenya Akkiba Magus was her name because someone had called it out as she glided ahead of them up Pinchbeck Alley, which parallels Gold Street, and she hesitated for an instant in that drawing-together fashion one only does when one's name is unexpectedly called out, before gliding on without looking around.

They never saw who called. Perhaps someone on a roof. They looked into Sequin Court as they passed, but it was empty. So was Fools Gold Court.

Slenya was two inches taller than the Gray Mouser and ten shorter than Fafhrd – a nice height for a girl.

'She's mine,' the Gray Mouser whispered with great authority.

'No, she's mine,' Fafhrd murmured back with crushing casualness.

'We *could* split her,' the Mouser hissed judiciously.

There was a zany logic to this suggestion for, quite amazingly, she was completely black on the right side and completely fair on the left side. You could see the dividing line down her back very distinctly. This was because of the extreme thinness of the dress of beige silk she was wearing. Her two colors split exactly at her buttocks.

On the fair side her hair was completely blonde. On the black side it was all brunette.

At this moment an ebony-black warrior appeared from nowhere and attacked Fafhrd with a brass scimitar.

Drawing his sword Graywand in a rush, Fafhrd parried at a square angle. The scimitar shattered, and the brazen fragments flew about. Fafhrd's wrist whipped Graywand in a circle and struck off his foe's head.

Meanwhile the Mouser was suddenly faced by an ivory-white warrior sprung from another nowhere and armed with a steel rapier, silver-plated. The Mouser whisked out Scalpel, laid a bind on the other's blade, and thrust him through the heart.

The two friends congratulated each other.

Then they looked around. Save for the corpses, Pinchbeck Alley was empty.

Slenya Akkiba Magus had disappeared.

The twain pondered this for five heartbeats and two inhalations. Then Fafhrd's frown vanished and his eyes widened.

'Mouser,' he said, 'the girl divided into the two villains! That explains all. They came from the same nowhere.'

'The same somewhere, you mean,' the Mouser quibbled. 'A most exotic mode of reproduction, or fission rather.'

'And one with a sex alternation,' Fafhrd added. 'Perhaps if we examined the corpses—'

They looked down to find Pinchbeck Alley emptier still. The two liches had vanished from the cobbles. Even the chopped-off head was gone from the foot of the wall against which it had rolled.

'An excellent way of disposing of bodies,' Fafhrd said with approval. His ears had caught the tramp and brozen clank of the approaching watch.

'They might have lingered long enough for us to search their pouches and seams for jewels and precious metal,' the Mouser demurred.

'But what was behind it all?' Fafhrd puzzled. 'A black-and-white magician—?'

'It's bootless to make bricks without straw,' said the Mouser, cutting him short. 'Let us hie to the Golden Lamphrey and there drink a health to the girl, who was surely a stunner.'

'Agreed. And we will drink to her appropriately in blackest stout laced with the palest bubbly wine of Ilthmar.'

III: TRAPPED IN
THE SHADOWLAND

Fafhrd and the Gray Mouser were almost dead from thirst. Their horses had died from the same Hell-throated ailment at the last waterhole, which had proved dry. Even the last contents of their waterbags, augmented by water of their own bodies, had not been enough to keep alive the dear dumb equine beasts. As all men know, camels are the only creatures who can carry men for more than a day or two across the almost supernaturally hot arid deserts of the World of Nehwon.

They tramped on south-westward under the blinding sun and over the burning sand. Despite their desperate plight and heat-fevered minds and bodies, they were steering a canny course. Too far south and they would fall into the cruel hands of the emperor of the Eastern Lands, who would find rare delight in torturing them before killing them. Too far east and they would encounter the merciless Mingols of the Steppes and other horrors. West and northwest were those who were pursuing them now. While north and northeast lay the Shadowland, the home of Death himself. So much they well knew of the geography of Nehwon.

Meanwhile, Death grinned faintly in his low castle in the heart of the Shadowland, certain that he had at last got the two elusive heroes in his bony grip. They had years ago had the nerve to enter his domain, visiting their first loves, Ivrian and Vlana, and even stealing from his very castle Death's favorite mask. Now they would pay for their temerity.

Death had the appearance of a tall, handsome young man, though somewhat cadaverous and of opalescent complexion. He was staring now at a large map of the Shadowland and its environs set in a dark wall of his dwelling. On this map Fafhrd and the Mouser were a gleaming speck, like an errant star or fire beetle, south of the Shadowland.

Death writhed his thin, smiling lips and moved his bony fingertips in tiny, cabalistic curves, as he worked a small but difficult magic.

His incantation done, he noted with approval that on the map a southern tongue of the Shadowland was visibly extending itself in pursuit of the dazzling speck that was his victims.

Fafhrd and the Mouser tramped on south, staggering and reeling now, their feet and minds aflame, their faces a-drip with precious sweat. They had been seeking, near the Sea of Monsters and the City of Ghouls, their strayed newest girls, Mouser's Reetha and Fafhrd's Kreeshkra, the latter a Ghoul herself, all her blood and flesh invisible, which made her bonny pink bones stand out the more, while Reetha believed in going naked and shaven from head to toe, a taste which gave the girls a mutual similarity and sympathy.

But the Mouser and Fafhrd had found nothing but a horde of fierce male Ghouls, mounted on equally skeletal horses, who had chased them east and south, either to slay them, or to cause them to die of thirst in the desert or of torture in the dungeons of the King of Kings.

It was high noon and the sun was hottest. Fafhrd's left hand touched in the dry heat a cool fence about two feet high, invisible at first though not for long.

'Escape to damp coolth,' he said in a cracked voice.

They eagerly clambered over the fence and threw themselves down on a blessed thick turf or dark grass two inches high, over which a fine mist was falling. They slept about ten hours.

In his castle Death permitted himself a thin grin, as on his map the south-trending tongue of the Shadowland touched the diamond spark and dimmed it.

Nehwon's greatest star, Astorian, was mounting the eastern sky, precursor of the moon, as the two adventurers awoke, greatly refreshed by their long nap. The mist had almost ceased, but the only star visible was vast Astorian.

The Mouser sprang up agitatedly in his gray hood, tunic,

and ratskin shoes. 'We must escape backward to hot dryth,' he said, 'for this is the Shadowland, Death's homeland.'

'A very comfortable place,' Fafhrd replied, stretching his huge muscles luxuriously on the thick greensward. 'Return to the briny, granular, rasping, fiery land-sea? Not I.'

'But if we stay here,' the Mouser countered, 'we will be will-lessly drawn by devilish and delusive will-o'-the-wisps to the low-walled Castle of Death, whom we defied by stealing his mask and giving its two halves to our wizards Sheelba and Ningauble, an action for which Death is not likely to love us. Besides, here we might well meet our two first girls, Ivrian and Vlana, now concubines of Death, and that would not be a pleasant experience.'

Fafhrd winced, yet stubbornly repeated, 'But it is comfortable here.' Rather self-consciously he writhed his great shoulders and restretched his seven feet on the deliciously damp turf. (The 'seven feet' refers to his height. He was by no means an octopus missing one limb, but a handsome, red-bearded, very tall barbarian.)

The Mouser persisted, 'But what *if* your Vlana should appear, blue-faced and unloving? Or my Ivrian in like state, for that matter?'

That dire image did it. Fafhrd sprang up, grabbing for the low fence. But – lo and behold – there was no fence at hand. In all directions stretched out the damp, dark green turf of the Shadowland. While the soft drizzle had thickened again, hiding Astorian. There was no way to tell directions.

The Mouser searched in his ratskin pouch and drew out a blue bone needle. He pricked himself finding it, and cursed. It was wickedly sharp at one end, round and pierced at the other.

'We need a pool or puddle,' he said.

'Where did you get that toy?' Fafhrd quizzed. 'Magic, eh?'

'From Nattick Nimblefingers the Tailor in vasty Lankhmar,' the Mouser responded. 'Magic, nay! Hast heard of compass needles, oh wise one?'

Not far off they found a shallow puddle atop the turf. The Mouser carefully floated his needle on the small mirror of clear, placid water. It spun about slowly and eventually settled itself.

'We go that way,' Fafhrd said, pointing out from the pierced end of the needle. 'South.' For he realized the pricking end must point toward the heart of the Shadowland – Nehwon's Death Pole, one might call it. For an instant he wondered if there were another such pole at the antipodes – perhaps a Life Pole.

'And we'll still need the needle,' the Mouser added, pricking himself again and cursing as he pouched it, 'for future guidance.'

'Hah! Wah-wah-wah-*wah*!' yelled three berserks, emerging like fleet statues from the mist. They had been long marooned in the skirts of the Shadowland, reluctant either to advance to the Castle of Death and find their Hell or Valhalla, or to seek escape, but always ready for a fight. They rushed at Fafhrd and the Mouser, bareskinned and naked-bladed.

It took the Twain ten heartbeats of clashing sword-fight to kill them, though killing in the domain of Death must be at least a misdemeanor, it occurred to the Mouser – like poaching. Fafhrd got a shallow slash wound across his biceps, which the Mouser carefully bound up.

'Wow!' said Fafhrd. 'Where did the needle point? I've got turned around.'

They located the same or another puddle-mirror, floated the needle, again found South, and then took up their trek.

They twice tried to escape from the Shadowland by changing course, once east, once west. It was no use. Whatever way they went, they found only soft-turfed earth and bemisted sky. So they kept on south, trusting Nattick's needle.

For food they cut out black lambs from the black flocks they encountered, slew, bled, skinned, dressed, and roasted the tender meat over fires from wood of the squat black trees and bushes here and there. The young flesh was succulent. They drank dew.

Death in his low-walled keep continued to grin from time to time at his map, as the dark tongue of his territory kept magically extending southwest, the dimmed spark of his doomed victims in its margin.

He noted that the Ghoulish cavalry originally pursuing the Twain had halted at the boundary of his marchland.

But now there was the faintest trace of anxiety in Death's smile. And now and again a tiny vertical frown creased his opalescent, unwrinkled forehead, as he exerted his faculties to keep his geographical sorcery going.

The black tongue kept on down the map, past Sarheenmar and thievish Ilthmar to the Sinking Land. Both cities on the shore of the Inner Sea were scared unto death by the dark invasion of damp turf and misty sky, and they thanked their degenerate gods that it narrowly bypassed them.

And now the black tongue crossed the Sinking Land, moving due west. The little frown in Death's forehead had become quite deep. At the Swamp Gate of Lankhmar the Mouser and Fafhrd found their magical mentors waiting, Sheelba of the Eyeless Face and Ningauble of the Seven Eyes.

'What have you been up to?' Sheelba sternly asked the Mouser.

'And what have *you* been doing?' Ningauble demanded of Fafhrd.

The Mouser and Fafhrd were still in the Shadowland, and the two wizards outside it, with the boundary midway between. So their conversation was like that of two pairs of people on opposite sides of a narrow street, on the one side of which it is raining cats and dogs, the other side dry and sunny, though in this instance stinking with the smog of Lankhmar.

'Seeking Reetha,' the Mouser replied, honestly for once.

'Seeking Kreeshkra,' Fafhrd said boldly, 'but a mounted Ghoul troop harried us back.'

From his hood Ningauble writhed out six of his seven eyes and regarded Fafhrd searchingly. He said severely, 'Kreeshkra, tired of your untameable waywardness, has gone back to the Ghouls for good, taking Reetha with her. I would advise you instead to seek Frix,' naming a remarkable female who had played no small part in the adventure of the rathordes, the

26

same affair in which Kreeshkra the Ghoul girl had been involved.

'Frix is a brave, handsome, remarkably cool woman,' Fafhrd temporized, 'but how to reach her? She's in another world, a world of air.'

'While I counsel that *you* seek Hisvet,' Sheelba of the Eyeless Face told the Mouser grimly. The unfeatured blackness in *his* hood grew yet blacker (with concentration) if that were possible. He was referring to yet another female involved in the rat-adventure, in which Reetha also had been a leading character.

'A great idea, Father,' responded the Mouser, who made no bones about preferring Hisvet to all other girls, particularly since he had never once enjoyed her favours, though on the verge of doing so several times. 'But she is likely deep in the earth and in her rat-size persona. How would I do it? How, how?'

If Sheel and Ning could have smiled, they would have.

However, Sheelba said only, 'It is bothersome to see you both bemisted, like heroes in smoke.'

He and Ning, without conference, collaborated in working a small but very difficult magic. After resisting most tenaciously, the Shadowland and its drizzle retreated east, leaving the Twain in the same sunshine as their mentors. Though two invisible patches of dark mist remained, entering into the flesh of the Mouser and Fafhrd and closing forever around their hearts.

Far eastaways, Death permitted himself a small curse which would have scandalized the high gods, had they heard it. He looked daggers at his map and its shortening black tongue. For Death, he was in a most bitter temper. Foiled again!

Ning and Sheel worked another diminutive wizardry.

Without warning, Fafhrd shot upwards in the air, growing tinier and tinier, until at last he was lost to sight.

Without moving from where he stood, the Mouser also grew tiny, until he was somewhat less than a foot high, of a size to cope with Hisvet, in or out of bed. He dove into the nearest rathole.

Neither feat was as remarkable as it sounds, since Nehwon is only a bubble rising through the waters of infinity.

The two heroes each spent a delightful weekend with his lady of the week.

'I don't know why I do things like this,' Hisvet said, lisping faintly and touching the Mouser intimately as they lay side by side supine on silken sheets. 'It must be because I loathe you.'

'A pleasant and even worthy encounter,' Frix confessed to Fafhrd in similar situation. 'It is my hang-up to enjoy playing, now and then, with the lower animals. Which some would say is a weakness in a queen of the air.'

Their weekend done, Fafhrd and the Mouser were automatically magicked back to Lankhmar, encountering one another in Cheap Street near Nattick Nimblefinger's narrow and dirty-looking dwelling. The Mouser was his right size again.

'You look sunburned,' he observed to his comrade.

'Space-burned, it is,' Fafhrd corrected. 'Frix lives in a remarkably distant land. But you, old friend, look paler than your wont.'

'Shows what three days underground will do to a man's complexion,' the Mouser responded. 'Come, let's have a drink at the Silver Eel.'

Ningauble in his cave near Ilthmar and Sheelba in his mobile hut in the Great Salt Marsh each smiled, though lacking the equipment for that facial expression. They knew they had laid one more obligation on their protégés.

IV: THE BAIT

Fafhrd the Northerner was dreaming of a great mound of gold.

The Gray Mouser the Southerner, ever cleverer in his forever competitive fashion, was dreaming of a heap of diamonds. He hadn't tossed out all of the yellowish ones yet, but he guessed that already his glistening pile must be worth more than Fafhrd's glowing one.

How he knew in his dream what Fafhrd was dreaming was a mystery to all beings in Nehwon, except perhaps Sheelba of the Eyeless Face and Ningauble of the Seven Eyes, respectively the Mouser's and Fafhrd's sorcerer-mentors. Maybe, a vast, black basement mind shared by the two was involved.

Simultaneously they awoke, Fafhrd a shade more slowly, and sat up in bed.

Standing midway between the feet of their cots was an object that fixed their attention. It weighed about eighty pounds, was about four feet eight inches tall, had long straight black hair pendant from head, had ivory-white skin, and was as exquisitely formed as a single chesspiece of the King of Kings carved from a single moonstone. It looked thirteen, but the lips smiled a cool self-infatuated seventeen, while the gleaming deep eye-pools were first blue melt of the Ice Age. Naturally, she was naked.

'She's mine!' the Gray Mouser said, always quick from the scabbard.

'No, she's mine!' Fafhrd said almost simultaneously, but conceding by that initial 'No' that the Mouser had been first, or at least he had expected the Mouser to be first.

'I belong to myself and to no one else, save two or three

virile demidevils,' the small naked girl said, though giving them each in turn a most nymphish lascivious look.

'I'll fight you for her,' the Mouser proposed.

'And I you,' Fafhrd confirmed, slowly drawing Graywand from its sheath beside his cot.

The Mouser likewise slipped Scalpel from its ratskin container.

The two heroes rose from their cots.

At this moment, two personages appeared a little behind the girl – from thin air, to all appearances. Both were at least nine feet tall. They had to bend, not to bump the ceiling. Cobwebs tickled their pointed ears. The one on the Mouser's side was black as wrought iron. He swiftly drew a sword that looked forged from the same material.

At the same time, the other newcomer – bone-white, this one – produced a silver-seeming sword, likely steel plated with tin.

The nine-footer opposing the Mouser aimed a skull-splitting blow at the top of his head. The Mouser parried in prime and his opponent's weapon shrieked off to the left. Whereupon, smartly swinging his rapier widdershins, the Mouser slashed off the black fiend's head, which struck the floor with a horrid clank.

The white afreet opposing Fafhrd trusted to a downward thrust. But the Northerner, catching his blade in a counter-clockwise bind, thrust him through, the silvery sword missing Fafhrd's right temple by the thinness of a hair.

With a petulant stamp of her naked heel, the nymphet vanished into thin air, or perhaps Limbo.

The Mouser made to wipe off his blade on the cotclothes, but discovered there was no need. He shrugged. 'What a misfortune for you, comrade,' he said in a voice of mocking woe. 'Now you will not be able to enjoy the delicious chit as she disports herself on your heap of gold.'

Fafhrd moved to cleanse Graywand on *his* sheets, only to note that it too was altogether unbloodied. He frowned. 'Too bad for you, best of friends,' he sympathized. 'Now you won't be able to possess her as she writhes with girlish abandon on your couch of diamonds, their glitter striking opalescent tones from her pale flesh.'

'Mauger that effeminate artistic garbage, how did you know that I was dreaming diamonds?' the Mouser demanded.

'How did I?' Fafhrd asked himself wonderingly. At last he begged the question with, 'The same way, I suppose, that you knew I was dreaming of gold.'

The two excessively long corpses chose that moment to vanish, and the severed head with them.

Fafhrd said sagely, 'Mouser, I begin to believe that supernatural forces were involved in this morning's haps.'

'Or else hallucinations, oh great philosopher,' the Mouser countered somewhat peevishly.

'Not so,' Fafhrd corrected, 'for see, they've left their weapons behind.'

'True enough,' the Mouser conceded, rapaciously eyeing the wrought-iron and tin-plated blades on the floor. 'Those will fetch a fancy price on Curio Court.'

The Great Gong of Lankhmar, sounding distantly through the walls, boomed out the twelve funereal strokes of noon, when burial parties plunge spade into earth.

'An after-omen,' Fafhrd pronounced. 'Now we know the source of the supernal force. The Shadowland, terminus of all funerals.'

'Yes,' the Mouser agreed. 'Prince Death, that eager boy, has had another go at us.'

Fafhrd splashed cool water onto his face from a great bowl set against the wall. 'Ah well,' he spoke through the splashes, ''Twas a pretty bait at least. Truly, there's nothing like a nubile girl, enjoyed or merely glimpsed naked, to give one an appetite for breakfast.'

'Indeed yes,' the Mouser replied, as he tightly shut his eyes and briskly rubbed his face with a palm full of white brandy. 'She was just the sort of immature dish to kindle your satyrish taste for maids newly budded.'

In the silence that came as the splashing stopped, Fafhrd inquired innocently, '*Whose* satyrish taste?'

V: UNDER THE THUMBS
OF THE GODS

Drinking strong drink one night at the Silver Eel, the Gray Mouser and Fafhrd became complacently, even luxuriously, nostalgic about their past loves and amorous exploits. They even boasted a little to each other about their most recent erotic solacings (although it is always very unwise to boast of such matters, especially out loud; one never knows who may be listening).

'Despite her vast talent for evil,' the Mouser said, 'Hisvet remains always a child. Why should that surprise me? — evil comes naturally to children, it is a game to them, they feel no shame. Her breasts are no bigger than walnuts, or limes, or at most small tangerines topped by hazelnuts — all eight of them.'

Fafhrd said, 'Frix is the very soul of the dramatic. You should have seen her poised on the battlement later that night, her eyes raptly agleam, seeking the stars. Naked save for some ornaments of copper fresh as rosy dawn. She looked as if she were about to fly — which she can do, as you know.'

In the Land of the Gods, in short in Godsland and near Nehwon's Life Pole there, which lies in the southron hemisphere at the antipodes from the Shadowland (abode of Death), three gods sitting together cross-legged in a circle picked out Fafhrd's and the Mouser's voices from the general mutter of their worshippers, both loyal and lapsed, which resounds eternally in any god's ear, as if he held a seashell to it.

One of the three gods was Issek, whom Fafhrd had once faithfully served as acolyte for three months. Issek had the appearance of a delicate youth with wrists and ankles broken, or rather permanently bent at right angles. During his Passion he had been severely racked. Another was Kos, whom Fafhrd

32

had revered during his childhood in the Cold Waste, rather a squat, brawny god bundled up in furs, with a grim, not to say surly, heavily bearded visage.

The third god was Mog, who resembled a four-limbed spider with a quite handsome, though not entirely human face. Once the girl Ivrian, the Mouser's first love, had taken a fancy to a jet statuette of Mog he had stolen for her and decided, perhaps roguishly, that Mog and the Mouser looked alike.

Now the Gray Mouser is generally believed to be and have always been complete atheist, but this is not true. Partly to humor Ivrian, whom he spoiled fantastically, but partly because it tickled his vanity that a god should choose to look like him, he made a game for several weeks of firmly believing in Mog.

So the Mouser and Fafhrd were clearly worshipers, though lapsed, and the three gods singled out their voices because of that and because they were the most noteworthy worshipers these three gods had ever had and because they were boasting. For the gods have very sharp ears for boasts, or for declarations of happiness and self-satisfaction, or for assertions of a firm intention to do this or that, or for statements that this or that must surely happen, or any other words hinting that a man is in the slightest control of his own destiny. And the gods are jealous, easily angered, perverse, and swift to thwart.

'It's them, all right – the haughty bastards!' Kos grunted, sweating under his furs – for Godsland is paradisial.

'They haven't called on me for years – the ingrates!' Issek said with a toss of his delicate chin. 'We'd be dead for all they care, except we've our other worshipers. But they don't know that – they're heartless.'

'They have not even taken our names in vain,' said Mog. 'I believe, gentlemen, it is time they suffered the divine displeasure. Agreed?'

In the meanwhile, by speaking privily of Frix and Hisvet, the Mouser and Fafhrd had aroused certain immediate desires in themselves without seriously disturbing their mood of complacent nostalgia.

33

'What say you, Mouser,' Fafhrd mused lazily, 'should we now seek excitement? The night is young.'

His comrade replied grandly, 'We have but to stir a little, to signify our interest, and excitement will seek us. We've loved and been forever adored by so many girls that we're bound to run into a pair of 'em. Or even two pair. They'll catch our present thoughts on the wing and come running. We will hunt girls – ourselves the bait!'

'So let's be on our way,' said Fafhrd, drinking up and rising with a lurch.

'Ach, the lewd dogs!' Kos growled, shaking sweat from his brow, for Godsland is balmy (and quite crowded). 'But how to punish 'em?'

Mog said, smiling lopsidedly because of his partially arachnid jaw structure, 'They seem to have chosen their punishment.'

'The torture of hope!' Issek chimed eagerly, catching on. 'We grant them their wishes—'

'—and then leave the rest to the girls,' Mog finished.

'You can't trust women,' Kos asserted darkly.

'On the contrary, my dear fellow,' Mog said, 'when a god's in good form, he can safely trust his worshipers, female and male alike, to do all the work. And now, gentlemen, on with our thinking caps!'

Kos scratched his thickly matted head vigorously, dislodging a louse or two.

Whimsically, and perhaps to put a few obstacles between themselves and the girls presumably now rushing toward them, Fafhrd and the Gray Mouser chose to leave the Silver Eel by its kitchen door, something they'd never done once before in all their years of patronage.

The door was low and heavily bolted, and when those were shot still wouldn't budge. And the new cook, who was deaf and dumb, left off his stuffing of a calf's stomach and came over to make gobbling noises and flap his arms in gestures of protest or warning. But the Mouser pressed two bronze agols into his greasy palm while Fafhrd kicked the door open. They

34

prepared to stride out into the dismal lot covered by the eroded ashes of the tenement where the Mouser had dwelt with Ivrian (and she and Fafhrd's equally dear Vlana had burned) and also the ashes of the wooden garden house of mad Duke Danius, which they'd once stolen and occupied for a space — the dismal and ill-omened lot which they'd never heard of anyone building on since.

But when they'd ducked their heads and gone through the doorway, they discovered that construction of a sort *had* been going on (or else that they'd always seriously underestimated the depth of the Silver Eel) for instead of on empty ground open to sky, they found themselves in a corridor lit by torches held in brazen hands along each wall.

Undaunted, they strode forward past two closed doors.

'That's Lankhmar City for you,' the Mouser observed. 'You turn your back and they've put up a new secret temple.'

'Good ventilation, though,' Fafhrd commented on the absence of smoke.

They followed the corridor around a sharp turn ... and stopped dead. The split-level chamber facing them had surprising features. The sunken half was close-ceilinged and otherwise gave the impression of being far underground, as if its floor were not eight finger-joints deeper than the raised section but eighty yards. Its furniture was a bed with a coverlet of violet silk. A thick yellow silk cord hung through a hole in the low ceiling.

The chamber's raised half seemed the balcony or battlement of a tower thrust high above Lankhmar's smog, for stars were visible in the black upper background and ceiling.

On the bed, silver-blonde head to its foot, slim Hisvet lay prone but upthrust on her straightened arms. Her robe of fine silk, yellow as desert sunlight, was outdented by her pair of small high breasts, but depended freely from the nipples of those, leaving unanswered the question of whether there were three more pairs arranged symmetrically below.

While against starry night (or its counterfeit), her dark hair braided with scrubbed copper wire, Frix stood magnificently tall and light-footed (though motionless) in her silken robe violet as a desert's twilight before dawn.

Fafhrd was about to say, 'You know, we were just talking about you,' and the Mouser was about to tread on his instep for being so guileless, when Hisvet cried to the latter, 'You again! – intemperate dirksman. I told you never even to *think* of another rendezvous with me for two years' space.'

Frix said to Fafhrd, 'Beast! I told you I played with a member of the lower orders only on *rare* occasions.'

Hisvet tugged sharply on the silken cord. A heavy door dropped down in the men's faces from above and struck its sill with a great and conclusive jar.

Fafhrd lifted a finger to his nose, explaining ruefully, 'I thought the door had taken off the tip. Not exactly a loving reception.'

The Mouser said bravely, 'I'm glad they turned us off. Truly, it would have been too soon, and so a bore. On with our girl hunt!'

They returned past the mute flames held in bronze hands to the second of the two closed doors. It opened at a touch to reveal another dual chamber and in it their loves Reetha and Kreeshkra, whom only short months ago they'd been seeking near the Sea of Monsters, until they were trapped in the Shadowland and barely escaped back to Lankhmar. To the left, in muted sunlight on a couch of exquisitely smoothed dark wood, Reetha reclined quite naked. Indeed, extremely naked, for as the Mouser noted, she'd kept up her habit, inculcated when she'd been slave of a finicky overlord, of regularly shaving all of herself, even her eyebrows. Her totally bare head, held at a pert angle, was perfectly shaped and the Mouser felt a surge of sweet desire. She was cuddling to her tender bosom a very emaciated-seeming but tranquil animal, which the Mouser suddenly realized was a cat, hairless save for its score of whiskers bristling from its mask.

To the right, in dark night a-dance with the light of camp-fire and on a smooth shale shore of what Fafhrd recognized to be, by the large white-bearded serpents sporting in it, the Sea of Monsters, sat his beloved Kreeshkra, more naked even than

Reetha. She might have been a disquieting sight to some (naught but an aristocratically handsome skeleton), except that the flames near which she sat struck dark blue gleams from the sweetly curved surfaces of her transparent flesh casing her distinguished bones.

'Mouser, why have you come?' Reetha cried out somewhat reproachfully. 'I'm happy here in Eevamarensee, where all men are as hairless by nature (our household animals too) as I am by my daily industry. I love you dearly still, but we can't live together and must not meet again. This is my proper place.'

Likewise, bold Kreeshkra challenged Fafhrd with 'Mud Man, avaunt! I loved you once. Now I'm a Ghoul again. Perhaps in future time . . . But now, begone!'

It was well neither Fafhrd nor Mouser had stepped across the threshold, for at those words this door slammed in their faces too, and this time stuck fast. Fafhrd forbore to kick it.

'You know, Mouser,' he said thoughtfully, 'We've been enamored of some strange ones in our time. But always most intensely interesting,' he hastened to add.

'Come on, come on,' the Mouser enjoined gruffly. 'There are other fish in the sea.'

The remaining door opened easily too, though Fafhrd pushed it somewhat gingerly. Nothing startling, however, came into view this time, only a long dark room, empty of persons and furniture, with a second door at the other end. Its only novel feature was that the right-hand wall glowed green. They walked in with returning confidence. After a few steps they became aware that the glowing wall was thick crystal enclosing pale green, faintly clouded water. As they watched, continuing to stroll, there swam into view with lazy undulations two beautiful mermaids, the one with long golden hair trailing behind her and a sheathlike garb of wide-meshed golden fishnet, the other with short dark hair parted by a ridgy and serrated silver crest. They came close enough for one to see the slowly pulsing gills scoring their necks where they merged into their sloping, faintly scaled shoulders, and farther down their bodies those discrete organs which contradict the contention, subject of many a crude jest, that a man is unable fully to enjoy an unbifurcated woman (though any pair of snakes in love tell us otherwise). They swam closer still, their dreamy eyes now wide and peering, and the Mouser and Fafhrd recognized the two queens of the sea they had embraced some years past while deep diving from their sloop *Black Treasurer*.

What the wide-peering fishy eyes saw evidently did not please the mermaids, for they made faces and with powerful flirts of their long finny tails retreated away from the crystal wall through the greenish water, whose cloudiness was increased by their rapid movements, until they could no longer be seen.

Turning to the Mouser, Fafhrd inquired, eyebrows alift, 'You mentioned other fish in the sea?'

With a quick frown the Mouser strode on. Trailing him, Fafhrd mused puzzledly, 'You said this might be a secret temple, friend. But if so, where are its porters, priests, and patrons other than ourselves?'

'More like a museum – scenes of distant life. And a piscesium, or piscatorium,' his comrade answered curtly over shoulder.

'I've also been thinking,' Fafhrd continued, quickening his steps, 'there's too much space here we've been walking through for the lot behind the Silver Eel to hold. What *has* been builded here? – or there?'

The Mouser went through the far door. Fafhrd was close behind.

In Godsland Kos snarled, 'The rogues are taking it too easily. Oh, for a thunderbolt!'

Mog told him rapidly, 'Never you fear, my friend, we have them on the run. They're only putting up appearances. We'll wear them down by slow degrees until they pray to us for mercy, groveling on their knees. That way our pleasure's greater.'

'Quieter, you two,' Issek shrilled, waving his bent wrists, 'I'm getting another girl pair!'

It was clear from these and other quick gesticulations and injunctions – and from their rapt yet tense expressions – that the three gods in close inward-facing circle were busy with something interesting. From all around other divinities large and small, baroque and classical, noisome and beautiful, came drifting up to comment and observe. Godsland *is* overcrowded, a veritable slum, all because of man's perverse thirst for variety. There are rumors among the packed gods there of other and (perish the thought!) superior gods, perhaps invisible, who enjoy roomier quarters on another and (oh woe!) higher level and who (abysmal deviltry!) even hear thoughts, but nothing certain.

Issek cried out in ecstasy, 'There, there, the stage is set! Now to search out the next teasing pair. Kos and Mog, help me. Do your rightful share.'

The Gray Mouser and Fafhrd felt they'd been transported to the mysterious realm of Quarmall, where they'd had one of their most fantastic adventures. For the next chamber seemed a cave in solid rock, given room-shape by laborious chipping. And behind a table piled with parchments and scrolls, inkwells and quills, sat the two saucy, seductive slave-girls they'd rescued from the cavern-world's monotonies and tortures: slender Ivivis, supple as a snake, and pleasantly plump Friska, light of foot. The two men felt relief and joy that they'd come home to the familiar and beloved.

Then they saw the room had windows, with sunlight suddenly striking in (as if a cloud had lifted), and was not solid rock but morticed stone, and that the girls wore not the scanty garb of slaves but rich and sober robes, while their faces were grave and self-reliant.

Ivivis looked up at the Mouser with inquiry but instant disapproval. 'What dost here, figment of my servile past? Tis true, you rescued me from Quarmall foul. For which I paid you with my body's love. Which ended at Tovilysis when we split. We're quits, dear Mouser, yes by Mog, we are!' (She wondered why she used that particular oath.)

Likewise Friska looked at Fafhrd and said, 'That goes for you too, bold barbarian. You also killed my lover Hovis, you'll recall – as Mouser did Ivivis' Klevis. We are no longer simple-minded slaves, playthings of men, but subtle secretary and present treasurer of the Guild of Free Women at Tovilysis. We'll never love again unless I choose – which I do not today! And so, by Kos and Issek, now begone!' (She wondered likewise why she invoked those particular deities, for whom she had no respect whatever.)

These rebuffs hurt the two heroes sorely, so that they had not the spirit to respond with denials, jests, or patient gallantries. Their tongues clove to their hard palates, their hearts and privates grew chilly, they almost cringed – and they rather swiftly stole from that chamber by the open door ahead ... into a large room shaped of bluish ice, or rock of the same hue and translucence and as cold, so that the flames dancing in the large fireplace were welcome. Before this was spread a rug looking wondrously thick and soft, about which were set scattered jars of unguents, small bottles of perfume (which made themselves known by their ranging scents), and other cosmetic containers and tools. Furthermore, the invitingly textured rug showed indentations as if made by two recumbent human forms, while about a cubit above it floated two living masks as thin as silk or paper or more thin, holding the form of wickedly pretty, pert girl faces, the one rosy mauvette, the other turquoise green.

Others would have deemed it a prodigy, but the Mouser and Fafhrd at once recognized Keyaira and Hirriwi, the invisible frost princesses with whom they'd once been separately paired for one long, long night in Stardock, tallest of Nehwon's northron peaks, and knew that the two gaysome girls were reclining unclad in front of the fire and had been playfully anointing each other's faces with pigmented salves.

Then the turquoise mask leapt up betwixt Fafhrd and the fire, so that dancing orange flames only shone through its staring eye holes and between its now cruel and amused lips as it spoke to him, saying, 'In what frowsty bed are you now dead asleep, gross one-time lover, that your squeaking soul can be blown halfway across the world to gape at me? Some day again climb Stardock and in your solid form importune me. I might hark. But now, phantom, depart!'

The mallow mask likewise spoke scornfully to the Mouser,

saying in tones as stinging and impelling as the flames seen through its facial orifices, 'And you remove too, wraith most pitiful. By Khahkht of the Black Ice and Gara of the Blue – and e'en Kos of the Green – I enjoin it! Blow winds! and out lights all!'

Fafhrd and the Mouser were hurt even more sorely by these new rebuffs. Their very souls were shriveled by the feeling that they were indeed the phantoms, and the speaking masks the solid reality. Nevertheless, they might have summoned the courage to attempt to answer the challenge (though 'tis doubtful), except that at Keyaira's last commands they were plunged into darkness absolute and manhandled by great winds and then dumped in a lighted area. A wind-slammed door crashed shut behind them.

They saw with considerable relief that they were not confronting yet another pair of girls (*that* would have been unendurable) but were in another stretch of corridor lit by clear-flaming torches held in brazen wall brackets in the form of gripping bird-talons, coiling squid-tentacles, and pinching crabclaws. Grateful for the respite, they took deep breaths.

Then Fafhrd frowned deeply and said, 'Mark me, Mouser, there's magic somewhere in all this. Or else the hand of a god.'

The Mouser commented bitterly, 'If it's a god, he's a thumb-fingered one, the way he sets us up to be turned down.'

Fafhrd's thoughts took a new tack, as shown by the changing furrows in his forehead. 'Mouser, I never squeaked,' he protested. 'Hirriwi said I squeaked.'

'Manner of speaking only, I suppose,' his comrade consoled. 'But gods! what misery I felt myself, as if I were no longer man at all, and *this* no more than broomstick.' He indicated his sword Scalpel at his side and gazed with a shake of his head at Fafhrd's scabbarded Graywand.

'Perchance we dream—' Fafhrd began doubtfully.

'Well, if we're dreaming, let's get on with it,' the Mouser said and, clapping his friend around the shoulders, started them down the corridor. Yet despite these cheerful words and actions, both men felt they were getting more and more into the toils of nightmare, drawing them on will-lessly.

They rounded a turn. For some yards the right-hand wall became a row of slender dark pillars, irregularly spaced, and between them they could see more random dusky slim shafts and at middle distance a long altar on which light showered softly down, revealing a tall, naked woman stretched on it, and by her a priestess in purple robes with dagger bared in one hand and large silver chalice in the other, who was intoning a litany.

Fafhrd whispered, 'Mouser! the sacrifice is the courtesan Lessnya, with whom I had some dealings when I was acolyte of Issek, years ago.'

'While the other is Ilala, priestess of the like-named goddess, with whom I had some commerce when I was lieutenant to Pulg the extortioner,' the Mouser whispered back.

Fafhrd protested, 'But we *can't* have already come all the way to the temple of Ilala, though this looks like it. It's half-way across Lankhmar from the Eel,' while the Mouser recalled tales he'd heard of secret passages in Lankhmar that connected points by distances shorter than the shortest distance between.

Ilala turned toward them in her purple robes and said with eyebrows raised, 'Quiet back there! You are committing sacrilege, trespassing on most holy ritual of the great goddess of all shes. Impious intruders, depart!' While Lessnya lifted on an elbow and looked at them haughtily. Then she lay back again and regarded the ceiling while Ilala plunged her dagger deep into her chalice and then with it flicked sprinkles of wine (or whatever other fluid the chalice held) on Lessnya's naked shape, wielding the blade as if it were as aspergillum. She aspersed her thrice – on bosom, loins, and knees – and then resumed her muttered litany, while Lessnya echoed her (or else snored) and the Mouser and Fafhrd stole on along the torchlit corridor.

But they had little time to ponder on the strange geometries and stranger religiosities of their nightmare progress, for now the left-hand wall gave way for a space to a fabulously decorated, large, dim chamber, which they recognized as the official residence room of the Grandmaster of the Thieves' Guild in

Thieves' House, half Lankhmar City back again from Ilala's fane. The foreground was filled with figures kneeling away from them in devout supplication toward a thick-topped ebony table, behind which there stood queenly tall a handsome red-haired woman dressed in jewels and behind her a trim second female in maid's black tunic collared and cuffed with white.

'' 'Tis Ivlis in her beauty from the past, for whom I stole Ohmphal's erubescent fingertips,' the Mouser whispered in stupefaction. 'And now she's got herself a peck more gems.'

'And that is Freg, her maid, looking no older,' Fafhrd whispered back hoarsely in dream-drugged wonderment.

'But what's she doing here in Thieves' House?' the Mouser pressed, his whisper feverish, 'where women are forbidden and contemned. As if *she* were grandmaster of the Guild ... grand-mistress ... goddess ... worshiped ... Is Thieves' Guild upside down? ... all Nehwon turvy-topsy ...?'

Ivlis looked up at them across the heads of her kneeling followers. Her green eyes narrowed. She casually lifted her fingers to her lips, then flicked them sideways twice, indicating to the Mouser that he should silently keep going in that direction and not return.

With a slow unloving smile, Freg made exactly the same gesture to Fafhrd, but even more idly seeming, as if humming a chorus. The two men obeyed, but with their gazes trailing behind them, so that it was with complete surprise, almost with starts of fear, that they found they had walked blindly into a room of rare woods embellished with intricate carvings, with a door before them and doors to either side, and in the one of the latter nearest the Mouser a freshly nubile girl with wicked eyes, in a green robe of shaggy toweling cloth, her black hair moist, and in the one nearest Fafhrd two slim blondes a-smile with dubious merriment and wearing loosely the black hoods and robes of nuns of Lankhmar. In nightmare's fullest grip they realized that this was the very same garden house of Duke Danius, haunted by their earliest deepest loves, impiously reconstituted from the ashes to which the sorcerer Sheelba had burned it and profanely refurbished with all the trinkets wizard Ningauble had magicked from it and scattered to the four winds; and that these three nightfillies were Ivmiss Ovarta-mortes, niece of Karstak like-named, Lankhmar's then over-lord, and Fralek and Fro, mirror-twin daughters of the death-crazed duke, the three she-colts of the dark to whom they'd madly turned after losing even the ghosts of their true loves in Shadowland. Fafhrd was wildly thinking in unvoiced sound, 'Fralek and Fro, and Freg, Friska and Frix – what is this Fr'-charm on me?' while through the Mouser's mind was skipping likewise, 'Ivlis, Ivmiss, Ivivis (*two* Iv's – and there's e'en an Iv in Hisvet) – who are these girl-lets of the Iv . . .?'

(Near the Life Pole, the gods Mog, Issek, and Kos were working at the top of their bent, crying out to each other new girl-discoveries with which to torment their lapsed worshipers. The crowd of spectator gods around them was now large.)

And then the Mouser bethought him with a shiver that he had not listed amongst his girl-lings of the Iv the archgirl of them all, fair Ivrian, forever lost in Death's demesne. And Fafhrd likewise shook. And the nightfillies flanking them pouted and made moues at them, and they were fairly cata-pulted into the midst of a pavilion of wine-dark silk, beyond whose unstirring folds showed the flat black horizons of the Shadowland.

Beauteous, slate-visaged Vlana spat full in Fafhrd's face, saying, 'I told you I'd do that if you came back,' but fair Ivrian only eyed the Mouser with never a sign or word.

And then they were back in the betorched corridor, more hurried along it than hurrying, and the Mouser envied Fafhrd death's spittle inching down his cheek. And girls were flashing by like ghosts, unheedingly – Mara of Fafhrd's youth, Atya who worshiped Tyaa, bovine-eyed Hrenlet, Ahura of Seleucia, and many many more – until they were feeling the utter despair that comes with being rejected not by one or a few loves, but by all. The unfairness of it alone was enough to make a man die.

Then in the rush one scene lingered awhile: Alyx the Pick-lock garbed in the scarlet robes and golden tiara a-swarm with rubies of the archpriest of an eastern faith, and kneeling before her costumed as clerk Lilyblack, the Mouser's girlish leman from his criminous days, intoning, 'Papa, the heathen rage, the civilized decay,' and the transvestite archpriestess pronouncing, 'All men are enemies . . .'

Almost Fafhrd and the Mouser dropped to their knees and prayed to whatever gods may be for surcease from their torment. But somehow they didn't, and of a sudden they found themselves on Cheap Street near where it crosses Crafts and turning in at a drab doorway after two females, whose backs were teasingly familiar, and following them up a narrow flight of stairs that stretched up so far in one flight that its crazy warpage was magnified.

In Godsland Mog threw himself back, blowing out his breath and saying, 'There! that gets them all,' while Issek likewise stretched himself out (so far as his permanently bent ankles and wrists would permit), observing, 'Lord, people don't appreciate how we gods work, what toil in sparrow-watching!' and the spectator gods began to disperse.

But Kos, still frowingly immersed in his task to such a degree that he wasn't aware of the pain in his short burly thighs from sitting cross-legged so long, cried out, 'Hold on! here's another pair: to wit, one Nemia of the Dusk, one Eyes of Ogo, women of lax morals and, to boot, receivers of stolen property – oh, that's vile!'

Issek laughed wearily and said, 'Quit now, dear Kos. I crossed those two off at the very start. They're our men's dearest enemies, swindled them out of a precious loot of jewels, as almost any god around could tell you. Sooner than seek them out (to be rebuffed in any case, of course) our boys would rot in hell,' while Mog yawned and added, 'Don't you ever know, dear Kos, when the game's done?'

So the befurred short god shrugged and gave over, cursing as he tried to straighten his legs.

Meanwhile, the Eyes of Ogo and Nemia of the Dusk reached the summit of the endless stairs and tiredly entered their pad, eyeing it with disfavor. (It *was* an impoverished, dingy, even noisome place – the two best thieves in Lankhmar had fallen on hard times, as even the best of thieves and receivers will in the course of long careers.)

Nemia turned round and said, 'Look what the cat dragged in.' Hardship had drastically straightened her lush curves. Her comrade Ogo-Eyes still looked somewhat like a child, but a very old and ill-used one. 'Wow,' she said wearily, 'you two look miserable, as if you'd just 'scaped death and sorry you had. Do yourselves a favor – fall down the stairs, breaking your necks.'

When Fafhrd and the Mouser didn't move, or change their woebegone expressions, she laughed shortly, dropped into a broken-seated chair, poked out a leg at the Mouser, and said, 'Well, if you're not leaving, make yourself useful. Remove my sandals, wash my feet,' while Nemia sat down before a rickety dressing table and, while surveying herself in the broken mirror, held out a broken-toothed instrument in Fafhrd's direction, saying, 'Comb my hair, barbarian. Watch out for snarls and knots.'

Fafhrd and the Mouser (the later preparing and fetching warm water) began solemn-faced to do those very things most carefully.

After quite a long time (and several other menial services rendered, or servile penances done) the two women could no longer keep from smiling. Misery, *after* it's comforted, loves company. 'That's enough for now,' Eyes told the Mouser. 'Come, make yourself comfortable.' Nemia spoke likewise to Fafhrd, adding, 'Later you men can make the dinner and go out for wine.'

After a while the Mouser said, 'By Mog, this is more like it.' Fafhrd agreed. 'By Issek, yes. Kos damn all spooked adventures.'

The three gods, hearing their names taken in vain as they rested in paradise from their toils, were content.

46

VI: TRAPPED IN THE
SEA OF STARS

Fafhrd the educated barbarian and his constant comrade the Gray (Grey?) Mouser, city-born but wizard-tutored in the wilds, had in their leopard-boat *Black Racer* sailed farther south in the Outer Sea along the Quarmallian or west coast of Lankhmar continent than they had ever ventured before, or any other honest mariner they knew.

They were lured on by a pair of shimmer-sprights, as they were called, a breed of will-o'-the-wisps which men deem infallible guides to lodgements of precious metals, if only one have a master hunter's patience and craft to track them down, by reason of which they are also called treasure-flies, silver-moths, and gold-bugs. This pair had a coppery pink seeming by day and a silvery black gleam by night, promising by those hues a trove of elektrum and still dearer, because massier, white gold. They most resembled restlessly flowing, small bedsheets of gossamer. They fluttered ceaselessly about the single mast, darting ahead, drifting behind. Sometimes they were almost invisible, faintest heat-blurs in the pelting fire of the near vertical sun, ghostliest shimmers in the dark of night and easily mistaken for reflections of the White Huntress' light on sea and sail, the moon now being near full. Sometimes they moved as sprightly as their name, sometimes they drooped and lagged, but ever moved on. At such times they seemed sad (or melancholy, Fafhrd said, one of his favorite moods). On other occasions they became (if ears could be trusted) vocal with joy, filling the air about the leopard-boat with faint sweet jargonings, whispers 'twixt wind and speech, and long ecstatic purrs.

By the Gray Mouser's and Fafhrd's calculations, *Black Racer* had now left behind Lankhmar continent to loadside, and the hypothetical Western continent far, far to steerside, and struck out due south into the Great Equatorial Ocean (sometimes called – but why? – the Sea of Stars) that girdles Nehwon and is deemed wholly dire and quite uncrossable by Lankhmarts and Easterners alike, who in their sailings hug the southern coasts of the northern continents, so that one would have thought the doughtiest sailors would have ere this turned back.

But there was, you see, another reason beside the hope of vast riches – and not chiefly their great courage either, by any means – that Fafhrd and the Mouser kept sailing on in the face of unknown perils and horrid legendry of monsters that crunched ships, and currents swifter than the hurricane, and craterous maelstroms that swallowed vastest vessels in one gulp and even sucked down venturesome islands. It was a reason they spoke of seldom to each other and then only most guardedly, in low tones after long silence in the long silent watches of the night. It was this: that on the edge of darkest sleep, or sluggishly rousing from sail-shadowed nap by day, they briefly saw the shimmer-sprights as beautiful, slim, translucent girls, mirror-image twins, with loving faces and great, glimmering wings. Girls with fine hair like gold or silver clouds and distant eyes that yet brimmed with thought and witchery, girls slim almost beyond belief yet not too slim for the act of love, if only they might wax sufficiently substantial, which was something their smiles and gazes seemed to promise might come to pass. And the two adventurers felt a yearning for these shimmer-girls such as they had never felt for mortal woman, so that they could no more turn back than men wholly ensorceled or stark lockjawed mad.

That morning as their treasure-sprights led them on, looking like rays of rainbow in the sun, the Mouser and Fafhrd were each lost in his secret thoughts of girls and gold, so that neither noted the subtle changes in the ocean surface ahead, from ripply to half smooth with odd little long lines of foam racing east. Suddenly the gold-bugs darted east and the next instant something seized the leopard-boat's keel so that she veered strongly east with a bound like that of the lithe beast for which her class of craft was named. The tall mast was almost snapped and the two heroes were nearly thrown to the deck, and by the time they had recovered from their surprise the *Black Racer* was speeding east, the twin shimmer-sprights winging ahead exultantly, and the two heroes knew that they were in the grip of the Great Eastward Equatorial Current and that it was no fable.

Momentarily forgetting their aerial maybe-girls, they moved to steer north out of it, Fafhrd leaning on the tiller while the Mouser saw to the large single sail, but at that moment a north-west wind struck from astern with gale force, almost driving the *Black Racer* under as it drove her deeper and deeper south into the current. This wind was no mere gust but steadily mounted to storm force, so that it would infallibly have torn their sail away ere they could furl it save that the current below was carrying them east almost as fast as the wind harried them on above.

Then a league to the south they saw three waterspouts traveling east together, gray pillars stretching halfway from earth to sky, at thrice *Black Racer*'s speed at least, indicating that the current was still swifter there. As the two still-astonished sailormen perforce accepted their plight – helpless in the twin grasp of furiously speeding water and air as if their craft were frozen to the sea – the Gray Mouser cried out, 'O Fafhrd, now I can well believe that metaphysical fancy that the whole universe is water and our world but one wind-haunted bubble in it.'

From where white-knuckled he gripped the tiller, Faf replied, 'I'll grant, what with those 'spouts and all this flying foam, it seems right now there's water everywhere. Yet still I can't believe that philosopher's dream of Nehwon-world a bubble, when any fool can see the sun and moon are massy orbs like Nehwon thousands of leagues distant in the high air, which must be very thin out there, by the by.

'But man, this is no time for sophistries. I'll tie the tiller, and while this weird calm lasts (born of near equal speeds of current and wind, and as if the air were cut away before and closing in behind) let's triple-reef the sail and make all snug.'

As they worked, the three waterspouts vanished in the distance ahead, to be replaced by a group of five more coming up fast from astern – somewhat nearer this time, for all the while *Black Racer* was being driven gradually but relentlessly south. From almost overhead the midday sun beat down fiercely, for the storm wind blowing near hurricane force had brought no clouds or opaque air with it – in itself a prodigy unparalleled in the recollection of the Mouser or even Fafhrd, a widely sailed man. After several futile efforts to steer north out of the mighty current (which resulted only in the following storm wind shifting perversely north a point or two, driving them deeper south) the two men gave over, thereby admitting their complete inability at present to influence their leopard boat's course.

'At this rate,' Fafhrd opined, 'we'll cross the Great Equatorial Ocean in a matter of month or two. Lucky we're well provisioned.'

The Mouser replied dolefully, 'If *Racer* holds together a day amidst those 'spouts and speeds, I'll be surprised.'

'She's a stout craft,' Fafhrd said lightly. 'Just think, Small Gloomy One, the southern continents unknown to man! We'll be the first to visit 'em!'

'If there are any such. And our planks don't split. Continents? – I'd give my soul for one small isle.'

'The first to reach Nehwon's south pole!' Fafhrd daydreamed on. 'The first to climb the southern Stardocks! The first to loot the treasures of the south! The first to find what land lies at antipodes from Shadowland, realm of Death! The first—'

The Mouser quietly removed himself to the other side of the shortened sail from Fafhrd and cautiously made his way to the prow, where he wearily threw himself down in a narrow angle of shadow. He was dazed by wind, spray, exertion, the needling sun, and sheer velocity. He dully watched the coppery pinkish shimmer-sprights, which were holding position with remarkable steadiness for them at mast height a ship's length ahead.

After a while he slept and dreamed that one of them detached itself from the other, and came down and hovered above him like a long rosy spectrum and then became a fond- and narrow-visaged green-eyed girl in his arms, who loosened his clothing with slim fingers cool as milk kept in a well, so that looking down closely he saw the nipples of her dainty breasts pressing like fresh-scoured copper thimbles into the curly dark hair on his chest. And she was saying softly and sweetly, head bent forward like his, lips and tongue brushing his ear, 'Press on, press on. This is the only way to Life and immortality and paradise.' And he replied, 'My dearest love, I will.'

He woke to Fafhrd's shout and to a fugitive but clear, though almost blinding vision of a female face that was narrow and beautiful, but otherwise totally unlike that of the douce girl of his dream. A sharp, imperious face, wildly alive, made all of red-gold light, the irises of her wide eyes vermilion.

He lifted up sluggishly. His jerkin was unlaced to his waist and pushed back off his shoulders.

'Mouser,' Fafhrd said urgently, 'when I first glimpsed you but now, you were all bathed in fire!'

Gazing stupidly down, the Mouser saw twin threads of smoke rising from his matted chest where the nipples of his dream had pressed into it. And as he stared at the gray threads, they died. He smelled the stink of burning hair.

He shook his head, blinked, and pushed himself to his feet. 'What a strange fancy,' he said to Fafhrd. 'The sun must have got in your eye. Say, look there!'

The five waterspouts had drawn far ahead and had been replaced by two groups (of three and four respectively) swiftly overtaking Black Racer from astern, the four rather distant, the three appallingly close, so that they could see clearly the structure of each: pillars of wild gray water almost a ship's length thick and towering up to thrice mast height, where each broke off abruptly.

And in the farther distance they could now see still more groups of speeding spouts, and most distant-dim yet speediest of all a gigantic single one that looked leagues thick. A-prow the twin shimmer-sprights led on.

' 'Tis passing strange,' Fafhrd averred.

'Does one speak of a covey of waterspouts?' the Mouser

wanted to know. 'Or a pride? A congeries? A fountain? Or –
yes! – a tower! A tower of waterspouts!'

The day passed and half the night, and their weird situation
of eastward speeding held – and *Black Racer* held together.
The sea was slick and moving in long low swells across which
blew thin, long, pale lines of foam. The wind was hurricane
force at very least, but the velocity of the Great Equatorial
Current had increased to match it.

Overhead, nearly at mast-top, the full moon shone down,
scantily scattered about with stars. Her White Huntress light
showed the smooth surface of the racing sea to be outdinted
near and far by towers of waterspouts racing by in majestical
array and yet with fantastical celerity, as if they somehow
profited far more from the speed of the current than did *Black
Racer*. At mast height and ship's length ahead, the twin
shimmer-sprights flew on like flags of silver lace against the
dark. All almost silently.

'Fafhrd,' the Gray Mouser spoke very softly, as if reluctant
to break the silver moonlight's spectral spell, 'Tonight I clearly
see that Nehwon *is* a vast bubble rising through waters of
eternity, with continents and isles afloat inside.'

'Yes, and they'd move around – the continents, I mean –
and bump each other,' Fafhrd said, softly too, albeit a little
gruffly. 'That is, providing they'd float at all. Which I most
strongly doubt.'

'They move all orderly, in pre-established harmony,' the
Mouser replied. 'And as for buoyancy, think of the Sinking
Land.'

'But then where'd be the sun and moon and stars and planets
nine?' Fafhrd objected. 'All in a jumble in the bubble's midst?
That's quite impossible – and ridiculous.'

'I'm getting to the stars,' the Mouser said. 'They're all afloat
in even stricter pre-established harmony in the Great Equatorial Ocean, which as we've seen this day and night, speeds
around Nehwon's waist once each day – that is, in its effects
on the waterspouts, not on *Black Racer*. Why else, I ask you,
is it called the Sea of Stars?'

Fafhrd blinked, momentarily impressed against his will.

Then he grinned. 'But if this ocean's all afloat with stars,' he demanded, 'why can't we see 'em all about our ship? Riddle me that, O Sage!'

The Mouser smiled back at him, very composedly. 'They're all of 'em inside the waterspouts,' he said, 'which are gray tubes of water pointing toward heaven – by which I mean, of course, the antipodes of Nehwon. Look up, bold comrade mine, at arching sky and heaven's top. You're looking at the same Great Equatorial Ocean we're afloat in, only halfway around Nehwon from *Black Racer*. You're looking *down* (or *up*, what skills it?) the tubes of the waterspouts there, so you can see the star at bottom of each.'

'I'm looking at the full moon too,' Fafhrd said. 'Don't try to tell me *that*'s at the bottom of a waterspout!'

'But I will,' the Mouser responded gently. 'Recall the gigantic spout like speeding mesa we briefly saw far south of us last noon? That was the moonspout, to invent a word. And now it's raced to sky ahead of us, in half day since.'

'Fry me for a sardine!' Fafhrd said with great feeling. Then he sought to collect his comprehension. 'And those folk on Nehwon's other side – up *there* – they're seeing a star at the bottom of each waterspout now around us here?'

'Of course not,' the Mouser said patiently. 'Sunlight drowns out their twinkles for those folk. It's *day* up there, you see.' He pointed at the dark near the moon. 'Up there, you see, they're bathed in highest noon, drenched in the light of the sun, which now is somewhere near us, but hid from us by the thick walls of his sunspout, to coin a word wholly analogous to moonspout.'

'Oh, monstrous!' Fafhrd cried. 'For if it's day up there, you little fool, why can't we see it here? Why can't we see up there Nehwon lands bathed in light with bright blue sea around 'em? Answer me that!'

'Because there are two different kinds of light,' the Mouser said with an almost celestial tranquility. 'Seeming the same by every local test, yet utterly diverse. First, there's *direct* light, such as we're getting now from moon and stars up there. Second, there is *reflected* light, which cannot make the really

53

longer journeys, and certainly can't recross – not one faint ray of it – Nehwon's central space to reach us here.'

'Mouser,' Fafhrd said in a very small voice, but with great certainty, 'you're not just inventing words, you're inventing the whole business – on the spur of the moment as you go along.'

'Invent the Laws of Nature?' the Mouser asked with a certain horror. 'That were far worse than darkest blasphemy.'

'Then in the name of all the gods at once!' Fafhrd demanded in a very large voice, 'how can the sun be in a waterspout and not boil it all away in an instant in an explosion vast? Tell me at once.'

'There are some things man was not meant to know,' the Mouser said in a most portentous voice. Then, swiftly switching to the familiar, 'or rather, since I am in no way superstitious, there are some things which have not yielded yet to our philosophy. An omission which in this instance I will remedy at once. There are, you see, two different kinds of *energy*, the one pure heat, the other purest light, which cannot boil the tiniest waterdrop – the direct light I've already told you of, which changes almost entirely to heat where e'er it hits, which in turn tells us why reflected light can't make the long trip back through Nehwon's midst. There, have I answered you?'

'Oh damn, damn, damn,' Fafhrd said weakly. Then managing to rally himself, if only desperately for a last time, he asked somewhat sardonically, 'All right, all right! But just where then is this floating sun you keep invoking, tucked in his vast adamantine-walled waterspout?'

'Look there,' the Mouser said, pointing due south, steerside abeam.

Across the moon-silvered gray field of the sea pricked out with speeding towers of waterspouts, almost at the dim distant horizon, Fafhrd saw a solitary gigantic waterspout huge as an island, taller than tallest mesa, moving east at least as swiftly as the rest and as ponderous-relentlessly as a juggernaut of the emperor of the Eastern Lands. The hair rose on the back of Fafhrd's neck, he was harrowed with fear and wonder, and he said not a word, but only stared and stared as the horrendous thing forged ahead in its immensity.

After a while he began also to feel a great weariness. He looked ahead and a little up at the stiffly flapping silver lace of the twin shimmer-sprights before the prow, taking comfort from their nearness and steadiness as if they were *Black Racer*'s flags. He slowly lowered himself until he lay prone on the narrow, snugly abutting planks of the deck, his head toward the prow, his chin propped on his hands, still observing the night-sprights.

'You know how groups of stars sometimes wink out mysteriously on clearest Nehwon nights?' the Mouser said lightly and bemusedly.

'That's true enough, they do,' Fafhrd agreed, somewhat sleepily.

'That must be because the tubes of their waterspout-walls are bent enough, by a strong gale perchance, to hide their light, keep it from getting out.'

Fafhrd mumbled, 'If you say so.'

After a considerable pause the Mouser asked in the same tones, 'Is it not passing strange to think that in the heart of each dark, gray 'spout out there dotting the main, there burns (without any heat) a jewel of blinding, purest diamond light?'

Fafhrd managed what might have been a weighty sigh of agreement.

After another long pause the Mouser said reflectively, as one who tidies up loose ends, 'It's easy now to see, isn't it, that the 'spouts small and great must all be tubes? For if they were solid water by some strange chance, they'd suck the oceans dry and fill the heavens with heaviest clouds – nay, with the sea! You get my point?'

But Fafhrd had gone to sleep. In his sleep he dreamed and in that dream he rolled over on his back and one of the shimmer-sprights parted from her sister and winged down to flutter close above him: a long and slender, black-haired form, moon pale, appareled in finest silver-shot black lace that witchingly enhanced her nakedness. She was gazing down at him tenderly yet appraisingly, with eyes that would have been violet had there been more light. He smiled at her. She slightly shook her head, her face grew grave, and she flowed down against him head to heel, her wraithlike fingers busy at the great bronze buckle of his heavy belt, while with long, night-cool cheek pressed 'gainst his fevered one, she whispered softly and yet most clearly in his ear, each word a symbol finely drawn in blackest ink on moon-white paper, 'Turn back, turn back, my dearest man, to Shadowland and Death, for that's the only way to stay alive. Trust only in the moon. Suspect all other prophecies but mine. So now, steer north, steer strongly strongly north.'

In his dream Fafhrd replied, 'I can't steer north, I've tried. Love me, my dearest girl,' and she answered huskily, 'That's as may hap, my love. Seek Death to 'scape from him. Suspect all flaming youth and scarlet shes. Beware the sun. Trust in the moon. Wait for her certain sign.'

At that instant Fafhrd's dream was snatched from him and he roused numbly to the Mouser's sharp cries and to the chilling fugitive glimpse of a face narrow, beauteous, and of most melancholy mien, pale violet-blue of hue and with eyes like black holes. This above wraithlike, like-complected figure, and all receding swift as thought amidst a beating of black wings.

Then the Mouser was shaking him by the shoulders and crying out, 'Wake up, wake up! Speak to me, man!'

Fafhrd brushed his face with the back of his hand and mumbled, 'Wha' happ'n?'

Crouched beside him, the Mouser narrated rapidly and somewhat breathlessly, 'The shimmer-sprights grew restless and 'gan play about the mast like corposants. One buzzed around me shrilly like a wasp, and when I'd driven it off, I saw the other nosing you from toe to waist to head, then nuzzling your neck. Your flesh grew silver-white, as white as death, the whiles the corposant became your glowing shroud. I greatly feared for you and drove it off.'

Fafhrd's muddied eyes cleared somewhat whilst the Mouser spoke and when the latter was done, he nodded and said knowingly, 'That would be right. She spoke me much of death and at the end she looked like it, poor sibyl.'

'Who spoke?' the Mouser asked. 'What sibyl?'

'The shimmer-girl, of course,' Fafhrd told him. 'You know what I mean.'

He stood up. His belt began to slip. He stared down wide-eyes at the undone buckle, then drew it up and hooked it together swiftly.

'Fafhrd, I don't know what you're talking of,' the Mouser denied, his expression suddenly hooded. 'Girl? What girl? Art seeing mirages? Has lack of erotic exercise addled your wits? Have you turned moon-mad lunatic?'

At this point Fafhrd had to speak most sharply and shrewdly to the Mouser to get him to admit that he – the Mouser – had suspected for days that the shimmer-sprights were girls, albeit girls with a strong admixture of the supernatural, insofar as any admixture of anything is able to affect the essential girlness of any such being, which isn't much.

But the Mouser did eventually make the admission although his mind had not the edge-of-sleep honesty of Fafhrd's and tended to drift off to musings on his bubble-cosmos. Yet under strong prompting by Fafhrd he even confessed to his encounter with the sun-red vermilion-eyed shimmer-girl last noon, when he'd looked afire, and upon Fafhrd's insistence recalled the exact words she'd said to him in dream.

'Your red girl spoke of Life and pressing on south to immortality and paradise,' Fafhrd summed up thoughtfully, 'whilst my dark dear talked of Death and turning back north toward Shadowland and Lankhmar and Cold Waste.' Then, with swift-growing excitement and utter amazement at his own insight, 'Mouser, I see it all! There are two different pairs of shimmer-girls! The daytime ones (you spoke with one of those) are children of the sun and messengers from the fabled Land of Gods at Nehwon's Life Pole. While the nighttimers, replacing them from dusk to dawn, are minions of the moon, White Huntress' daughters, owing allegiance to the Shadowland, which lies across the world from the Life Pole.'

'Fafhrd, hast thou thought,' the Mouser spoke from a brown study, 'how nicely calculated must be the height and diameter of each waterspout-tube, so that the star at its bottom is seen from every spot in other half of Nehwon (up there, when it's night there) but from no spot in our half down here? – which incidentally explains why stars are brightest at zenith, you see all of each, not just a lens or biconvex meniscus. It seems to argue that some divinity must—' At that point the impact of Fafhrd's words at last sank in and he said in tones less dreamy, 'Two different sets of girls? Four girls in all? Fafhrd, I think you're overcomplicating things. By Ildritch's Scimitar—'

'There are two sets of girl twins,' Fafhrd overrode him. 'That much is certain though all else be lies. And mark you this, Small Man, your sun-girls mean us ill though seeming to promise good, for how reach immortality and paradise except by dying? How reach Godsland except by perishing? The whiles the sun, pure light or no, is baleful, hot, and deadly. But my moon-girls, seeming to mean us ill, intend good only – being at once as cool and lovely as the moon. She said to me in dream, "Turn back to Death," which sounds dire. But you and I have lived with Death for dozen years and ta'en no lasting hurt – just as she said herself, "for that's the only way to stay alive. Seek Death to 'scape from him!" So steer we north at once! – as she directed. For if we keep on south, deeper and deeper into torrid realm of sun ("Beware the sun," she said!) we'll die for sure, betrayed by your false, lying girls of fire. Recall, her merest touch made your chest smoke. While my girl said, "Suspect all flaming youth and scarlet shes," capping my argument.'

'I don't see that at all,' the Mouser said. 'I *like* the sun myself, I always have. His searching warmth is best of medicines. It's you who love the cold and clammy dark, you Cold Waste savage! My girl was sweet and fiery pink with life, while yours was gloomy-spoken and as livid as a corpse, on your own admission. Take her word for things? Not I. Besides, by Ildritch's Scimitar – to get back to that – the simplest explanation is always the best as well as the most elegant. There are *two* shimmer-girls only, the one I spoke in dream and the one you spoke – not four buzzing about bewilderingly and changing guard at dawn and dusk, to our confusion. The two girls – only two! – look the same in outward seeming – copper by day, silver by night – but inwardly mine is angel, yours deadly valkyr. As was revealed in dream, your surest guide.'

'Now you are quibbling,' Fafhrd said decisively, 'and are making my head spin, to boot, with 'wildering words. This much is clear to me: We now get ready, and ready *Black Racer*, to steer north, as my poor lovely moon-girl strongly advised me more than once.'

'But Fafhrd,' the Mouser protested, 'we tried again and again to steer north yesterday and failed each time. What reason have you to suppose, you big lug—'

Fafhrd cut in with, ' "Trust only in the moon," she said. "Wait for her certain sign." So wait we, for the nonce, and watch. Look at the sea and sky, idiot boy, and be amazed.'

The Mouser was indeed. While they had been disputing, intent only on the cuts and thrusts and parries and ripostes of their word-duel, the smooth surface of the racing Sea of Stars had changed from sleek and slick to mat yet ripply. Great vibrations were speeding across it, making the leopard-boat quiver. The moon-silvered lines of foam were blowing over it less predictably – the hurricane itself, though diminished no whit, was getting flukey, the wind now hot, now cold about their necks. While in the sky were clouds at last, coming in swiftly from northwest and east at once and mounting toward the moon. All of nature seemed to cringe apprehensively, as if in anticipation of some dire event about to hap, heralding war in heaven. The two silvery shimmer-sprights appeared to share this foreboding or presentiment, for they 'gan fly about most erratically, their lace wildly aflow, uttering high cheeping cries and whistlings of alarm against the unnatural silence and at last parting so that one hovered agitatedly to the southeast above the prow, the other near the stern to the northwest.

The rapidly thickening clouds had blotted out most of the stars and mounted almost to the moon. The wind held still, exactly equalling the current's speed. *Black Racer* poised, as if at crest of a gigantic wave. For an instant the sea seemed to freeze. Silence was absolute.

The Mouser looked straight up and uttered from the back of his throat a half choked, high pitched, little scream that froze his comrade's blood. After mastering that shock, Fafhrd looked up too — at just which instant it grew very dark. The hungry clouds had blotted out the moon.

'Why did you so cry out?' he demanded angrily.

The Mouser answered with difficulty, his teeth chattering, 'Just before the clouds closed on her, *the moon moved*.'

'How could you know that, you little fool, when the clouds were moving? — which always makes the moon seem to move.'

'I don't know, but as sure as I stand firm-footed here, I saw it! *The moon began to move*.'

'Well, if the moon be in a waterspout, as you claim, she's subject to all whims of wind and wave. So what's so blood-curdling strange in her moving?' Fafhrd's frantic voice belied the reasonableness of his question.

'I don't know,' the Mouser repeated in a curiously small, strained voice, his teeth still clinking together, '*but I didn't like it*.'

The shimmer-spright at the stern whistled thrice. Her nervously twisting, lacy, silver luminescence stood out plainly in the black night, as did her sister's at the prow.

'It is the sign!' Fafhrd cried hoarsely. 'Ready to go about!' And he threw his full weight against the tiller, driving it steerside and so the rudder loadside, to steer them north. *Black Racer* responded most sluggishly, but did break the grip of current and wind to the extent of swinging north a point or two, no more.

A long flat lightning flash split the sky and showed the gray sea to the horizon's rim, where they now saw *two* giant waterspouts, the one due south, the other rushing in from the west. Thunder crashed like armies or armadas meeting at an iron-sonorous Armageddon.

Then all was wildfire and chaos in the night, great crashing waves, and winds that fought like giants whose heads scraped heaven. Whilst round about the ship the shimmer-sprights fought too, now two, now seeming four of them at least as they circled and dipped at and about each other. The frozen sea was ripped, great rags of it thrown skyward, pits opening that seemed to go down to the black, mucky seabottom unknown to man. Lightning and deafening thunderclaps became almost continuous, revealing all. And through that all, *Black Racer* somehow lived, a chip in chaos, Fafhrd and Mouser performing prodigies of seamanship.

And now from the southwest the second giant waterspout drove in like a moving mountain, sending great swells before it that mightily aided Fafhrd's tillering, driving them north, and north again, and again still north. While from the south the first giant 'spout turned back, or so it seemed, and those two (moonspout and sunspout?) battled.

And then of a sudden it was as if *Black Racer* had struck a wall. Fafhrd and Mouser were thrown to the deck and when they had madly struggled to their feet they found to their utter astonishment that their leopard-boat was floating in calm water, while in the distance lightning and thunder played, almost inaudible and unseen to their numbed ears and half-blinded eyes. There were no stars and moon, only thick night. There were no shimmer-sprights. Their sail was split to ribbons, the faint lightning showed. Under his hand Fafhrd felt a looseness in the tiller, as if the whole steering assemblage had been strained to breaking point and only survived by a miracle.

The Mouser said, 'She lists a little to stern and steerside, don't you think? She's taking water, I trow. Perhaps there's stuff shifted below. Man we the pump. Later we can bend on a new sail.'

So they fell to and for some hours worked together silently as in many old times, nursing the leopard-boat and making all new, by light of two lanterns Fafhrd rigged from the mast that burned purest leviathan-oil, for the storm had entirely gone with its lightnings and the dark clouds pressed down.

As the cloud ceiling did, indeed, over all Nehwon that night (and day on other side). Over the subsequent months and years reports drifted in of the Great Dark, as it came mostly to be called, that had shrouded all Nehwon for a space of hours, so that it was never truly known whether the moon had monstrously traveled halfway round the world that time to battle with the sun and then back again to her appointed spot, or no, though there were scattered but persistent disquieting rumors of such a dread journeying glimpsed through fugitive gaps in the cloud-cover, and even that the sun himself had briefly moved to war with her.

After long while Fafhrd said quietly as they took a break from their labors, 'It's lonely without the shimmer-sprights, don't you think?'

The Mouser said, 'Agreed. I wonder if they'd ever have led us to treasure, or ever so intended? Or would have led us, or one of us, somewhere, either your spright, or mine?'

'I still firmly believe there were four sprights,' Fafhrd said. 'So either pair of twins might have led us somewhere together without parting us.'

'No, there were only two sprights,' the Mouser said, 'and they were set on leading us in very different directions, anti-podean, off from each other.' And when Fafhrd did not reply he said after a time, 'Part of me wishes I'd gone with my fiery girl to find what's like to dwell in paradise bathed by the splendid sun.'

Fafhrd said, 'Part of me wishes I'd followed my melancholy maid to dwell in the pale moon, spending the summer months mayhap in Shadowland.' Then after a silent space, 'But man was not meant for paradise, I trow, whether of warmth or coolth. No, never, never, never, never.'

'Never shares a big bed with once,' the Mouser said.

While they were speaking it had grown light. The clouds had all lifted. The new sail shone. The leviathan lamps burned wanly, their clear beam almost invisible against the paling sky. Then in the farthest distance north the two adventurers made out the loom of a great aurochs couchant, unmistakable sign of the southernmost headland of the Eastern Lands.

'We've weathered Lankhmar continent in a single day and night,' the Mouser said.

A breeze sprang up from the south, stirring the still air. They set course north up the long Sea of the East.

VII: THE FROST MONSTREME

'I am tired, Gray Mouser, of these little brushes with Death,' Fafhrd the Northerner said, lifting his dinted, livid goblet and taking a measured sup of sweet ferment of grape laced with bitter brandy.

'Want a big one?' his comrade scoffed, drinking likewise.

Fafhrd considered that, while his gaze traveled slowly yet without stop all the way round the tavern, whose sign was a tarnished and serpentine silver fish. 'Perhaps,' he said.

'It's a dull night,' the other agreed.

True indeed, the interior of the Silver Eel presented a tavern visage as leaden-hued as its wine cups. The hour was halfway between midnight and dawn, the light dim without being murky, the air dank yet not chill, the other drinkers like moody statues, the faces of the barkeep and his bully and servers paralyzed in expressions of petulant discontent, as if Time herself had stopped.

Outside, the city of Lankhmar was silent as a necropolis, while beyond that the world of Nehwon had been at peace – unwar, rather – for a full year. Even the Mingols of the vasty Steppes weren't raiding south on their small, tough horses.

Yet the effect of all this was not calm, but an unfocused uneasiness, a restlessness that had not yet resulted in the least movement, as if it were the prelude to an excruciating flash of cold lightning transfixing every tiniest detail of life.

This atmosphere affected the feelings and thoughts of the tall, brown-tunicked barbarian and his short, gray-clad friend.

'Dull indeed,' Fafhrd said. 'I long for some grand emprise!'

'Those are the dreams of untutored youth. Is that why you've shaved your beard? – to match your dreams? Both bare-faced lies!' the Mouser asked, and answered.

'Why have you let yours grow these three days?' Fafhrd countered.

'I am but resting the skin of my face for a full tweaking of its hairs. And you've lost weight. A wistfully youthful fever?'

'Not that, or any ill or care. Of late you're lighter, too. We are changing the luxuriant musculature of young manhood for a suppler, hardier, more enduring structure suited to great mid-life trials and venturings.'

'We've had enough of those,' the Mouser asserted. 'Thrice around Nehwon at the least.'

Fafhrd shook his head morosely. 'We've never really lived. We've not owned land. We've not led men.'

'Fafhrd, you're gloomy-drunk!' the Mouser chortled. 'Would you be a farmer? Have you forgot a captain is the prisoner of his command? Here, drink yourself sober, or at least glad.'

The Northerner let his cup be refilled from two jars, but did not change his mood. Staring unhappily, he continued, 'We've neither homes nor wives.'

'Fafhrd, you need a wench!'

'Who spoke of wenches?' the other protested. 'I mean women. I had brave Kreeshkra, but she's gone back to her beloved Ghouls. While your pet Reetha prefers the hairless land of Eevamarensee.'

The Mouser interjected *sotto voce*, 'I also had imperious, insolent Hisvet, and you her brave, dramatic queen-slave Frix.'

Fafhrd went on, 'Once, long ago, there were Friska and Ivivis, but they were Quarmall's slaves and then became free women at Tovilysis. Before them were Keyaira, Hirriwi, but they were princesses, invisibles, loves of one long, long night, daughters of dread Oomforafor and sib of murderous Faroomfar. Long before all of those, in Land of Youth, there were fair Ivrian and slender Vlana. But they were girls, those lovely in-betweens (or actresses, those mysteries), and now they dwell with Death in Shadowland. So I'm but half a man. I need a *mate*. And so do you, perchance.'

'Fafhrd, you're mad! You prate of world-spanning wild

adventures and then babble of what would make them impossible: wife, home, henchmen, duties. One dull night without girl or fight, and your brains go soft. Repeat, you're mad.'

Fafhrd reinspected the tavern, and its stodgy inmates. 'It stays dull, doesn't it,' he remarked, 'as if not one nostril had twitched or ear wiggled since I last looked. And yet it is a calm I do not trust. I feel an icy chill. Mouser—'

That one was looking past him. With little sound, or none at all, two slender persons had just entered the Silver Eel and paused appraisingly inside the lead-weighted iron-woven curtains that kept out fog and could turn sword thrusts. The one was tall and rangy as a man, blue-eyed, thin-cheeked, wide-mouthed, clad in jerkin and trousers of blue and long cloak of gray. The other was wiry and supple-seeming as a cat, green-eyed, compact of feature, short thick lips compressed, clothed similarly save the hues were rust red and brown. They were neither young nor yet near middle age. Their smooth unridged brows, tranquil eyes, evenly curving jaws, and long cheek-molding hair – here silvery yellow, there black shot with darkest brown (in turn gold-shotten, or were those golden wires braided in?) – proclaimed them feminine.

That last attribute broke the congealed midnight trances of the assembled dullards, a half dozen of whom converged on the newcomers, calling low invitations and trailing throaty laughs. The two moved forward as if to hasten the encounter, with gaze unwaveringly ahead.

And then – without an instant's pause or any collision, except someone recoiled slightly as if his instep had been trod on and someone else gasped faintly as if his short ribs had encountered a firm elbow – the two were past the six. It was as if they had simply walked through them, as a man would walk through smoke with no more fuss than the wrinkling of a nostril. Behind them, the ignored smoke fumed and wove a bit.

Now there were in their way the Gray Mouser and Fafhrd, who had both risen and whose hands still indicated the hilts of their scabbarded swords without touching them.

'Ladies—' the Mouser began.

'Will you take wine—?' Fafhrd continued.

65

'Strengthened against night's chill,' the Mouser concluded, sketching a bow, while Fafhrd courteously indicated the four-chaired table from which they'd just risen.

The slender women halted and surveyed them without haste. 'We might—' the smaller purred.

'Provided you let Rime Isle pay for the drinks,' the taller concluded in tones bright and swift as running snow water.

At the words 'Rime Isle,' the faces of the two men grew thoughtful and wondering, as if in another universe someone had said Atlantis or El Dorado or Ultima Thule. Nevertheless they nodded agreement and drew back chairs for the women.

'Rime Isle,' Fafhrd repeated conjuringly, as the Mouser did the honors with cups and jars. 'As a child in the Cold Waste and later in my adolescent piratings, I've heard it and Salthaven City whispered of. Legend says the Claws point at it – those thin, stony peninsulas that tip Nehwonland's last northwest corner.'

'For once legend speaks true,' the electrum-haired woman in blue and gray said softly yet crisply. 'Rime Isle exists today. Salthaven, too.'

'Come,' said the Mouser with a smile, ceremoniously handing her her cup, 'it's said Rime Isle's no more real than Simorgya.'

'And is Simorgya unreal?' she asked, accepting it.

'No,' he admitted with a somewhat startled, reminiscent look. 'I once watched it from a very small ship when it was briefly risen from the deeps of the Outer Sea. My more venturesome friend' – he nodded towards Fafhrd – 'trod its wet shale for a short space to see some madmen dance with devilfish which had the aspect of black fur cloaks awrithe.'

'North of Simorgya, westward from the Claws,' briskly said the red- and brown-clad woman with black hair shot with glistening dark bronze and gold. Her right hand holding steady in the air her brimming wine cup where she'd just received it, she dipped her left beneath the table and swiftly slapped it down on the arabesquery of circle-stained oak, then lifted it abruptly to reveal four small rounds gleaming pale as moons. 'You agreed Rime Isle would pay.'

With nods abstracted yet polite, the Mouser and Fafhrd each took up one of the coins and closely studied it.

'By the teats of Titchubi,' the former breathed, 'this is no *sou marque*, black dog, no *chien noir*.'

'Rime Isle silver?' Fafhrd asked softly, lifting his gaze, eyebrows a-rise, from the face of the coin toward that of the taller woman.

Her gaze met his squarely. There was the hint of a smile at the ends of her long lips, back in her cheeks. She said sincerely yet banteringly, 'Which never tarnishes.'

He said, 'The obverse shows a vast sea monster menacing out of the depths.'

She said, 'Only a great whale blowing after a deep sound.'

The Mouser said to the other woman, 'Whilst the reverse depicts a ship-shaped, league-long square rock rising from miles-long swells.'

She said, 'Only an iceberg hardly half that size.'

Fafhrd said, 'Well, drink we what this bright, alien coinage has bought. I am Fafhrd, the Gray Mouser he.'

The tall woman said, 'And I Afreyt, my comrade Cif.'

After deep draughts, they put down their cups, Afreyt with a sharp double tap of pewter on oak. 'And now to business,' she said cliptly, with the faintest of frowns at Fafhrd (it was arguable if there was any frown at all) as he reached for the wine jars. 'We speak with the voice of Rime Isle—'

'And dispurse her golden monies,' Cif added, her green eyes glinting with yellow flecks. Then, flatly, 'Rime Isle is straitly menaced.'

Her voice going low, Afreyt asked, 'Hast ever heard of the Sea Mingols?' and, when Fafhrd nodded, shifted her gaze to the Mouser, saying, 'Most Southrons misdoubt their sheer existence, deeming every Mingol a lubber when off his horse, whether on land or sea.'

'Not I,' he answered. 'I've sailed with Mingol crew. There's one, now old, named Ourph—'

'And I've met Mingol pirates,' Fafhrd said. 'Their ships are few, each dire. Arrow-toothed water rats — Sea Mingols, as you say.'

'That's good,' Cif told them both. 'Then you'll more like believe me when I tell you that in response to the eldritch prophecy, "Who seizes Nehwon's crown, shall win her all—"'

'For crown, read north polar coasts,' Afreyt interjected.

'And supremely abetted by the Wizard of Ice, Khahkht, whose very name's a frozen cough—'

'Perchance the evilest being ever to exist—' Afreyt supplemented, her eyes a sapphire moon shining frosty through two narrowed, crosswise window slits.

'The Mingols have ta'en ship to harry Nehwon's northmost coasts in two great fleets, one following the sun, the other – the Widdershin Mongols – going against it—'

'For a few dire ships, believe armadas,' Afreyt put in, still gazing chiefly at Fafhrd (just as Cif favored the Mouser), and then took up the main tale with, 'Till Sunwise and Widdershins meet at Rime Isle, overwhelm her, and fan out south to rape the world!'

'A dismal prospect,' Fafhrd commented, setting down the brandy jar with which he'd laced the wine he'd poured for all.

'At least an overlively one,' the Mouser chimed in. 'Mingols are tireless raptors.'

Cif leaned forward, chin up. Her green eyes flamed. 'So Rime Isle is the chosen battleground. Chosen by Fate, by cold Khahkht, and the Gods. The place to stop the Steppe horde turned sea raiders.'

Without moving, Afreyt grew taller in her chair, her blue gaze flashing back and forth between Fafhrd and his comrade, 'So Rime Isle arms, and musters men, and hires mercenaries. The last's my work and Cif's. We need two heroes, each to find twelve men like himself and bring them to Rime Isle in the space of three short moons. You are the twain!'

'You mean there's any other one man in Nehwon like me – let alone a dozen?' the Mouser asked incredulously.

'It's an expensive task, at very least,' Fafhrd said judiciously.

Her biceps swelling slightly under the close-fitting rust-red cloth, Cif brought up from beneath the table two tight-packed pouches as big as oranges and set one down before each man.

The small thuds and swiftly damped chinkings were most satisfying sounds.

'Here are your funds!'

The Mouser's eyes widened, though he did not yet touch his globular sack. 'Rime Isle must need heroes sorely. And heroines? – if I might make suggestion.'

'That has been taken care of,' Cif said firmly.

Fafhrd's middle finger feather-brushed his bag and came away.

Afreyt said, 'Drink we.'

As the goblets lifted, there came from all around a tiny tinkling as of faery bells; a minute draft, icy chill, stole past from the door; and the air itself grew very faintly translucent, very slightly softening and pearling all things seen – all of which portents grew light-swift by incredible tiger leaps into a stunning, sense-raping clangor of bells big as temple domes and thick as battlements, an ear-splittingly roaring and whining polar wind that robbed away all heat in a trice and blew out flat the iron-and-lead-weighted door drapes and sent the inhabitants of the Silver Eel sailing and tumbling, and an ice fog thick as milk, through which Cif could be heard to cry, ' 'Tis icy breath of Khahkht!' and Afreyt, 'It's tracked us down!' before pandemonium drowned out all else.

Fafhrd and the Mouser each desperately gripped money bag with one hand and with the other, table, glad it was bolted down to stop its use in brawls.

The gale and the tumult died and the fog faded, not quite as swiftly as it all had come. They unclenched their hands, wiped ice crystals from brows and eyes, lit lamps, and looked around.

The place was a bloodless shambles, silent too as death until the frightened moaning began, the cries of pain and wonder. They scanned the long room, first from their tables, then afoot. Their slender tablemates were not among the slowly recovering victims.

The Mouser intoned, somewhat airily, 'We're such folk here as we've been searching for? Or have we drunk some drug that—'

He broke off, Fafhrd had taken up his fat little moneybag and headed for the door. 'Where away?' Mouser called.

Fafhrd stopped and turned. He called back unsmiling, 'North of the Trollsteps, to hire my twelve berserks. Doubtless you'll find your dozen swordsmen-thieves in warmer clime. In three moons less three days, we rendezvous at sea midway between Simorgya and Rime Isle. Till then, fare well.'

The Mouser watched him out, shrugged, rummaged up a cup and the brandy jar overset but unbroken, bedewed by the magic blast. The liquor that hadn't spilled made a gratifyingly large slug. He fingered his moneybag a moment, then teased open the hard knot in its thong. Inside, the leather had a faint amber glow. 'A golden orange indeed,' he said happily, unmindful of the forms mewling and crawling and otherwise crippling around him, and plucked out one of the packed yellow coins. Reverse, a smoking volcano, possibly snow-clad; obverse, a great cliff rising from the sea and looking not quite like ice or any ordinary rock. What drollery! He gazed again at the iron-curtained doorway. What a huge fool, he thought, to take seriously a quite impossible task set by vanished females most likely dead or at best sorceled beyond reach! Or to make rendezvous at distant date in uncharted ocean betwixt a sunken land and a fabulous one – Fafhrd's geography was even more hopeful than his usual highly imaginative wont.

And just think what rare delights – nay, what whole sets of ecstasies and blisses – this much gold would buy. How fortunate that metal was mindless slave of the man who held it!

He returned the coin, thonged shut the gold and its glow, stood up decisively, then looked back at the table top, near an edge of which the four silver coins still lay cozily flat.

While he regarded them, the grubby hand of a fat server who'd been wedged under the table by the indoor blizzard reached up and whisked them down.

With another shrug, the Mouser ambled rather grandly toward the door, whistling between his teeth a Mingol march.

Inside a sphere half again as tall as a man, a skinny old being was busy. On the interior of the sphere was depicted a world map of Nehwon, the seas in blackest blues, the lands in blackest greens and browns, yet all darkly agleam like blued, greened, and browned iron, creating the illusion that the sphere was a giant bubble rising forever through infinite murky, oily waters – as some Lankhmar philosophers assert is veriest truth about Nehwon-world itself. South of the Eastern Lands in the Great Equatorial Ocean there was even depicted a ring-shaped water wall a span across and three fingers high, such as those same philosophers say hides the sun from the half of Nehwon it is floating across, though no blinding solar disk now lay in the bottom of the liquid crater, but only a pale glow sufficient to light the sphere's interior.

Where they were not hid by a loose, light robe, the old being's four long, ever-active limbs were covered by short, stiff black hairs either grizzled or filmed with ice, while Its narrow face was nasty as a spider's. Now It lifted Its leathery lips and nervously questing long-nailed fingers toward an area of the map where a tiny, gleaming black blotch south of blue and amidst brown signified Lankhmar City on the southron coast of the Inner Sea. Was it Its breath that showed frosty, or did Its will conjure up the white wisp that streaked across the black blotch? Whichever, the vapor vanished.

It muttered high-pitched in Mingolish, 'They're gone, the bitches. Khahkht sees each fly die, and sends Its shriveling breath where'er It will. Mingols harry, world unwary. Harlots fumble, heroes stumble. And now 'tis time, 'tis time, 'tis time to gin to build the frost monstreme.'

It opened a circular trap door in the South Polar Regions and lowered Itself out on a thin line.

Three days short of three moons later, the Mouser was thoroughly disgusted, bone weary, and very cold. His feet and toes were very, very cold inside fine, fur-lined boots, which slowly rose and fell under his soles as the frosty deck lifted and sank with the long, low swell. He stood by the short mainmast, from the long yard of which (longer than the boom) the loosely furled mainsail hung in frozen festoons. Beyond dimly discerned low prow and stern and mainyard top, vision was utterly blotted out by a fog of tiniest ice crystals, like cirrus cloud come down from Stardock heights, through which the light of an unseen gibbous moon, still almost full swollen, seeped out dark pearl gray. The windlessness and general stillness, contrary to all experience, seemed to make the cold bite deeper.

Yet the silence was not absolute. There was the faint wash and drip – perhaps even tiniest crackling of thinnest ice film – as the hull yielded to the swell. There were the resultant small creakings of the timbers and rigging of *Flotsam*. And beneath or beyond these, still fainter sounds lurked in the fringes of the inaudible. A part of the Mouser's mind that worked without being paid attention strained ceaselessly to hear those last. He was of no mind to be surprised by a Mingol flotilla, or single craft even. *Flotsam* was transport, not warship, he repeatedly warned himself. Very strange some of those last real or fancied sounds were that came out of the frigid fog – shatterings of massive ice leagues away, the thump and splash of mighty oars even farther off, distant doleful shriekings, still more distant deep minatory growlings, and a laughter as of fiends beyond the rim of Nehwon. He thought of the invisible fliers that had troubled the snowy air halfway up Stardock when Fafhrd and he had climbed her, Nehwon's loftiest peak.

The cold snapped that thought chain. The Mouser longed to stamp his feet, flail his hands cross-front against his sides, or – best! – warm himself with a great burst of anger, but he perversely held off, perhaps so ultimate relief would be greater, and set to analyze his disgusted weariness.

First off, there'd been the work of finding, winning, and mastering twelve fighter-thieves – a rare breed to begin with. And training 'em! – half of 'em had to be taught the art of the sling, and two (Mog help him!) swordsmanship. And the choosing of the likeliest two for corporals – Pshawri and Mikkidu, who were now sleeping snug below with their double squad, damn their hides!

Concurrent with that, there'd been the searching out of Old Ourph and gathering of his Mingol crew of four. A calculated risk, that. Would Mingol mariners fight fiercely 'gainst their own in the pinch? Mingols were ever deemed treacherous. Yet 'twas always good to have some of the enemy on your side, the better to understand 'em. And from them he might even get wider insight into the motives behind the present Mingol excursions naval.

Concurrent with *that*, the selection, hire, patching, and provisioning of *Flotsam* for its voyage.

And then the study needed! Beginning with poring over ancient charts filched from the library of the Lankhmar Starsmen and Navigators Guild, the refreshing of his knowledge of wind, waves, and celestial bodies. And the responsibility!! for no fewer than seventeen men, with no Fafhrd to share it and spell him while he slept – to lick 'em into shape, doctor their scurvies, probe under water for 'em with boathook when they tumbled overboard (he'd almost lost thumb-footed Mikkidu that way the first day out), keep 'em in good spirits but in their places too, discipline 'em as required. (Come to think of it, that last was sometimes delight as well as duty. How quaintly Pshawri squealed when shrewdly thwacked with Cat's-Claw's scabbard! – and soon would again, by Mog!)

Lastly, the near moon-long perilous voyage itself!!! Northwest from Lankhmar across the Inner Sea. Through a treacherous gap in the Curtain Wall (where Fafhrd had once sought sequined sea-queens) into the Outer Sea. Then a swift, broad reach north with the wind on their load side until they sighted the black ramparts of No-Ombrulsk, which shared the latitude of sunken Simorgya. There he had nosed *Flotsam* due west, away from all land and almost into the teeth of the west wind, which blew a little on their steer side. After four days of that weary, close reach, they had arrived at the undistinguished patch of troubled ocean that marked Simorgya's grave, according to the independent cipherings of the Mouser and Ourph, the one working from his stolen charts, the other counting knots in grimy Mingol calculating cords. Then a swift two-day broad reach north again, while air and sea grew rapidly colder, until by their reckonings they were half-journey to the latitude of the Claws. And now two days of dismal beating about in one place await for Fafhrd, with the cold increasing steadily until, this midnight, clear skies had given way to the ice fog in which *Flotsam* lay becalmed. Two days in which to wonder if Fafhrd would manage to find this spot, or even come at all. Two days in which to get bored with and maddened by his scared, rebellious crew and dozen soldier-thieves – all snoring warm below, Mog flog 'em! Two days to wonder *why* in Mog's name he'd spent all but four of his Rime Isle doubloons on this insane voyage, on *work* for himself, instead of on wine and women, rare books and art objects, in short on sweet bread and circuses for himself alone.

And finally, superlastly, the suspicion growing toward conviction that Fafhrd had never started out from Lankhmar at all!!!! that he'd strode so nobly, so carkingly high-minded, out of the Silver Eel with his bag of gold – and instantly begun to spend it on those very same delights which the Mouser (inspired by Fafhrd's seeming-good example) had denied himself.

In a pinnacle of exasperation, a mountaintop of rage, the Mouser seized the padded striker from its mainmast hook and smote the ship's gong a blow mighty enough to shatter the gelid bronze. In fact, he was mildly surprised that *Flotsam*'s frosty deck wasn't showered with sharp-edged frozen shards of brown metal. Whereupon he smote it again and again and again, so that the gong swung like a signboard in a hurricane, and meanwhile he jumped up and down, adding to the general alarm the resounding thuds of his feet (and haply warming them).

The forward hatch was flung back from below and Pshawri shot up out of it like a jack-in-the-box, to scurry to the Mouser and stand before him mad-eyed. The corporal major was followed in a pouring rush by Mikkidu and the rest of the two squads, most of them half-naked. After them – and far more leisurely – came Gavs and the other Mingol crewman off watch, thonging their black hoods closely under their yellow chins, while Ourph came ghosting up behind his captain, though the two other Mingols properly kept to their stations at tiller and prow. The Mouser was vastly surprised. So his scabbard thwackings had actually done some good!

Measuredly beating the padded striker head in the cupped

palm of his right hand, the Mouser observed, 'Well, my small stealers' — (all of the thieves were in fact at least a finger-breadth shorter than the Gray One) — 'it appears you've missed a beating, *barely*,' his face in a hideous grin as he closely surveyed the large areas of bare flesh exposed to the icy air.

He went on, 'But now we must keep you warm — a sailorly necessity in this clime, for which each of you is responsible on pain of flogging, I'll have you know.' His grin became more hideous still. 'To evade night ramming attack, *man the sweeps!*'

The ragged dozen poured past him to snatch up the long, slender oars from their rack between mainmast and mizzen, and drop their looms into the ten proper locks, and stand facing prow at the ready, feet braced against sweeping studs, oar handles against chests, blades poised overside in the fog. Pshawri's squad was stationed steer-side, Mikkidu's load-side, while major and minor corporals supervised fore and aft.

After a quick glance at Pshawri, to assure himself every man was at his station, the Mouser cried, 'Flotsamers! One, two, three — sweep!' and tapped the gong, which he steadied and damped by its edge gripped in his right hand. The ten sweeps-men dipped blades into the unseen salt water and thrust heavily forward against the tholes.

'Recover!' the Mouser growled slowly, then gave the gong another tap. The ship began to move forward and the wash of the swell became tiny slaps against the hull.

'And now keep to it, you clownish, ill-clad cutpurses!' he cried. 'Master Mikkidu! Relieve me at the gong! Sir Pshawri, keep 'em sweepin' evener!' And as he handed the striker to the gasping corporal minor, he dipped his lips toward the cryptic wrinkled face of Ourph and whispered, 'Send Trenchi and Gib below to fetch 'em their warm duds on deck.'

Then he allowed himself a sigh, generally pleased yet perversely dissatisfied because Pshawri hadn't given him excuse to thwack him. Well, one couldn't have everything. Odd to think of a Lankhmar second-story man and Thieves Guild malcontent turned promising soldier-sailor. Yet natural enough – there wasn't that much difference between climbing walls and rigging.

Feeling warmer now, he thought more kindly of Fafhrd. Truly, the Northerner had not yet missed rendezvous; it was *Flotsam*, rather, that'd been early. Now was the time appointed. His face grew somber as he permitted himself the coldly realistic thought (of the sort no one likes) that it would indeed be miracle if he and Fafhrd did find each other in this watery waste, not to mention the icy fog. Still, Fafhrd was resourceful.

The ship grew silent again except for the brush and drip of the sweeps, the clink of the gong, and the small commotions as Pshawri briefly relieved oarsmen hurrying into the clothes the Mingols had fetched. The Mouser turned his attention to the part of his mind that kept watch on the fog's hiddenmost sounds. Almost at once he turned questioningly toward Old Ourph. The dwarfish Mingol flapped his arms slowly up and down. Straining his ears, the Mouser nodded. Then the beat of approaching wings became generally audible. Something struck the icy rigging overhead and a white shape hurtled down. The Mouser threw up his right arm to fend it off and felt his wrist and forearm strongly gripped by something that heaved and twisted. After a moment of breathless fear, in which his left hand snatched at his dirk, he reached it out instead and touched the horny talons tight as gyves around his wrist, and found rolled around a scaly leg a small parchment, the threads of which he cut with sharpened thumbnail. Whereupon the large white hawk left his wrist and perched on the short, round rod from which the ship's gong hung.

Then by flame of fat candle a Mingol crewman fetched after lighting it from the firebox, the Mouser read in Fafhrd's huge script writ very small:

Ahoy, Little Man! – for 'tis unlike there's vessel closer in this wavy wilderness. Burn a red flare and I'll be there.

F.

And then in blacker but sloppier letters suggesting hurried afterthought:

Let's feign mutual attack when we meet, to train our crews. Agreed!

The white flame, burning steady and bright in the still air, showed the Mouser's delighted grin and also the added expression of incredulous outrage as he read the postscript. Northerners as a breed were battle-mad, and Fafhrd the feyest.

'Gib, get quill and squid ink,' he commanded. 'Sir Pshawri, take slow-fire and a red flare to the mainmast top and burn it there. Yarely! But if you fire *Flotsam*, I'll nail you to the burning deck!'

Some moments later, as the Mouser-enlisted small cat-burglar steadily mounted the rigging, though additionally encumbered by a boathook, his captain reversed the small parchment, spread it flat against the mast, and neatly inscribed on its back by light of candle, which Gib held along with the inkhorn:

Madman Most Welcome! – I'll burn them one each bell. I do *not* agree. *My* crew is trained already.

                                                                M.

He shook the note to dry it, then gingerly wrapped it closely around the glaring hawk's leg, just above talons and threaded it tight. As his fingers came away, the bird bated with a shriek and winged off into the fog without command. Fafhrd had at least his avian messengers well trained.

A red glare, surprisingly bright, sprang forth from the fog at the masthead and rose mysteriously a full ten cubits above the top. Then the Mouser saw that, for safety's sake, his own and his ship's, the little corporal major had fixed the flare to the boathook's end and thrust it aloft, thereby also increasing the distance at which it could be seen – by at least a Lankhmar league, the Mouser hurriedly calculated. A sound thought, he had to admit, almost a brilliancy. He had Mikkidu reverse *Flotsam*'s course for practice, the steerside sweepsmen pulling water to swing the ship their way. He went to the prow to assure himself that the heavily muffled Mingol there was steadily scanning the fog ahead, next he returned to the stern, where Ourph stood by his tillerman, both equally thick-cloaked against the cold.

Then, as the red flare glowed on and the relative quiet of steady sweeping returned, the Mouser's ears unwilled resumed their work of searching the fog for strange sounds, and he said softly to Ourph without looking at him, 'Tell me now, Old One, what you really think about your restless nomad brotheren and why they've ta'en to ship instead of horse.'

'They rush like lemmings, seeking death . . . for others,' the ancient croaked reflectively. 'Gallop the waves instead of flinty steppes. To strike down cities is their chiefest urge, whether by land or sea. Perhaps they flee the People of the Ax.'

'I've heard of those,' the Mouser responded doubtfully. 'Think you they'd league with Stardock's viewless fliers, who ride the icy airs above the world?'

'I do not know. They'll follow their clan wizards anywhere.'

The red flare died. Pshawri came down rather jauntily from the top and reported to his dread captain, who dismissed him with a glare which was unexpectedly terminated by a broad wink and the command to burn another flare at the next bell, or demihour. Then turning once more to Ourph, the Mouser spoke low: 'Talking of wizards, do you know of Khahkht?'

The ancient let five heartbeats go by, then croaked, 'Khahkht is Khahkht. It is no tribal sorcerer, 'tis sure. It dwells in farthest north within a dome – some say a floating globe – of blackest ice, from whence It watches the least deeds of men, devising evil every chance It gets, as when the stars are right – better say wrong – and all the Gods asleep. Mingols dread Khahkht and yet . . . whene'er they reach a grand climacteric they turn to It, beseech It ride ahead before their greatest, bloodiest centaurings. Ice is Its favored quarter, ice Its tool, and icy breath Its surest sign save blink.'

'Blink?' the Mouser asked uneasily.

'Sunlight or moonlight shining back from ice,' the Mingol replied. 'Ice blink.'

A soft white flash paled for an instant the dark, pearly fog, and through it the Mouser heard the sound of oars – mightier strokes than those of *Flotsam*'s sweeps and set in a more ponderous rhythm, yet oars or sweeps indubitably, and swiftly growing louder. The Mouser's face grew gladsome. He peered about uncertainly. Ourph's pointing finger stabbed dead ahead. The Mouser nodded, and pitching his voice trumpet-shrill to carry, he hailed forward, 'Fafhrd! Ahoy!'

There was a brief silence, broken only by the beat of *Flotsam*'s sweeps and of the oncoming oars, and then there came out of the fog the heart-quickening though still eerie cry, 'Ahoy, small man! Mouser, well met in wildering waters! And now – on guard!'

The Mouser's glad grin grew frantic. Did Fafhrd seriously intend to carry out *in fog* his fey suggestion of a feigned ships-battle? He looked with a wild questioning at Ourph, who shrugged hugely for one so small.

A brighter white blink momentarily lightened the fog ahead. Without pausing an instant for thought, the Mouser shouted his commands. 'Load-side sweeps! pull water! Yarely! Steerside, push hard!' And unmindful of the Mingol manning it, he threw himself at the tiller and drove it steer-side so that *Flotsam*'s rudder would strengthen the turning power of the load-side sweeps.

It was well he acted as swiftly as he did. From out the fog ahead thrust a low, thick, sharp-tipped, glittering shaft that would otherwise have rammed *Flotsam*'s bow and split her twain. As it was, the ram grazed *Flotsam*'s side with shuddering rasp as the small ship veered abruptly load-side in response to the desperate sweeping of its soldier-thieves.

And now, following its ram, the white, sharp prow of Fafhrd's ship parted the gleam-shot fog. Almost incredibly lofty that prow was, high as a house and betokening ship as huge, so that *Flotsam*'s men had to crane necks up at it and even the Mouser gasped in fear and wonder. Fortunately it was yards to steerward as *Flotsam* continued to veer loadward, or else the smaller ship had been battered in.

Out of the fog dead ahead there appeared a flatness traveling sideways. A yard above the deck, it struck the mast, which might have snapped except that the flatness broke off first and there dropped with a clash at the Mouser's feet something which further widened his eyes: the great ice-crusted blade and some of the loom of an oar twice the size of *Flotsam*'s sweeps, and looking for all the world like a dead giant's fingernail.

The next huge oar missed the mast, but struck Pshawri a glancing blow and sent him sprawling. The rest missed *Flotsam* by widening margins. From the vast and towering, white, glittering bulk already vanishing in the fog there came a mighty cry: 'Oh coward! To turn aside from battle challenge! Oh, crafty coward! But go on guard again! I'll get you yet, small one, howe'er you dodge!'

Those huge, mad words were followed by an equally insane laughter. It was the sort of laughter the Mouser had heard before from Fafhrd in perilous battle plights, now madder than ever, fiendish even, but it was loud as if there were a dozen Fafhrds voicing it in unison. Had he trained his berserks to echo him?

A clawlike hand gripped the Mouser's elbow hard. Then Ourph was pointing at the big, broken oar end on the deck. 'It's nought but ice.' The old Mingol's voice resonated with superstitious awe. 'Ice forged in Khahkht's chill smithy.' He let go Mouser and, swiftly stooping, raised the thing in black-mitted hands widely spaced, as one might a wounded deadly serpent, and of a sudden hurled it overboard.

Beyond him, Mikkidu had lifted Pshawri's shoulders and bloodied head from the deck. But now he was peering up at his captain over his still, senseless comrade. In his wild eyes was a desperate questioning.

The Mouser hardened his face. 'Sweep on, you sluggards,' he commanded measuredly. 'Push strongly. Mikkidu, let crewmen see to Pshawri, you chink gong for the sweeps. Swiftest beat! Ourph, arm your crew. Send down for arrows and your bows of horn – and for my soldiers their slings and ammunition. Leaden ball, not rock. Gavs, keep close watch astern, Trenchi at prow. Yarely all!'

The Gray One looked grimly dangerous and was thinking

thoughts he hated. A thousand years ago in the Silver Eel, Fafhrd had announced he'd hire twelve berserks, madmen in battle. But had his dear friend, now demon-possessed, guessed then just how mad his dozen dements would be, and that their craziness would be catching? and infect himself?

Above the ice fog, the stars glittered like frost candles, dimmed only by the competing light of the gibbous moon low in the southwest, where in the distance the front of an approaching gale was rolling up the thick carpet of ice crystals floating in air.

Not far above the pearly white surface, which stretched to all horizons save the southwest, the messenger hawk the Mouser had released was winging east. As far as eye could see, no other living thing shared its vast-arched loneliness, yet the bird suddenly veered as if attacked, then frantically beat its wings and came to a twisting stop in mid-air, as if it had been seized and held helpless. Only there was nothing to be seen sharing the clear air with the thrashing bird.

The scrap of parchment around its leg unrolled like magic, lay flat in the air for a space, then rolled itself around the scaly leg again. The white hawk shot off desperately to the east, zigzagging as if to dodge pursuit and flying very close to the white floor, as if ready at any moment to dive into it.

A voice came out of the empty air at the point where the bird had been released, soliloquizing, 'There's profit enow and more in this league of Oomforafor of Stardock and the Khahkht of the Black Ice, if my ruse works – and it will! Dear devilish sisters, weep! – your lovers who defiled you are dead men already, though they still breathe and walk awhile. Delayed revenge savored and denied is sweeter than swift. And sweetest of all when the ones you hate love, but are forced to kill, each other. For if my notes effect not that mebliss, my name's not Faroomfar! And now, wing sound-swift! my flat steed of air, my viewless magic rug.'

The strange, low fog stayed thick and bitter cold, but Fafhrd's garb of reversed snow-fawn fur was snug. Gauntleted hand on the low figurehead – a hissing snow serpent – he gazed back with satisfaction from *Sea Hawk*'s prow at his oarsmen, still rowing as strongly as when he'd first commanded them on sighting Mouser's red flare from the masthead. They were staunch lads, when kept busy and battered as needed. Nine of them tall as he, and three taller – his corporals Skullick and Mannimark and sergeant Skor, the last two hid by the fog where Skor clinked time at the stern. Each petty officer immediately commanded a squad of three men.

And *Sea Hawk* was a staunch sailing galley! – a little longer and narrower of beam and with much taller mast, rigged fore and aft, than the Gray Mouser's ship (though Fafhrd could not know that, never having seen *Flotsam*).

Yet he frowned slightly. Pelly should be back by now, provided Mouser had sent a return message, and the little gray man never lost a chance to talk, whether by tongue or pen. It was time he visited the top anyhow – the Mouser might burn another flare, and Skullick wake-dream on watch. But as he neared the mast, a seven-foot ghost loomed up – a ghost in turned gray otter's fur.

'How now, Skullick?' Fafhrd rasped, looking up their half span's difference in height. 'Why have you left your station? Speak swiftly, scum!' And without other warning or preparation, he struck his corporal major a short-traveling jolt in the midriff that jarred him back a step and (rather illogically) robbed him of most of the breath he had to speak with.

'It's cold . . . as witch's womb . . . up there,' Skullick gasped with pain and difficulty. 'And my relief's . . . o'erdue.'

'From now on you'll wait on station for your relief until Hell freezes over, and haply you too. But you're relieved.' And Fafhrd struck him again in the same crucial spot. 'Now water the rowers, four measures of water to one of usquebaugh – and if you take more than two gulps of the last, I'll surely know!'

He turned away abruptly, reached the mast in two strides, and climbed it rhythmically by the pins of its bronze collars, past the mainyard, to which the big sail was snugly furled, past the peak, until his gloved hands gripped the short, horizontal bar of the crow's-perch. As he drew himself up by them, it was a wonder how the fog gave way without gradation to starceilinged air, as though a fine film, impalpable yet tough, confined the ice motes, held them down. When he stood on the bar and straightened himself, he was waist-deep in fog so thick he could barely see his feet. He and the mast top were scudding through a pearly sea, strongly propelled by the invisible rowers below. The stars told him *Sea Hawk* was still headed due west. His sense of direction had worked truly in the fog below. Good!

Also, the feckless Skullick had spoken true. It was cold indeed as a she-demon's privies, yet wonderfully bracing. He noted the new wind sweeping up the fog in the southwest, and north of that the spot where he'd picked up the Mouser's flare on the horizon's brim. The deformed fat moon was there now, almost touching it, yet still most bright. If the Mouser burned another flare, it ought to be higher, because Fafhrd's rowing should be bringing the ships together. He searched the west closely to make sure another red spark wasn't being drowned by Nehwon's strong moonlight.

He saw a black speck against the lopsided, bright pearl orb. As he watched, it rapidly increase in size, grew wings, and with a white beat of them landed with jolting twin-talon grip on Fafhrd's gauntleted wrist.

'You're ruffled, Pelly. Who has troubled you?' he asked as he snapped threads and unrolled from leg the parchment scrap. He recognized the start of his own note, flipped it over, and by the flat moonlight read the Mouser's.

Madman Most Welcome! – I'll burn them one each bell. I do *not* agree. *My* crew is trained already.

M.

No feigned attack, you cur once my friend, but earnest deadly. I want no less than your destruction, dog. To the death!

Fafhrd read the salutation and first sentence with great relief and joy. The next two sentences made him frown in puzzlement. But with the dire postscript, his face fell, and his expression became one of deep dread and utter dolefulness.

He hurriedly rescanned the script to see how the letters and words were formed. They were the Mouser's unquestionably, the postscript slightly scrawled 'cause writ more swift. Something he'd missed nagged briefly at his mind, then was forgot. He crumpled the parchment and thrust it deep in his pouch.

He said to himself in the naked, low tones of a man plunged into nightmare, 'I can't believe and yet cannot deny. I know when Mouser jests and when speaks true. There must be swift-striking madness in these polar seas, perhaps loosed by that warlock Afreyt named ... Ice Wizard ... It ... Khahkht. And yet ... and yet I must ready *Sea Hawk* for total war, howe'er it grieve me. A man must be prepared for *all* events, no matter how they chill and tear his heart.'

He gave the west a final glance. The front of the southwest gale was close now, sweeping up the ice crystals ahead of it. It was a chord that cut off a whole sector of the circular white fog-sea, replacing it with naked black ocean. From that came a fleeting white glow that made Fafhrd mutter, 'Ice blink.'

Then closer still, hardly a half-score bowshots away, still in the fog yet near its wind-smitten edge, a redness flared bright, then died.

Fafhrd sank swiftly into the fog, going down the mast in swift hand-over-hand drops, his boots hardly touching the bronze collar pins.

Inside the dark-mapped globular vacuity, It ceased Its dartings, held Itself rigidly erect, facing away from the water-walled equatorial sun disk, and intoned in voice like grinding ice floes, 'Heed me, smallest atomies, that in rime seas seethe and freeze. Hear me, spirits of the cold, then do straightway what you're told. Ships are meeting, heroes greeting; gift to each, from each, of death. Monstreme lurk, in icy murk, picket of the Mingol work 'gainst each city, hearth, and kirk. If they 'scape the Viewless' ruse, make yourself of direst use. Vessels shatter! Manbones scatter! Bloody flesh, bones darkness splatter! – every splinter, every tatter! Deeds of darkness, darkness merit – so, till's done, put out the sun!'

And with reptilian swiftness It whipped around and clapped

a blacked-iron lid over the softly flaring, walled solar disk, which plunged the spherical cavity into an absolute blackness, wherein It whispered grindingly and chucklesome, '... and the Ghouls conjured the sun out of Heaven, quotha! Ghouls, indeed! – ever o'er-boastful. Khahkht never boasts, but does!'

At the foot of *Flotsam's* mainmast the Gray Mouser gripped Pshawri by the throat, but forbore to shake him. Beneath bloody head-circling bandage, his corporal major's white-circled pupils stared at him defiantly from bloodless face.

'Was one light battle-tap enough to make a crack for all your brains to leak out?' the Mouser demanded. '*Why did you fire that flare*, and so reveal us to our enemy?'

Pshawri winced but continued to oppose his gaze to the captain's glare. 'You ordered it – and did not countermand,' he stated stubbornly.

The Mouser sputtered, but had to allow the truth of that. The fool had been obedient, even if utterly lacking in judgment. Soldiers and their blind devotion to duty! especially spoken order! Most odd to think that his faithful idiot was yesterday a burglar-thief, child of treachery and lies and blinkered selfishness. The Mouser had also guiltily to admit he could have countermanded his command, paying lip service to logic and making allowance for stupidity, and particularly have noted what the fool was up to when he mounted the mast a second time. Pshawri was clearly still shaken from his head blow, poor devil, and at least he had been quick enough in casting boathook and flare into the sea when the Mouser'd roared at him from below.

'Very well,' he said gruffly, releasing his grip. 'Next time think too – if there's time – and there was! – as well as act. Ask Ourph for a noggin of white brandy. Then be forward lookout with Gavs – I'm doubling them bow and stern.'

And with that, the Mouser himself took up the general work of trying to pierce the stilly fog with eyes and ears, wondering the while unhappy and uneasy about the nature of Fafhrd's madness and of the vast, fell vessel he'd built, bought, commandeered, or perchance got from Ningauble or other sorcerer.

Or sorcerers? – it had surely been big and weird enough to be the chattel of several archimages! Conceivably a refitted prison hulk from rimy No-Ombrulsk. Or, illest thought of all (stemming from Ourph's fears 'bout the vanished oar shard), was the sorcerer Khahkht? – and some link 'twixt that warlock and mad Fafhrd?

Flotsam ghosted on, the sweepsmen pushing only enough to keep her under way. Mouser had early ordered slowest beat to conserve their strength.

'Three bells,' Ourph softly called.

Dawn nighs, the Mouser thought.

Pshawri could not have been long at the bow when his cry came back, 'Clear sea ahead! And wind!'

The fog thinned to wisps torn and tossed aft by the eddying, frosty air. The gibbous moon was firmly bedded on the western horizon, yet still sent an eerie white glare, while south of her a few lonely stars hung in the sky. That was uncanny, the Mouser thought, for the imminent dawn should already have extinguished them. He faced east – and almost gasped. Above the low, moonlit fog bank, the heavens were darker than ever, the night was starless, while due east on the fog bank rested a sliver of blackness blacker than any night could be, as if a black sun were rising that shot out beams of a darkness powerful and active as light – not light's absence, but its enemy-opposite. And from that same thickening sliver, along with potent darkness, there seemed to come a cold more intense and different in kind from that of the bitter southwest wind striking behind his right ear.

'Ship on our load-side beam!' Pshawri cried shrilly.

At once the Mouser dropped his gaze and sighted the stranger vessel, about three bowshots distant, just emerged from the fog bank and equally illumined by the moon glare, and headed straight at *Flotsam*. At first he took it for Fafhrd's icy leviathan come again, then saw it was small as his own ship, maybe narrower of beam. His thoughts zigzagged wildly – did mad Fafhrd command a fleet? was it a Sea Mingol warcraft? or still other pirate? or from Rime Isle? He forced himself to think more to the purpose.

His heart pulsed twice. Then, 'Make sail, my Mingols all!' he commanded. 'Odd-numbered sweepsmen! rack your long tools, then arm! Pshawri! command 'em!' And he grasped the tiller as the steersman let it go.

Aboard *Sea Hawk*, Fafhrd saw *Flotsam*'s low hull and short masts and long, slantwise main and mizzen yards blackly silhouetted against the spectrally white, misshapen moon awash in the west. In the same instant he at last realized what it was that had nagged his mind at the mast top. He whipped gauntlet from his right hand, plunged the latter into his pouch, plucked out the parchment scrap, and this time reread his own note — and saw below it the damning postscript he knew he'd never written. Clearly both postscripts, penned in deceptive scrawls, were cunning forgeries, however done o'erhead in birds' realm.

So even as he felt the wind and commanded, 'Skor! Take your squad. Prepare to make sail!' he drew a favorite arrow from the quiver ready beside him on the deck, threaded the note around it in studied haste, swiftly uncased and strung his great bow, and with a curt prayer to Kos bent it to its muscle-cracking extreme and sent the pet arrow winging high into the black sky toward the moon and the black two-master.

Aboard *Flotsam*, the Mouser felt a shiver of superadded apprehension which mounted while he watched his Mingols purposefully struggling with frozen lines and ties in the freshening chilly wind, until it culminated in the *chunk* of an arrow almost vertically into the deck scarce a cubit from his foot. So the small, moonlit sailing galley (for he had meanwhile identified it as such a craft) was signaling attack! Yet the range was still so great that he knew of only one bowman in Nehwon who could have made that miraculous shot. Not letting go the tiller, he stooped and severed the threads of the pale parchment wrapped tightly just behind the arrow's half-buried head, and read (or rather mostly reread) the two notes, his with the devilish postscript he'd never seen before. Even as he finished, the characters became unreadable from the black beams of antisun fighting down the moon rays and beginning to darken that orb. Yet he made the same deduction as had Fafhrd, and hot tears of joy were squeezed from his chilled eye sockets as he realized that whatever impossible-seeming sleights of ink and voice had been worked this night, his friend was sane and true.

There was a protracted sharp crackling as the last ties of the sails were loosed and wind filled them, breaking their frozen folds and festoons. The Mouser bore on the tiller, heading *Flotsam* into what was now a strengthening gale. But at the same time he sharply commanded, 'Mikkidu! burn three flares, two red, one white!'

Aboard *Sea Hawk*, Fafhrd saw the blessed treble sign flare up in gathering unnatural murk, even as his reefed sails filled and he turned his craft into the wind. He ordered, 'Manni-mark! answer those flares with like. Skullick, you dolt! slack your squad's bows. Those to the west are friends!' Then he said to Skor beside him, 'Take the helm. My friend's ship is on close-hauled southron course like ours. Work over to her. Lay us alongside.'

Aboard *Flotsam*, the Mouser was giving like directions to Ourph. He was cheered by sight of Fafhrd's flares matching his own, though he did not need their testimony. Now he longed for talk with Fafhrd. Which would be soon. The gap of black water between ships was narrowing rapidly. He wasted a moment musing whether mere chance or else some goddess had steered his comrade's arrow aside from his heart. He thought of Cif.

Aboard both ships, almost in unison, Pshawri and Manni-mark cried out fearfully, 'Ship close astern!'

Out of the torn and darkening fog bank, driving with preter-natural rapidity into the teeth of the gale on a course to smash them both, there had silently come a craft monstrous in size and aspect. It might well have remained unseen until collision, save that the weird rays of the rising black sun striking its load side engendered there a horrid, pale reflection, not natural white light at all, but a loathy, colorless luminescence – a white to make the flesh crawl, a cave-toad, fish-belly white. And if the substance making the reflection had any texture at all, it was that of ridged and crinkled gray horn – dead men's finger-nails.

The leprous Hel-glow showed the demonic craft to have thrice the freeboard of any natural ship. Its towering prow and sides were craggy and jagged, as if it were cast entire of ice in a titanic rough mold left over from the Age of Chaos, or else hacked by jinn into crude ship-likeness from a giant berg broken off from glacier vast. And it was driven by banks of oars long and twitchy as insect legs or limbs of myriapod, yet big as jointed yards or masts, as they sent it scuttling monstrously across black ocean vast. And from its lofty deck, as if hurled by demon ballistas, catapults, and mangonels, there now came hurtling down around *Flotsam* and *Sea Hawk* great blocks of ice which sent up black, watery volcanoes. While from the jagged top of its foremast – pale, big, and twisted as a thunder-blasted pine long dead – there shot out two thin beams of blackest black, like rays of antisun but more intense, which smote the Gray Mouser and Fafhrd each in the chest with deep-striking chill and sick, spreading dizziness and weakening of will.

Nevertheless they each managed to give rapid, stinging commands, and the two ships turned away in time's nick from each other and the oared deathberg striking between them. *Flotsam* had had only to turn further into the wind and so come round smoothly and swiftly. But *Sea Hawk* perforce must jibe. Its sail shivered a space, then filled abruptly on the other side with noise like thunder crack, but the stout Ool Krut canvas did not split. Both ships scudded north before the gale.

Behind them the eldritch bergship slowed and turned with supernatural celerity, spider-walked by its strange oars, and came in monstrous pursuit, gigantically oared on. And although no word was voiced or sign given by the pursued – almost as if by taking no notice of it, the menacing tangle of ghostly white evil astern could be made not to be – a collective shudder nevertheless went through the crews and captains of the sailing galley and the long-yarded two-master.

With that began a time of trial and tension, a Reign of Terror, an Eternal Night, such as no one amongst them had ever known before. First, there was the darkness, which grew greater the higher the antisun climbed in the black heavens.

Even candle flames below and the cook fires sheltered from the blast grew blue and dim. While the pustulant white glow hunting them had this quality: that its light illumined nothing it fell on, but rather darkened it, as if it carried the essence of the antilight along with it, as if it existed solely to make visible the terror of the bergship. Although the bergship was real as death and ever inching nearer, that eerie light sometimes seemed to Fafhrd and the Mouser most akin to the glows seen crawling on the inside of closed eyelids in darkness absolute.

Second, there was the cold that was a part of the antisunlight and struck deep with it, that penetrated every cranny of *Sea Hawk* and *Flotsam*, that had to be fought with both protective huddlings and violent movement, and also with drink and food warmed very slowly and with difficulty over the enfeebled flames – a cold that could paralyze both mind and body, and then kill.

Third, there was the potent silence that came with the unnatural dark and cold, the silence that made almost inaudible the constant creakings of rigging and wood, that muffled all foot-stampings and sideflailings against the cold, that turned all speech to whispers and changed the pandemonium of the great gale itself driving them north to the soft roaring of a sea-shell held forever to the ear.

And then there was that great gale itself, no whit weaker that it had no great noise – the gale that blew icy spume over the stern, the murderous gale that had always to be struggled against and kept watch on (gripping with fingers and thumbs like gyves to hopefully firm handholds when a man was anywhere on deck above), the gale near hurricane force that was driving them ever north at an unprecedented pace. None of them had ever before sailed before such a wind, even in the Mouser's and Fafhrd's and Ourph's first passage of the Outer Sea. Any of them would have long since hove to with bare masts and likely sea anchor, save for the menace of the bergship behind.

Last, there was that monstrous craft itself, deathberg or bergship, ever gaining on them, its leggy oars ever more strongly plied. Rarely, a jagged ice block crashed in black sea beside them. Rarely, a black ray teased at hero's heart. But those were but cackling reminders. The monster craft's main menace: it did nothing (save close the distance to its fleeting foes). The monster craft's intent: grapple and board! (or so it seemed).

Each on his ship, Fafhrd and Mouser fought weariness and chill; insane desire to sleep; strange, fleeting dreads. Once Fafhrd fancied unseen fliers battling overhead, as if in fabulous aerial extension of the sea war of his and Mouser's craft 'gainst iceship huge. Once Mouser seemed to see black sails of two great fleets. Both masters cheered their men, kept them alive.

Sometimes *Sea Hawk* and *Flotsam* were far apart in their parallel flight north, quite out of sight and hail. Sometimes they came together enough to see glints of each other. And once so close their captains could trade words.

Fafhrd hailed in bursts (they were whispers in Mouser's ears), 'Ho, Small One! Heard you Stardock's fliers? Our mountain princesses . . . fighting with Faroomfar?'

The Mouser shouted back, 'My ears are frostbit. Have you sighted . . . other foe ships . . . besides monstreme?'

Fafhrd: Monstreme? What's that?

Mouser: That ill astern. My word's analogous . . . to bireme . . . quadrireme. Monstreme! – rowed by monsters.

Fafhrd: A monstreme in full gale. An awful thought! (He looked astern at it.)

Mouser: Monstreme in monsoon . . . would be awfuler.

Fafhrd: Let's not waste breath. When will we raise Rime Isle?

Mouser: I had forgot we had a destination. What time think you?

Fafhrd: First bell in second dogwatch. Sunset season.

Mouser: It should get lighter . . . when this black sun sets.

Fafhrd: It ought to. Damn the double dark!

Mouser: Damn the dimidiate halved white astern! What's its game?

Fafhrd: Freeze fast to us, I wot. Then kill by cold, else board us.

Mouser: That's great, I must say. They should hire you.

So their shouts trailed off – a joy at first, but soon a tired-ness. And they had their men to care for. Besides, it was too risky, ships so close.

There passed a weary and nightmarish time. Then to the north, where nought had changed all the black day of plunging into it, Fafhrd marked a dark red glow. Long while he doubted it, deemed it some fever in his frozen skull. He noted Afreyt's slender face bobbing among his thoughts. At his side Skor asked him, 'Captain, is that a distant fire dead ahead? Our lost sun about to rise in north?' At last Fafhrd believed in the red glow.

Aboard *Flotsam*, the Mouser, racked by the poisons of ex-haustion and barely aware, heard Fafhrd whisper, 'Mouser, ahoy. Look ahead. What do you see?' He realized it was a mighty shout diminished by black silence and the gale, and that *Sea Hawk* had come close again. He could see glints from the shields affixed along her side, while astern the monstreme was close too, looming like a leprously opalescent cliff arock. Then he looked ahead.

After a bit, 'A red light,' he wheezed, then forced himself to bellow the same words alee, adding, 'Tell me what is it. And then let me sleep.'

'Rime Isle, I trow,' Fafhrd replied across the gap.

'Are they burning her down?' the Mouser asked.

The answer came back faintly and eerily, 'Remember . . . on the gold pieces . . . a volcano?'

The Mouser didn't believe he'd heard aright his comrade's next cry after that one, until he'd made him repeat it. Then, 'Sir Pshawri!' he called sharply, and when that one came limping up, hand to bandaged head, he ordered, 'Heave bucket overside on line and haul it up. I want waves' sample. Swiftly, you repulsive cripple!'

Somewhat later, Pshawri's eyebrows rose as his captain took the sloshing bucket he proffered and set it to his lips and uptilted it, next handed it back to Pshawri, swished around his teeth the sample he'd taken into his mouth, made a face, and spat to lee.

The fluid was far less icy than the Mouser had expected, almost tepid – and saltier than the water of the Sea of Monsters, which lies just west of the Parched Mountains that hide the Shadowland. He wondered for a mad moment if they'd been magicked to that vast, dead lake. 'Twould fit with monstreme. He thought of Cif.

There was impact. The deck tilted and did not rock back. Pshawri dropped the bucket and screamed.

The monstreme had thrust between the smaller ships and instantly frozen to them with its figurehead (living or dead?) of sea monster hacked or born of ice, its jaws agape betwixt their masts, while from the lofty deck high overhead there pealed down Fafhrd's laughter, monstrously multiplied.

The monstreme visibly shrank.

At one stride went the dark. From the low west the true sun burst forth, warmly lighting the bay in which they lay and striking an infinitude of golden gleams from the great, white, crystalline cliff to steerside, down which streaming water rushed in a thousand streams and runnels. A league or so beyond it rose a conical mountain down whose sides flowed glaring scarlet and from whose jaggedly truncated summit brilliant vermilion flames streamed toward the zenith, their dark smoke carried off northeastward by the wind.

Pointing at it with outthrown arm, Fafhrd called, 'See, Mouser, the red glow.'

Straight ahead, nearer than the cliff and drifting steadily still nearer, was a town or small unwalled city of low buildings hugging gentle hills, its waterfront one long low wharf, where a few ships were docked and a small crowd was assembled quietly. While to the west, rounding out the bay, there were more cliffs, the nearer bare dark rock, the farther robed in snow.

Facing the city, Fafhrd said, ᶠSalthaven.'

Studying the steaming, streaming, glittering white cliff and fiery peak beyond, the Mouser remembered the two scenes on his golden coins, all spent. This reminded him of the four silver coins he'd not been able to spend because they'd been snatched from his table at the Eel by the battered server, and of the two scenes on *their* faces: an iceberg and a monster. He turned round.

The monstreme was gone. Or rather, its last dissolving shards were sinking into the tranquil waters of the bay without sound or commotion, save that a little steam was rising.

Half-hurled, half-self-magicked from the monstreme's bridge, where It had been gazing out in triumph over the welter of dire, frigid forms on the decks below, Its mind obsessed with evil, back into Its cramped black sphere, Khahkht cursed in voice like Fafhrd's which midway became again a croak, 'Damn to the depths of Hell Rime Isle's strange gods! Their day will come, their dooms! Which now devise I whilst I snugly sleep . . .' It whipped the lid off the water-walled sun and spoke a spell that rotated the sphere until the sun was topmost, the Great Subequatorial Desert nethermost. It briefly fanned the former hot and then curled up in the latter and closed Its eyes, muttering, '. . . for even Khahkht is cold.'

While on tall Stardock, Great Oomforafor listened to the news of the defeat, or setback rather, and of his dear daughters' further treacheries, as told him by his furious, bedraggled son Prince Faroomfar, who'd been hurled back much as Khahkht.

As the Mouser turned back to the great white cliff, he realized that it must be made entire of salt – hence the seaport's name – and that the hot, volcanic waters coursing down it were dissolving it, which did much to account for the warm saltiness of ocean hereabouts and the swift melting of the frost monstreme. The last made all of magic ice, he mused, both stronger and weaker than the ordinary – as magic itself than life.

Fafhrd and he, looking toward the long wharf as they experienced sweetest relief and their ships drew steadily closer to it, saw two slender figures of different heights standing somewhat apart from the other seaside welcomers, who by that token and their proud attitudes and quietly rich garb – blue-gray the one, rust-red the other – must be individuals high in the councils of Rime Isle.

VIII: RIME ISLE

Fafhrd and the Gray Mouser supervised the mooring of *Sea Hawk* and *Flotsam* by bow and stern lines made fast round great wooden bollards, then sprang nimbly ashore, feeling unutterably weary, yet knowing that as captains they should not show it. They made their way to each other, embraced, then turned to face the crowd of Rime Isle men who had witnessed their dramatic arrival standing in a semicircle around the length of dock where their battered and salt-crusted ships were now moored.

Beyond the crowd stretched the houses of Salthaven port – small, stout and earth-hugging, as befitted this most northerly clime – in hues of weathered blue and green and a violet that was almost gray, except for those in the immediate neighborhood, which seemed rather squalid, where they were all angry reds and plague yellow.

Beyond Salthaven the low rolling land went off, gray-green with moss and heather, until it met the gray-white wall of a great glacier, and beyond that the old ice stretched until it met in turn the abrupt slopes of an active and erupting volcano, although the red glow of its lava and the black volume of its flamy smoke seemed to have diminished since they first glimpsed it from their ships.

The foremost of the crowd were all large, burly, quiet-faced men, booted, trousered, and smocked as fishers. Most of them bore quarterstaves, handling them as if they knew well how to use these formidable weapons. They curiously yet composedly eyed the twain and their ships, the Mouser's broad-beamed and somewhat lubberly trader *Flotsam* with its small Mingol crew and squad of disciplined (a wonder!) thieves, Fafhrd's trimmer galley *Sea Hawk* with its contingent of disciplined (if that can be imagined at all) berserkers. On the dock near the bollards where they'd made fast were Fafhrd's lieutenant Skor, the Mouser's – Pshawri – and two other crew members.

It was the quietness and composure of the crowd that puzzled and now began even to nettle the Mouser and Fafhrd. Here they'd sailed all the distance and survived almost unimaginable black hurricane-dangers to help save Rime Isle from a vast invasion of maddened and piratical Sea-Mingols bent on world-conquest, and there was no gladness to be seen anywhere, only stolidly appraising looks. There should be cheering and dancing and some northerly equivalent of maidens throwing flowers! True, the two steaming cauldrons of chowder borne on a shoulder-yoke by one of the fishermen seemed to betoken thoughtful welcome – but they hadn't yet been offered any!

The mouth-watering aroma of the fish-stew now reached the nostrils of the crewmen lining the sides of the two vessels in various attitudes of extreme weariness and dejection – for they were at least half as spent as their captains and had no urge to conceal it – and their eyes slowly brightened and their jaws began to work sympathetically. Behind them the sun-dancing snug harbor, so recently black-skyed, was full of small ships riding at anchor, local fishing craft chiefly with the lovely lines of porpoises, but near at hand several that were clearly from afar, including a small trading galleon of the Eastern Lands and (wonder!) a Keshite junk, and one or two modest yet unfamiliar craft that had the disquieting look of coming from seas beyond Nehwon's. (Just as there was a scatter of sailors from far-off ports in the crowd, peering here and there from between the tall Rime Islanders.)

And now the Rime Isler nearest the Twain walked silently toward them, flanked a pace behind by two others. He stopped a bare yard away, but still did not speak. In fact, he still did not seem so much to be looking at them as past them at their ships and crews, while working out some abstruse reckoning in his head. All three men were quite as tall as Fafhrd and his berserkers.

Fafhrd and the Mouser retained their dignity with some difficulty. Never did to speak first when the other man was supposed to be your debtor.

Finally the other seemed to terminate his calculations and he spoke, using the Low Lankhmarese that is the trade jargon of the northern world.

'I am Groniger, harbor master of Salthaven. I estimate your ships will be a good week repairing and revictualling. We will feed and board your crew ashore in the traders' quarters.' He gestured toward the squalid red and yellow buildings.

'Thank you,' Fafhrd said gravely, while the Mouser echoed coolly, 'Indeed, yes.' Hardly an enthusiastic welcome, but still one.

Groniger thrust out his hand, palm uppermost. 'The charge,' he said loudly, 'will be five gold pieces for the galley, seven for the tub. Payment in advance.'

Fafhrd's and the Mouser's jaws dropped. The latter could not contain his indignation, captain's dignity or no.

'But we're you're sworn allies,' he protested, 'come here as promised, through perils manifold, to be your mercenaries and help save you from the locust-swarm invasion of the raptorial Sea-Mingols counseled and led by evilest Khahkht, the Wizard of Ice.'

Groniger's eyebrows lifted. 'What invasion?' he queried. 'The Sea-Mingols are our friends. They buy our fish. They may be pirates to others, but never to Rime Isle ships. Khahkht is an old wives' tale, not to be credited by men of sense.'

'Old wives' tale?' the Mouser exploded. 'When we were but now three endless nights harried by Khahkht's monstrous galley and sank it at last on your very doorstep. His invasion came that close to success. Did you not observe the universal blackness and hell-wind when he conjured the sun out of heaven three days running?'

'We saw some dark clouds blowing up from the south,' Groniger said, 'under whose cover you approached Salthaven. They vanished when they touched Rime Isle – as all things superstitious are like to do. As for invasion, there were rumors of such an eruption some months back, but our council sifted

97

'em and found 'em idle gossip. Have any of you heard aught of a Sea-Mingol invasion since?' he asked loudly, looking from side to side at his fellow Rime Islers. They all shook their heads.

'So pay up!' he repeated, jogging his outthrust palm, while those behind him wagged their quarterstaves, firming their grips.

'Shameless ingratitude!' the Mouser rebuked, taking a moral tone as a leader of men. 'What gods do you worship here on Rime Isle, to be so hard-hearted?'

Groniger's answer rang out distinct and cool. 'We worship no gods at all, but do our business in the world clearheadedly, no misty dreams. We leave such fancies to the so-called civilized people – decadent cultures of the hothouse south. Pay up, I say.'

At that moment Fafhrd, whose height permitted him to see over the crowd, cried out, 'Here are those coming who hired us, harbor master, and will give the lie to your disclaimers.'

The crowd parted respectfully to let through two slender, trousered women with long knives at their belts in jeweled scabbards. The taller was clad all in blue, with like eyes, and fair hair. Her comrade was garmented in dark red, with green eyes and black hair that seemed to have gold wires braided in it. Skor and Pshawri, still stupid with fatigue, took note of them and it was impossible to mistake the message in the sea-dogs' kindling eyes: Here were the northern angels come at last!

'The eminent councilwomen Afreyt and Cif,' Groniger intoned. 'We are honored by their presence.'

They approached with queenly smiles and looks of amiable curiosity.

'Tell them, Lady Afreyt,' said Fafhrd courteously to the one in blue, 'how you commissioned me to bring Rime Isle twelve—' Suppressing the word 'berserk', he smoothly made it, '—stout northern fighters of the fiercest temper.'

'And I twelve ... nimble and dextrous Lankhmar sworders and slingers, sweet Lady Cif,' the Mouser chimed in airily, avoiding the word 'thief'.

Afreyt and Cif looked at them blankly. Then their gazes became at once anxious and solicitous.

Afreyt commented, 'They've been tempest-tossed, poor lads, and doubtless it has disordered their memories. Our little northern gales come as a surprise to southerners. They seem gentle. Use them well, Groniger.' Looking intently at Fafhrd, she lifted her hand to adjust her hair and in lowering it hesitated a finger for a moment crosswise to her tightly shut long lips.

Cif added, 'Doubtless privation has temporarily addled their wits. Their ships have seen hard use. But what a tale! I wonder who they are? Nourish them with hot soup – after they've paid, of course.' And she winked at the Mouser a green dark-lashed eye on the side away from Groniger. Then the two ladies wandered on.

It is a testimony to the fundamental levelheadedness and growing self-control of the Mouser and Fafhrd (now having, as captains, to control others) that they did not expostulate at this astounding and barely-tempered rebuff, but actually each dug a hand into his purse – though they did look after the two strolling females somewhat wonderingly. So they saw Skor and Pshawri, who had been dazedly following the two apparitions of northernly delight, now approach these houris with the clear intent of establishing some sort of polite amorous familiarity.

Afreyt struck Skor aside in no uncertain fashion, but only after leaning her face close enough to his head to hiss a word or two into his ear and grasp his wrist in a way that would have permitted her to slip a token or note into his palm. Cif treated Pshawari's advances likewise.

Groniger, pleased at the way the two captains were now dragging gold pieces from their purses, nevertheless admonished them, 'And see to it that your crewmen offer no affront to our Salthaven women, nor stray one step beyond the bounds of the traders' quarter.'

Paying up took the last of the Rime Isle gold that Cif had given them back at the Silver Eel in Lankhmar, while the Mouser had to piece out his seven with two Lankhmar rilks and a Sarheenmar dubloon.

Groniger's eyebrows rose as he scanned the take. 'Rime Isle coinage! So you'd touched here before and knew our harbor rules and were only seeking to bargain? But what made you invent such an unbelievable story?'

Fafhrd shrugged and said shortly, 'Not so. Had 'em off an Eastern trading galley in these waters,' while the Mouser only laughed.

Nevertheless, a thought struck Groniger, and he looked after the two Rime Isle councilwomen speculatively as he said shortly, 'Now you may feed your men.'

The Mouser called toward *Flotsam*, 'Ho, lads! Fetch your bowls, cups, and spoons. These most hostful Rime Islanders have provided a feast for you. Orderly now! Pshawri, attend me.'

While Fafhrd commanded likewise, adding, 'Forget not they're our friends. Do 'em courtesies. A word with you, Skor.' Never do to show resentment, though that 'tub' still rankled with the Mouser, despite it being a very fair description of the broad-beamed, sweep-propelled *Flotsam*.

When the Mouser and Fafhrd had seen all their men eating and served a measure of grog to celebrate safe arrival, they turned to their somewhat doleful lieutenants, who with only a show of reluctance yielded up the notes they'd been slipped – as the Twain had surmised – along with the words, 'For your master!'

Unfolded, Afreyt's read, 'Another faction controls the Rime Isle council, temporarily. You do not know me. At dusk tomorrow seek me at the Hill of the Eight-Legged Horse,' while Cif's message was, 'Cold Khahkht has sowed dissension in our council. We never met – play it that way. You'll find me tomorrow night at the Flame Den if you come alone.'

'So she does not speak with the voice of Rime Isle after all,' Fafhrd commented softly. 'To what fiery female politicians have we joined our destinies?'

'Her gold was good,' the Mouser answered gruffly. 'And now we've two new riddles to solve.'

'Flame Den and Eight-Legged Horse,' Fafhrd echoed.

'Tub, he called her,' the Mouser mused bitterly, his mind

veering. 'What godless literal-minded philosophers are we now supposed to succor in spite of themselves?'

'You're a godless man too,' Fafhrd reminded him.

'Not so, there was once Mog,' the Mouser protested with a touch of his old playful plaintiveness, referring to a youthful credulity, when he had briefly believed in the spider god to please a lover.

'Such questions can wait, along with the two riddles,' Fafhrd decided. 'Now let's curry favor with the atheist fishermen while we can.'

And accompanied by the Mouser, he proceeded ceremoniously to offer Groniger white brandy fetched from *Flotsam* by old Ourph the renegade Mingol. The harbor master was prevailed upon to accept a drink, which he took in slow sips, and by way of talk of repair docks, watering, crew dormitories ashore, and the price of salt fish, the conversation became somewhat more general. With difficulty Fafhrd and the Mouser won license to venture outside the traders' quarter, but only by day, and not their men. Groniger refused a second drink.

Inside Its icy sphere, which would have cramped a taller being, Khahkht roused, muttering, 'Rime Isle's new gods are treacherous — betray and re-betray — yet stronger than I guessed.'

It began to study the dark map of the world of Nehwon depicted on the sphere's interior. Its attention moved to the northern tongue of the Outer Sea, where a long peninsula of the Western Continent reached toward the Cold Waste, with Rime Isle midway between. Leaning Its spidery face close to the tip of that peninsula, It made out on the northern side tiny specks in the dark blue waters.

'The armada of the Widdershins Sea-Mingols invests Sayend,' It chuckled, referring to the easternmost city of the ancient Empire of Eevamarensee. 'To work!'

It wove Its thickly black-bristled hands incantingly above the gathered specks and droned, 'Harken to me, slaves of death. Hear my word and feel my breath. Every least instruction learn. First of all, Sayend must burn! Against Nehwon your horde be hurled, next Rime Isle and then the world.' One spider-hand drifted sideways toward the small green island in ocean's midst. 'Round Rime Isle let fishes swarm, provisioning my Mingol storm.' The hand drifted back and the passes became swifter. 'Blackness seize on Mingol mind, bend it 'gainst humankind. Madness redden Mingol ire, out of cold come death by fire!'

It blew strongly as if on cold ashes and a tiny spot on the peninsula tip glowed dark red like an uncovered ember.

'By will of Khahkht these weirds be locked!' It grated, sealing the incantment.

The ships of the Widdershins Sea-Mingols rode at anchor in Sayend harbor, packed close together as fish in a barrel, and as silvery white. Their sails were furled. Their midships decks, abutting abeam, made a rude roadway from the precipitous shore to the flagship, where Edumir, their chief paramount, sat enthroned on the poop, quaffing the mushroom wine of Quarmall that fosters visions. Cold light from the full moon south in the wintry sky revealed the narrow horse-cage that was the forecastle of each ship and picked out the mad eyes and rawboned head of the ship's horse, a gaunt Steppe-stallion, thrust forward through the wide-set irregular bars and all confronting the east.

The taken town, its sea-gate thrown wide, was dark. Before its walls and in its sea-street its small scatter of defenders sprawled as they'd fallen, soaked in their own blood and scurried over by the looting Sea-Mingols, who did not, however, bother the chief doors behind which the remaining inhabitants had locked and barred themselves. They'd already captured the five maidens ritual called for and dispatched them to the flagship, and now they sought oil of whale, porpoise, and scaly fish. Puzzlingly, they did not bring most of this treasure-trove down to their ships, but wasted it, breaking the casks with axes and smashing the jars, gushing the precious stuff over doors and wooden walls and down the cobbled street.

The lofty poop of the great flagship was dark as the town

in the pouring moonlight. Beside Edumir his witchdoctor stood above a brazier of tinder, holding aloft a flint and a horseshoe in either hand, his eyes wild as those of the ship-horses. Next him crouched a wiry-thewed warrior naked to the waist, bearing the Mingol bow of melded horn that is Nehwon's most feared, and five long arrows winged with oily rags. While to the other side was an ax-man with five casks of the captured oil.

On the next level below, the five Sayend maidens cowered wide-eyed and silent, their pallor set off by their long dark braided hair, each in the close charge of two grim she-Mingols who flashed naked knives.

While on the main deck below that, there were ranked five young Mingol horsemen, chosen for this honor because of proven courage, each mounted on an iron-disciplined Steppe-mare, whose hoofs struck random low drum-notes from the hollow deck.

Edumir cast his wine cup into the sea and very deliberately turned his long-jawed, impassive face toward his witchdoctor and nodded once. The latter brought down horseshoe and flint, clashing them just above the brazier, and then nurtured the sparks so engendered until the tinder was all aflame.

The bowman laid his five arrows across the brazier and then, as they came alight, plucked them out and sent them winging successively toward Sayend with such miraculous swiftness that the fifth was painting its narrow orange curve upon the midnight air before the first had struck.

They lodged each in wood and with a preternatural rapidity the oil-drenched town flared up like a single torch, and the muffled, despairing cries of its trapped inhabitants rose like those of Hell's prisoners.

Meanwhile the she-Mingols guarding her had slashed the garments from the first maiden, their knives moving like streaks of silver fire, and thrust her naked toward the first horseman. He seized her by her dark braids and swung her across his saddle, clasping her slim, naked back to his leather-cuirassed chest. Simultaneously the ax-man struck in the head of the first cask and upended it above horse, rider, and maiden, drenching them all with gleaming oil. Then the rider twitched reins and dug in his spurs and set his mare galloping across the close-moored decks towards the flaming town. As the maiden became aware of the destination of the wild ride, she began to scream, and her screams rose higher and higher, accompanied by the rhythmic, growling shouts of the rider and the drum-beat of the mare's hoofs.

All these actions were repeated once, twice, thrice, quarce – the third horse slipped sideways in the oil, stumbled, recovered – so that the fifth rider was away before the first had reached his goal. The mares had been schooled from colthood to face and o'erlap walls of flame. The riders had drunk deep of the same mushroom wine as Edumir. The maidens had their screams.

One by one they were briefly silhouetted against the red gateway, then joined with it. Five times the flame of Sayend rose higher still, redly illuminating the small bay and the packed ship and the staring Mingol faces and glazed Mingol eyes, and Sayend expired in one unending scream and shout of agony.

When it was done, Edumir rose up tall in his fur robes and cried in trumpet voice, 'East away now. Over ocean. To Rime Isle!'

Next day the Mouser and Fafhrd got their ships pumped out, warped to the docks assigned them, and work began on them early. Their men, refreshed by a long night's sleep ashore, set to work at repairs after a little initial grumbling, the Mouser's thieves under the direction of his chief lieutenant Pshawri and small Mingol crew. Presently there was the muffled thud of mallets driving in tow, and the stench of tar, as the loosened seams of *Flotsam* were caulked from within, while from the deck of *Sea Hawk* came the brighter music of hammers and saws, as Fafhrd's vikings mended upper works damaged by the icy projectiles of Khahkht's frost monstreme. Others reaved new rigging where needed and replaced frayed stays.

The traders' quarter, where they'd been berthed, duplicated

in small the sailors' quarter of any Nehwon port, its three taverns, two brothels, several stores and shrines and loosely administered by a small permanent population of ill-assorted foreigners, their unofficial mayor a close-mouthed, scarred captain named Bomar, from the Eight Cities, and their chief banker a dour black Keshite. It was borne in on Fafhrd and the Mouser that one of these fisherfolks' chief concerns, and that of the traders too, was to keep Rime Isle a valuable secret from the rest of Nehwon. Or else they had caught the habit of impassivity from their fisher-hosts, who tolerated, profited from them, and seldom omitted to enforce a bluff discipline. The foreign population had heard nothing of a Sea-Mingol eruption, either, or so they claimed.

The Rime Islanders seemed to live up to first impressions: a large-bodied, sober-clad, quiet, supremely practical and supremely confident people, without eccentricities or crochets or even superstitions, who drank little and lived by the rule of 'Mind your own business'. They played chess a good deal in their spare time and practiced with their quarterstaves, but otherwise they appeared to take little notice of each other and none at all of foreigners, though their eyes were not sleepy.

And today they had become even more inaccessible, ever since an early-sailing fishing boat had returned almost immediately to harbor with news that had sent the entire fleet of them hurrying out. And when the first of these came creaming back soon after noon with hold full of new-caught fish, swiftly salted them down (there was abundance of salt – the great eastern cliff, which no longer ran with hot volcanic waters), and put out to sea again, clapping on all sail, it became apparent that there must be a prodigious run of food fish just outside the harbor mouth – and the thrifty fishers determined to take full advantage of it. Even Groniger was seen to captain a boat out.

Individually busy with their supervisings and various errands (since only they could go outside the traders' quarter), the Mouser and Fafhrd met each other by a stretch of seawall north of the docks and paused to exchange news and catch a breather.

'I've found the Flame Den,' the former said. 'At least I think I have. It's an inner room in the Salt Herring tavern. The Ilthmart owner admitted he sometimes rents it out of a night – that is, if I interpreted his wink aright.'

Fafhrd nodded and said, 'I just now walked to the north edge of town and asked a grandad if he ever heard of the Hill of the Eight-Legged Horse. He gave a damned unpleasant sort of laugh and pointed across the moor. The air was very clear (you've noticed the volcano's ceased to smoke? I wonder that the Islers take so little note of it), and when I'd located the one heathered hill of many that was his finger's target (about a league northwest), I made out what looked like a gallows atop it.'

The Mouser grunted feeling fully at that grim disclosure and rested his elbows on the seawall, surveying the ships left in the harbor, 'foreigners' all. After a while he said softly, 'There's all manner of slightly strange things here in Salthaven, I trow. Things slightly off-key. That Ool Plerns sailing-dory now – saw you ever one with so low a prow at Ool Plerns? Or a cap so oddly-visored as that of the sailor we saw come off the Gnampf Nor cutter? Or that silver coin with an owl on it Groniger gave me in change for my dubloon? It's as if Rime Isle were on the edge of other worlds with other ships and other men and other gods – a sort of rim . . .'

Gazing out likewise, Fafhrd nodded slowly and started to speak when there came angry voices from the direction of the docks, followed by a full-throated bellow.

'That's Skullick, I'll be bound!' Fafhrd averred. 'Got into what sort of idiot trouble, the gods know.' And without further word he raced off.

'Likely just broken bounds and got a drubbing,' the Mouser called out, trotting after. 'Mikkidu got a touch of the quarter-staff this morn for trying to pick an Isler's pouch – and serve him right! I could not have whacked him more shrewdly myself.'

That evening Fafhrd strode north from Salthaven toward Gallows Hill (it was an honester name), resolutely not looking back at the town. The sun, set in the far southwest a short while ago, gave a soft violet tone to the clear sky and the pale knee-high heather through which he trod and even to the black slopes of the volcano Darkfire where yesterday's lava had cooled. A chill breeze, barely perceptible, came from the glacier ahead. Nature was hushed. There was a feeling of immensity.

Gradually the cares of the day dropped away and his thoughts turned to the days of his youth, spent in similar clime – to Cold Corner with its tented slopes and great pines, its snow serpents and wolves, its witchwomen and ghosts. He remembered Nalgron his father and his mother Mor and even Mara, his first love. Nalgron had been an enemy of the gods, somewhat like these Rime Isle men (he was called the Legend Breaker) but more adventurous – he had been a great mountain climber, and in climbing one named White Fang had got his death. Fafhrd remembered an evening when his father had walked with him to the lip of Cold Canyon and named to him the stars as they winked on in a sky similarly violet.

A small sound close by, perhaps that of a lemming moving off through the heather, broke his reverie. He was already mounting the gentle slope of the hill he sought. After a moment he continued to the top, stepping softly and keeping his distance from the gibbet and the area that lay immediately beneath its beam. He had a feeling of something uncanny close at hand and he scanned around in the silence.

On the northern slope of the hill there was a thick grove of gorse more than man-high, or bower rather, since there was a narrow avenue leading in, a door of shadows. The feeling of an uncanny presence deepened and he mastered a shiver.

As his eyes came away from the gorse, he saw Afreyt standing just uphill and to one side of the grove and looking at him steadily without greeting. The darkening violet of the sky gave its tone to her blue garb. For some reason he did not call out to her and now she lifted her narrow hand crosswise to her lips, enjoining silence. Then she looked toward the grove.

Slowly emerging from the shadow door were three slender girls barely past childhood. They seemed to be leading and looking up at someone Fafhrd could not make out at first. He blinked twice, widening his eyes, and saw it was the figure of a tall, pale-bearded man wearing a wide-brimmed hat that shadowed his eyes, and either very old or else enfeebled by sickness, for he took halting steps and though his back was straight he rested his hands heavily on the shoulders of two of the girls.

And then Fafhrd felt an icy chill, for the suspicion came to him that this was Nalgron, whose ghost he had not seen since he had left Cold Corner. And either the figure's skin, beard and robe were alike strangely mottled, or else he was seeing the pale needle-clumps of the gorse through them.

But if it were a ghost, Nalgron's or another's, the girls showed no fear of it, rather a dutiful tenderness, and their shoulders bowed under its hands as they supported it along, as if its weight were real.

They slowly mounted the short distance to the hilltop, Afreyt silently following a few paces behind, until the figure stood directly beneath the end of the gallow's beam.

There the old man or ghost seemed to gain strength (and perhaps greater substantiality too) for he took his hands from the girls' shoulders and they retreated a little toward Afreyt, still looking up at him, and he lifted his face toward the sky, and Fafhrd saw that although he was a gaunt man at the end of middle age with strong and noble features not unlike Nalgron's, he had thinner lips, their ends downturning like a knowing schoolmaster's, and he wore a patch on his left eye.

He scanned around uncertainly, o'erpassing Fafhrd, who stood motionless and afraid, and then the old man turned north and lifted an arm in that direction and said in a hoarse voice that was like the soughing of the wind in thick branches, 'The Widder-Mingol fleet comes on from the west. Two raiders harry ahead, make for Cold Harbor.' Then he rapidly turned back his head through what seemed an impossibly great angle, as though his neck were broken yet somehow still serviceable, so that he looked straight at Fafhrd with his single eye, and said, 'You must destroy them!'

Then he seemed to lose interest, and weakness seized him

again, or perhaps a sort of sensuous languor after task completed, for he stepped a little more swiftly as he returned toward the bower, and when the girls came in around him, his resting hands seemed to fondle their young necks lasciviously as well as take support from their slim shoulders until the shadow door, darker now, swallowed them.

Fafhrd was so struck with this circumstance, despite his fear, that when Afreyt now came stepping toward him saying in a low but businesslike voice, 'Didst mark that? Cold Harbor is Rime Isle's other town, but far smaller, easy prey for even a single Mingol ship that takes it by surprise. It's on the north coast, a day's journey away, ice-locked save for these summer months. You must—' his interrupting reply was 'Think you the girl'll be safe with him?'

She broke off, then answered shortly, 'As with any man. Or male ghost. Or god.'

At that last word, Fafhrd looked at her sharply. She nodded and continued, 'They'll feed him and give him drink and bed him down. Doubtless he'll play with their breasts a little and then sleep. He's an old god and far from home, I think, and wearies easily, which is perhaps a blessing. In any case, they serve Rime Isle too and must run risks.'

Fafhrd considered that and then, clearing his throat, said, 'Your pardon, Lady Afreyt, but your Rime Isle men, judging not only from Groniger but from others I've met, some of them councilmen, do not believe in any gods at all.'

She frowned. 'That's true enough. The old gods deserted Rime Isle long years ago and our folk have had to learn to fend for themselves in the cruel world – in this clime merciless. It's bred hard-headedness.'

'Yet,' Fafhrd said, recalling something, 'my gray friend judged Rime Isle to be a sort of rim-spot, where one might meet all manner of strange ships and men and gods from very far places.'

'That's true also,' she said hurriedly. 'And perhaps it's favored the same hard-headedness: how, where there are so many ghosts about, to take account only of what the hand can firmly grasp and can be weighed in scales. Money and fish.

It's one way to go. But Cif and I have gone another – where phantoms throng, to learn to pick the useful and trustworthy ones from the flibbertigibbets and flimflammers – which is well for Rime Isle. For these two gods we've found—'

'*Two* gods?' Fafhrd questioned, raising his eyebrows. 'Cif found one too? Or is another in the bower?'

'It's a long story,' she said impatiently. 'Much too long to tell now, when dire events press upon us thick and fast. We must be practical. Cold Harbor's in dismal peril and—'

'Again your pardon, Lady Afreyt,' Fafhrd broke in, raising his voice a little. 'But your mention of practicality reminds me of another matter upon which you and Cif appear to differ most sharply with your fellow councilmen. They know of no Mingol invasion, they say, and certainly nothing of you and Cif hiring us to help repel it – and you've asked us in your notes to keep that secret. Now, I've brought you the twelve berserkers you wanted—'

'I know, I know,' she said sharply, 'and I'm pleased. But you were paid for that – and shall get further pay in Rime Isle gold as services are rendered. As for the council, the wizardries of Khahkht have lulled their suspicions – I doubt not that today's fish-run in his work, tempting their cupidity.'

'And my comrade and I have suffered from his wizardries too, I trow,' Fafhrd said. 'Nevertheless, you told us at the Silver Eel in Lankhmar that you spoke with the voice of Rime Isle, and now it appears that you speak only for Cif and yourself in a council of – what is it, twelve?'

'Did you expect your task to be all easy sailing?' she flared at him. 'Art unacquainted with set-backs and adverse gales in quests? Moreover, we *do* speak with the voice of Rime Isle, for Cif and I are the only councilpersons who have the old glory of Rime Isle at heart – and we are both full council members, I assure you, only-daughters inheriting house, farms and council membership from fathers after (in Cif's case) sons died. We played together as children in these hills, she and I, reviving Rime Isle's greatness in our games. Or sometimes we'd be pirate queens and rape the Isle. But chiefly we'd imagine ourselves seizing power in the council, forcibly putting down all the other members—'

'So much violence in little girls?' Fafhrd couldn't help putting in. 'I think of little girls as gathering flowers and weaving garlands whilst fancying themselves little wives and mothers—'

'—and put them all to the sword and cut their wives' throats!' Afreyt finished. 'Oh, we gathered flowers too, sometimes.'

Fafhrd chuckled, then his voice grew grave. 'And so you've inherited full council membership – Groniger always mentions you with respect, though I think he has suspicions of something between us – and now you've somehow discovered a stray old god or two whom you think you can trust not to betray you, or delude you with senile ravings, and he's told you of a great two-pronged Mingol invasion of Rime Isle preparatory to world conquest, and on the strength of that you went to Lankhmar and hired the Mouser and me to be your mercenary captains, using your own fortunes for the purpose, I fancy—'

'Cif is the council treasurer,' she assured him with a meaningful crook of her lips. 'She's very good at figures and accounts – as I am with the pen and words, the council's secretary.'

'And yet you trust this god,' Fafhrd pressed on, 'this old god who loves gallows and seems to draw strength from them. Myself, I'm very suspicious of all old men and gods. In my experience they're full of lechery and avarice – and have a long lifetime's experience of evil to draw on in their twisty machinations.'

'Agreed,' Afreyt said. 'But when all's said and done a god's a god. Whatever nasty itches his old heart may have, whatever wicked thoughts of death and doom, he must first be true to his god's nature: which is, to hear what we say and hold us to it, to speak truth to man about what's going on in distant places, and to prophecy honestly – though he may try to trick us with words if we don't listen to him very carefully.'

'That does agree with my experience of the breed,' Fafhrd admitted. 'Tell me, why is this called the Hill of the Eight-Legged Horse?'

Without a blink at the change of subject, Afreyt replied,

'Because it takes four men to carry a coffin or the laid-out corpse of one who's been hanged – or died any other way. Four men – eight legs. You might have guessed.'

'And what is this god's name?'

Afreyt said: 'Odin.'

Fafhrd had the strangest feeling at the gong-beat sound of that simple name – as if he were on the verge of recalling memories of another lifetime. Also, it had something of the tone of the gibberish spoken by Karl Treuherz, that strange other-worlder who had briefly come into the lives of Fafhrd and the Mouser astride the neck of a two-headed sea serpent whilst they were in the midst of their great adventure-war with the sapient rats of Lankhmar Below-Ground. Only a name – yet there was the feeling of walls between world disturbed.

At the same time he was looking into Afreyt's wide eyes and noting that the irises were violet, rather than blue as they had seemed in the yellow torchlight of the Eel – and then wondering how he could see any violet at all in anything when that tone had some time ago faded entirely from the sky, which was now full night except that the moon a day past full had just now lifted above the eastern highland.

From beyond Afreyt a light voice called tranquilly, attuned to the night, 'The god sleeps.'

One of the girls was standing before the mouth of the bower, a slim white shape in the moonlight, clad only in simple frock that was hardly more than a shift and left one shoulder bare. Fafhrd marvelled that she was not shivering in the chill night air. Her two companions were dimmer shapes behind her.

'Did he give any trouble, Mara?' Afreyt called. (Fafhrd felt a strange feeling at that name, too.)

'Nothing new,' the girl responded.

Afreyt said, 'Well, put on your boots and hooded cloak – May and Gale, you also – and follow me and the foreign gentleman, out of earshot, to Salthaven. You'll be able to visit the god at dawn, May, to bring him milk?'

'I will.'

'Your children?' Fafhrd asked in a whisper.

Afreyt shook her head. 'Cousins. Meanwhile,' she said in a

voice that was likewise low, but businesslike, 'you and I will discuss your instant expedition with the berserks to Cold Harbor.'

Fafhrd nodded, although his eyebrows rose a little. There was a fugitive movement in the air overhead and he found himself thinking of his and the Mouser's one-time loves, the invisible mountain-princesses Hirriwi and Keyaira, and of their night-riding brother, Prince Faroomfar.

The Gray Mouser saw his men fed and bedded down for the night in their dormitory ashore, not without some fatherly admonitions as to the desirability of prudent behavior in the home port of one's employers. He briefly discussed the morrow's work with Ourph and Pshawri. Then, with a final enigmatic scowl all around, he threw his cloak over his left shoulder, withdrew into the chilly evening, and strolled toward the Salt Herring.

Although he and Fafhrd had had a long refreshing sleep aboard the *Flotsam* (declining the shore quarters Gronigen had offered them, though accepting for their men), it had been a long, exactingly busy, and so presumably tiring day – yet now, somewhat to his surprise, he felt new life stirring in him. But this new life invading him did not concern itself with his and Fafhrd's many current problems and sage plans for future contingencies, but rather with a sense of just how preposterous it was that for the past three moons he should have been solemnly playing at being captain of men, fire-breathing disciplinarian, prodigious navigator, and the outlandishly heroic rest of it. He, a thief, captaining thieves, drilling them into sailorly and warlike skills that would be of no use to them whatever when they went back to their old professions – ridiculous! All because a small woman with golden glints in her dark hair and in her green eyes had set him an unheard-of task. Really, most droll.

Moonlight striking almost horizontally left the narrow street in shadow but revealed the cross-set beams above the Salt Herring's door. Where did they get so much wood in an island so far north? That question at least was answered for him when he pressed on inside. The tavern was built of the gray beams and planks of wrecked or dismantled ships – one wall still had a whaleback curve and he noted in another the borings and embedded shells of sea creatures.

A slow eyesweep around showed a half dozen oddly sorted mariners quietly drinking and two youngish Islers even more quietly playing chess with chunky stone pieces. He recalled having seen this morning with Groniger the one playing the black.

Without a word he marched toward the inner room, the low doorway to which was now half occupied by a brawny and warty old hag, sitting bowed over on a low stool, who looked the witch-mother of all unnatural giants and other monsters.

His Ilthmart host came up beside him, wiping his hands on the towel that was his apron and saying softly, 'Flame Den's taken for tonight – a private party. You'd only be courting trouble with Mother Grum. What's your pleasure?'

The Mouser gave him a hard, silent look and marched on. Mother Grum glowered at him from under tangled brows. He glowered back. The Ilthmart shrugged.

Mother Grum moved back from her stool, bowing him into the inner room. He briefly turned his head, favoring the Ilthmart with a cold superior smile as he moved after her. One of the Islers, lifting a black rook to move it, swung his eyes motionless and bent over the board as if in deepest thought.

The inner room had a small fire in it, at any rate, to provide movement to entertain the eye. The large hearth was in the center of the room, a stone slab set almost waist high. A great copper flue (the Mouser wondered what ship's bottom it had helped cover) came down to within a yard of it from out of the low ceiling, and into this flue the scant smoke twistingly flowed. Elsewhere in the room were a few small, scarred tables, chairs for them, and another doorway.

Sidewise together on the edge of the hearth sat two women who looked personable, but used by life. The Mouser had seen one of *them* earlier in the day (the late afternoon) and judged her a whore. Their somewhat provocative attire now, and the red stockings of one, were consonant with his theory.

The Mouser went to a table a quarter way around the fire from them, cast his cape over one chair and sat down in another, which commanded both doorways. He knit his fingers together and studied the flames impassively.

Mother Grum returned to her stool in the doorway, presenting her back to all three of them.

One of the two whorish-looking women stared into the fire and from time to time fed it with driftwood that sang and sometimes tinged the flames with green and blue and with thorny black twigs that spat and crackled and burned hot orange. The other wove cat's cradles between the spread fingers of her outheld hands on a long loop of black twine. Now and then the Mouser looked aside from the fire at her severe angular creations.

Neither of the women took notice of the Mouser, but after a while the one feeding the fire stood up, brought a wine jar and two small tankards to his table, poured into one, and stood regarding him.

He took up the tankard, tasted a small mouthful, swallowed it, set down the tankard, and nodded curtly without looking at her.

She went back to her former occupation. Thereafter the Mouser took an occasional swallow of wine while studying and listening to the flames. What with their combination of crackling and singing, they were really quite vocal in that rather small, silent room – resembling an eager, rapid, youthful voice, by turns merry and malicious. Sometimes the Mouser could have sworn he heard words and phrases.

While in the flames, continually renewed, he began to see faces, or rather one face which changed expression a good deal – a youthful handsome face with very mobile lips, sometimes open and amiable, sometimes convulsed by hatreds and envies (the flames shone green a while), sometimes almost impossibly distorted, like a face seen through hot air above a very hot fire. Indeed once or twice he had the fancy that it was the face of an actual person sitting on the opposite side of the fire from him, sometimes half rising to regard him through the flames, sometimes crouching back. He was almost tempted to get up and walk around the fire to check on that, but not quite.

The strangest thing about the face was that it seemed familiar to the Mouser, though he could not place it. He gave up racking his brains over that and settled back, listening more closely to the flame-voice and trying to attune its fancied words to the movements of the flame-face's lip.

Mother Grum got up again and moved back, bowing. There entered without stooping a lady whose russet cloak was drawn across the lower half of her face, but the Mouser recognized the gold-shot green eyes and he stood up. Cif nodded to Mother Grum and the two harlots, walked to the Mouser's table, cast her cloak atop his, and sat down in the third chair. He poured for her, refilled his own tankard, and sat down also. They drank. She studied him for some time.

Then, 'You've seen the face in the fire and heard its voice?' she asked.

His eyes widened and he nodded, watching her intently now.

'But have you guessed why it seems familiar?'

He shook his head rapidly, sitting forward, his expression a most curious and expectant frown.

'It resembles you,' she said flatly.

His eyebrows went up and his jaw dropped, just a little. That was true! It did remind him of himself – only when he was younger, quite a bit younger. Or as he saw himself in mirror these days only when in a most self-infatuated and vain mood, so that he saw himself as unmarked by age.

'But do you know why?' she asked him, herself intent now.

He shook his head.

She relaxed. 'Neither do I,' she said. 'I thought you might know. I marked it when I first saw you in the Eel, but as to why – it is a mystery within mysteries, beyond our present ken.'

'I find Rime Isle a nest of mysteries,' he said meaningfully, 'not the least your disapproval of myself and Fafhrd.'

She nodded, sat up straighter, and said, 'So now I think it's high time I told you why Afreyt and I are so sure of a Mingol invasion of Rime Isle while the rest of the council disbelieves it altogether. Don't you?'

He nodded emphatically, smiling.

'Almost a year ago to the day,' she said, 'Afreyt and I were walking alone upon the moor north of town, as has been our habit since childhood. We were lamenting Rime Isle's lost glories and lost (or man-renounced) gods and wishing for their return, so that the Isle might have surer guidance and fore-knowledge of perils. It was a day of changeable winds and weather, the end of spring, not quite yet summer, all the air alive, now bright, now gloomed-over, as clouds raced past the sun. We had just topped a gentle rise when we came upon the form of a youth sprawled on his back in the heather with eyes closed and head thrown back, looking as if he were dying or in the last stages of exhaustion – as though he has been cast ashore by the last great waves of some unimaginably great storm on high.

'He wore a simple tunic of homespun, very worn, and the plainest sandals, worn thin, with frayed thongs, and a very old belt dimly pricked out with monsters, yet from first sight I was almost certain that he was a god.

'I knew it in three ways. From his insubstantiality – though he was there to the touch, I could almost see the crushed heather through his pale flesh. From his supernal beauty – it was ... the flame-face, though tranquil-featured, almost as if in death. And from the adoration I felt swelling in my heart.

'I also knew it from the way Afreyt acted, kneeling at once like myself beside him across from me – though there was something unnatural in her behavior, betokening an amazing development when we understood it aright, which we did not then. (More of that later.)

'You know how they say a god dies when his believers utterly fail him? Well, it was as if this one's last worshiper were dying in Nehwon. Or as if – this is closer to it – all his wor-shipers had died in his own proper world and he whirled out into the wild spaces between the worlds, to sink or swim, sur-vive or perish according to the reception he got in whatever new world whereon chance cast him ashore. I think it's within the power of gods to travel between the worlds, don't you? – both involuntarily and also by their own design. And who knows what unpredictable tempests they might encounter in dark mid-journey?

'But I was not wasting time in speculations on that day of miracles a year ago. No, I was chafing his wrist and chest, pressing my warm cheek against his cold one, prising open his lips with my tongue (his jaw was slack) and with my open lips clamped upon his (and his nostrils clipped between my finger and thumb) sending my fresh, new-drawn breaths deep into his lungs, the meanwhile fervently praying to him in my mind, though I know they say the gods hear only our words, no thoughts. A stranger, happening upon us, might have judged us in the second or third act of lovemaking, I the more feverish seeking to rekindle his ardor.

'Meanwhile Afreyt (again here's that unnatural thing I mentioned) seemed to be as busy as I across from me – and yet somehow I was doing all the work. The explanation of that came somewhat later.

'My god showed signs of life. His eyelids quivered, I felt his chest stir, while his lips began to return my kisses.

'I uncapped my silver flask and dribbled brandy between his lips, alternating the drops with further kisses and words of comfort and endearment.

'At last he opened his eyes (brown shot with gold, like yours) and with my help raised up his head, meanwhile muttering words in a strange tongue. I answered in what languages I know, but he only frowned, shaking his head. That's how I knew he was not a Nehwon god – it's natural, don't you think, that a god, all-knowing in his own world, would be at a loss at first, plunged into another? He'd have to take it in.

'Finally he smiled and lifted his hand to my bosom, looking at me questioningly. I spoke my name. He nodded and shaped his lips, repeated it. Then he touched his own chest and spoke the name "Loki."'

At that word the Mouser knew feelings and thoughts similar to those of Fafhrd hearing 'Odin' – of other lives and worlds, and of Karl Treuherz's tongue and his little Lankhmarese-German, German-Lankhmarese dictionary that he'd given Fafhrd. At the same moment, though for that moment only, he saw the fire-face so like his own in the flames, seeming to wink at him. He frowned wonderingly.

Cif continued, 'Thereafter I fed him crumbs of meat from my script, which he accepted from my fingers, eating sparingly and sipping more brandy, the whiles I taught him words, pointing to this and that. That day Darkfire was smoking thick and showing flames, which interested him mightily when I named it. So I took flint and iron from my script and struck them together, naming "fire". He was delighted, seeming to gather strength from the sparks and smouldering straws and the very word. He'd stroke the little flames without seeming to take hurt. That frightened me.

'So passed the day – I utterly lost in him, unaware of all else, save what struck his fancy moment by moment. He was a wondrously apt scholar. I named objects both in our Rime tongue and Low Lankhmarese, thinking it'd be useful to him as he got his vision for lands beyond the Isle.

'Evening drew in. I helped the god to his feet. The wan light washing over him seemed to dissolve a little his pale flesh.

'I indicated Salthaven, that we should walk there. He assented eagerly (I think he was attracted by its evening smokes, being drawn to fire, his trumps) and we set out, he leaning on me lightly.

'And now the mystery of Afreyt was made clear. She would by no means go with us! And then I saw, though only very dimly, the figure *she* had been succoring, tending and teaching all day long, as I had Loki – the figure of a frail old man (god, rather), bearded and one-eyed, who'd been lying close alongside Loki at the first, and I empowered to see only the one and she the other!'

'A most marvelous circumstance indeed,' the Mouser commented. 'Perhaps like drew to like and so revealed itself. Say, did the other god by any chance resemble Fafhrd? – but for being one-eyed, of course.'

She nodded eagerly. 'An older Fafhrd, as 'twere his father. Afreyt marked it. Oh, you must know something of this mystery?'

The Mouser shook his head, 'Just guessing,' and asked, 'What was *his* name – the older god's?'

(She told him.)

'Well, what happened next?'

'We parted company. I walked the god Loki to Salthaven, he leaning on my arm. He was still most delicate. It seems one worshiper is barely enough at best to keep a god alive and visible, no matter how active his mind – for by now he was pointing out things to me (and indicating actions and states) and naming them in Rimic, Low Lankhmarese – and High as well! – before I named them, sure indication of his god's intellect.

'At the same time he was, despite his weakness, beginning to give me indications of a growing interest in me (I mean, my person) and I was fast losing all doubts as to how I'd be expected to entertain him when I got him home. Now, I was very happy to have got, hopefully, a new god for Rime Isle. And I must needs adore him, if only to keep him alive. But as for making him free of my bed, I had a certain reluctance, no matter how ghostly-insubstantial his flesh turned out to be in closest contact (and if it stayed that way)!

'Oh, I suppose I'd have submitted if it had come to that; still, there's something about sleeping with a god – a great honor, to be sure, but (to name only one thing) one surely couldn't expect faithfulness (if one wanted that) – certainly not from the whimsical, merry and mischievous god this Loki was showing himself to be! Besides, I wanted to be able to weigh clearheadedly the predictions and warnings for Rime Isle I hoped to get from him – not with a mind dreamy with lovemaking and swayed by all the little fancies and fears that come with full infatuation.

'As things fell out, I never had to make the decision. Passing this tavern, he was attracted by a flickering red glow and slipped inside without attracting notice (he was still invisible to all but me). I followed (that got me a look or two, I being a respectable councilwoman) and pressed on after him as he followed the pulsing fire-glow into this inner room, where a great bawdy party was going on and the hearth was ablaze. Before my eyes he melted into the flames and joined with them!

'The revelers were somewhat taken aback by my intrusion, but after looking them over with a smile I merely turned and went out, waving my hand at them and saying, "Enjoy!" – that was for Loki too. I'd guessed he'd got where he wanted to be.'

And she waved now at the dancing flames, then turned back to the Mouser with a smile. He smiled back, shaking his head in wonder.

She continued, 'So I went home, well content, but not before I'd reserved the Flame Den (as I then learned this place is called) for the following night.

'Next day I hired two harlots for the evening (so there'd be entertainment for Loki) and Mother Grum to be our door-woman and ensure our privacy.

'That night went as I guessed it would. Loki had indeed taken up permanent residence in the fire here and after a while I was able to talk with him and get some answers to questions, though nothing of profit to Rime Isle as yet. I made arrangements with the Ilthmart for the Flame Den to be reserved one night each week, and like bargains with Hilsa and Rill to come on those nights and entertain the god and keep him happy. Hilsa, has the god been with you tonight?' she called to the woman feeding the fire, the one with red stockings.

'Twice,' that one replied matter-of-factly in a husky voice. 'Slipped from the fire invisibly and back again. He's content.'

'Your pardon, Lady Cif,' the Mouser interposed, 'but how do these professional women find such close commerce with an invisible god to be? What's it like? I'm curious.'

Cif looked toward them where they sat by the fire.

'Like having a mouse up your skirt,' Hilsa replied with a short chuckle, swinging a red leg.

'Or a toad,' her companion amended. 'Although he dwells in the flames, his person is cold.' Rill had laid aside her cat's cradle and joined her hands, fingers interweaving, to make shadow-faces on the wall, of prick-eared gigantic werewolves, great sea serpents, dragons, and long-nosed, long-chinned witches. 'He likes these hobgoblins,' she commented.

The Mouser nodded thoughtfully, watching them for a while, and then back to the fire.

Cif continued, 'Soon the god, I could tell, was beginning to get the feel of Nehwon, fitting his mind to her, stretching it out to her farthest bounds, and his oracles became more to the point. Meantime Afreyt, with whom I conferred daily, was caring for old Odin out on the moor in much the same way (though using girls to comfort and appease him 'stead of full-grown women, he being an older god), eliciting prophecies of import.

'Loki it was who first warned us that the Mingols were on the move, mustering horse-ships against Rime Isle, mounting under Khahkht's urgings toward a grand climacteric of madness and rapine. Afreyt put independent question to Odin and he confirmed it – they were together in the tale at every point.

'When asked what we must do, they both advised – again independently – that we seek out two certain heroes in Lankhmar and have them bring their bands to the Isle's defence. They were most circumstantial, giving your names and haunts, saying you were their men, whether or not you knew it in this life, and they did not change their stories under repeated questioning. Tell me, Gray Mouser, have you not known the god Loki before? Speak true.'

'Upon my word, I haven't, Lady Cif,' he averred, 'and am no more able than you to explain the mystery of our resemblance. Though there is a certain weird familiarity about the name, and Odin's too, as if I'd heard them in dreams or nightmares. But however I rack my brains, it comes no clearer.'

'Well,' she resumed after a pause, 'the two gods kept up their urgings that we seek you out and so half a year ago Afreyt and I took ship for Lankhmar on Hlal – with what results you know.'

'Tell me, Lady Cif,' the Mouser interjected, rousing himself from his fire-peerings, 'how did you and tall Afreyt get back to Rime Isle after Khahkht's wizardrous blizzard snatched you out of the Silver Eel?'

'It transpired as swiftly as our journey there was long,' she said. 'One moment we were in his cold clutch, battered and blinded by wind-driven ice, our ears assaulted by a booming laughter. The next we had been taken in charge by two feminine flying creatures who whirled us at dizzying speed through darkness to a warm cave where they left us breathless. They said they were a mountain king's two daughters.'

'Hirriwi and Keyaira, I'll be bound!' the Mouser exclaimed. 'They must be on our side.'

'Who are those?' Cif inquired.

'Mountain princesses Fafhrd and I have known in our day. Invisibles like our revered fire-dweller here.' He nodded toward the flames. 'Their father rules in lofty Stardock.'

'I've heard of that peak and dread Oomforafor, its king, whom some say is with his son Faroomfar an ally of Khahkht. Daughters against father and brother – that would be natural. Well, Afreyt and I after we'd recovered our breath made our way to the cavern's mouth – and found ourselves looking down on Rime Isle and Salthaven from a point midway up Darkfire. With some difficulty we made our way home across rock and glacier.'

'The volcano,' the Mouser mused. 'Again Loki's link with fire.' His attention had been drawn back to the hypnotic flames.

Cif nodded. 'Thereafter Loki and Odin kept us informed of the Mingols' progress toward Rime Isle – and your own. Then four days ago Loki began a running account of your encounters with Khahkht's frost monstreme. He made it most vivid – sometimes you'd have sworn he was piloting one of the ships himself. I managed to reserve the Flame Den the succeeding nights (and have it now for the next three days and nights also), so we were able to follow the details of the long flight or long pursuit – which, truth to tell, became a bit monotonous.'

'You should have been there,' the Mouser murmured.

'Loki made me feel I was.'

'Incidentally,' the Mouser said casually, 'I'd think you'd have rented the Flame Den every night once you'd got your god here.'

'I'm not made of gold,' she informed him without rancor. 'Besides, Loki likes variety. The brawls that others hold here amuse him – were what attracted him in the first place.

Furthermore, it would have made the council even more suspicious of my activities.'

The Mouser nodded. 'I thought I recognized a crony of Groniger's playing chess out there.'

'Hush,' she counseled him. 'I must now consult the god.' Her voice had grown a little singsong in the later stages of her narrative and it became more so as, without transition, she invoked, 'And now, O Loki god, tell us about our enemies across the seas and in the realms of ice. Tell us of cruel, cold Khahkht, of Edumir of the Widdershin Mingols and Gonov of the Sunwise. Hilsa and Rill, sing with me to the god.' And her voice became a somnolent two-toned, wordless chant in which the other women joined: Hilsa's husky voice, Rill's slightly shrill one, and a soft growling that after a bit the Mouser realized came from Mother Grum – all tuned to the fire and its flame-voice.

The Mouser lost himself in this strange medley of notes and all at once, the crackling flame-voice, as if by some dream magic, became fully articulate, murmuring rapidly in Low Lankhmarese with occasional words slipped in that were as hauntingly strange as the god's own name.

'Storm clouds thicken round Rime Isle. Nature brews her blackest bile. Monsters quicken, nightmares foal, niss and nicor, drow and troll.' (Those last four nouns were all strange ones to the Mouser, specially the bell-toll sound of 'troll'.) 'Sound alarms and strike the drum – in three days the Mingols come, Sunwise Mingols from the east, horse-head ship and human beast. Trick them all most cunningly – lead them to the spinning sea, to down-swirling dizzy bowl. Trust the whirlpool, 'ware the troll! Mingols to their deaths must go, down to weedy hell below, never draw an easy breath, suffer an unending death, everlasting pain and strife, everlasting death in life. Mingol madness ever burn! Never peace again return!'

And the flame-voice broke off in a flurry of explosive crackles that shattered the dream-magic and brought the Mouser to his feet with a great start, his sleepy mood all gone. He stared at the fire, walked rapidly around it, peered at it closely from the other side, then swiftly scanned the entire room. Nothing!

He glared at Hilsa and Rill. They eyed him blandly and said in unison, 'The god has spoken,' but the sense of a presence was gone from the fire and the room as well, leaving behind not even a black hole into which it might have retired – unless perchance (it occurred to the Mouser) it had retired into *him*, accounting for the feeling of restless energy and flaming thought which now possessed him, while the litany of Mingol doom kept repeating itself over and over in his memory. 'Can such things be?' he asked himself and answered himself with an instant and resounding 'Yes!'

He paced back to Cif, who had risen likewise. 'We have three days,' she said.

'So it appears,' he said, then, 'Know you aught of trolls? What are they?'

'I was about to ask you that,' she replied. 'The word's as strange to me as it appears to be to you.'

'Whirlpools, then,' he queried, his thoughts racing. 'Any of them about the isle? Any sailors' tales—?'

'Oh, yes – the Great Maelstorm off the isle's rock-fanged east coast with its treacherous swift currents and tricky tides, the Great Maelstrom from whence the island gets what wood it owns, after it's cast up on the Beach of Bleached Bones. It forms regularly each day. Our sailors know it well and avoid it like no other peril.'

'Good! I must put to sea and seek it out and learn its every trick and how it comes and goes. I'll need a small sailing craft for that while *Flotsam*'s laid up for repairs – there's little time. Aye, and I'll need more money too – shore silver for my men.'

'Wherefore to sea?' her breath catching, she asked. 'Wherefore must you dash yourself at such a maw of danger?' – but in her widening eyes he thought he could see the dawning of the answer to that.

'Why, to put down your foes,' he said ringingly. 'Heard you not Loki's prophecy? We'll expedite it. We'll drown at least one branch of the Mingols e'er ever they set foot on Rimeland! And if, with Odin's aid, Fafhrd and Afreyt can scupper the Widder-Mingols half as handily, our task is done!'

The triumphant look flared up in her eyes to match that in his own.

The waning moon rode high in the southwest and the brightest stars still shone, but in the east the sky had begun to pale with the dawn, as Fafhrd led his twelve berserks north out of Salthaven. Each was warmly clad against the ice ahead and bore longbow, quiver, extra arrow-pack, belted ax, and bag of provender. Skor brought up the rear, keen to enforce Fafhrd's rule of utter silence while they traversed the town, so that this breach of port regulations might go unnoticed. And for a wonder they had not been challenged. Perhaps the Rimelanders slept extra sound because so many of them had been up to all hours salting down the monster fish-catch, the last boatloads of which had come in after nightfall.

With the berserks tripped along the girls May and Mara in their soft boots and hooded cloaks, the former with a jar of fresh-drawn milk for the god Odin, the latter to be the expeditions's guide across central Rime Isle to Cold Harbor, at Afreyt's insistence – 'for she was born on a Cold Harbor farm and knows the way – and can keep up with any man.'

Fafhrd had nodded dubiously on hearing that. He had not liked accepting responsibility for a girl with his childhood sweetheart's name. Nor had he liked leaving the management of everything in Salthaven to the Mouser and the two women, now that there was so much to do, and besides all else the new task of investigating the Grand Maelstrom and spying out its ways, which would occupy the Mouser for a day at least, and which more befitted Fafhrd as the more experienced ship-conner. But the four of them had conferred together at midnight in *Flotsam*'s cabin behind shrouded portholes, pooling their knowledge and counsels and the two gods' prophecies, and it had been so decided.

The Mouser would take Ourph with him, for his ancient sea-wisdom, and Mikkidu, to discipline him, using a small fishing craft belonging to the women. Meanwhile, Pshawri would be left in sole charge of the repairs on *Flotsam* and *Sea Hawk* (subject to the advisements of the three remaining Mingols), trying to keep up the illusion that Fafhrd's berserks were still aboard the latter. Cif and Afreyt would take turns in standing by at the docks to head off inquiries by Groniger and deal with any other matters that might arise unexpectedly.

Well, it should work, Fafhrd told himself, the Rime Islers being such blunt, unsubtle types, hardy and simple. Certainly the Mouser had seemed confident enough – restless and driving, eyes flashing, humming a tune under his breath.

Onwinging dawn pinkened the low sky to the east as Fafhrd tramped ahead through the heather, lengthening his stride, an ear attuned to the low voices of the men behind and the lighter ones of the girls. A glance overshoulder told him they were keeping close order, with Mara and May immediately behind him.

As Gallows Hill showed up to the left, he heard the men mark it with grim exclamations. A couple spat to ward off ill omen.

'Bear the god my greeting, May,' he heard Mara say.

'If he wakes enough to attend to aught but drink his milk and sleep again,' May replied as she branched off from the expedition and headed for the hill with her jar through the dissipating shadows of night.

Some of the men exclaimed gloomily at that, too, and Skor called for silence.

Mara said softly to Fafhrd, 'We bear left here a little, so as to miss Darkfire's icefall, which we skirt through the Isle's center until it joins the glacier of Mount Hellglow.'

Fafhrd thought, what cheerful names they favor, and scanned ahead. Heather and gorse were becoming scantier and stretches of lichened, shaly rock beginning to show.

'What do they call this part of Rime Isle?' he asked her.

'The Deathlands,' she answered.

More of the same, he thought. Well, at any rate the name fits the mad, death-bent Mingols and this gallows-favoring Odin god too.

The Mouser was tallest of the four short, wiry men waiting at the edge of the public dock. Pshawri close beside him looked resolute and attentive, though still somewhat pale. A neat bandage went across his forehead. Ourph and Mikkidu rather resembled two monkeys, the one wizened and wise, the other young and somewhat woebegone.

The salt cliff to the east barely hid the rising sun, which glittered along its crystalline summit and poured light on the farther half of the harbor and on the fishing fleet putting out to sea. The Mouser gazed speculatively after the small vessels – you'd have thought the Islanders would have been satisfied with yesterday's monster catch, but no, they seemed even more in a hurry today, as if they were fishing for all Nehwon or as if some impatient chant were beating in their heads, driving them on, such as was beating in the Mouser's now: *Mingols to their deaths must go, down to weedy hell below* – yes, to hell they must go indeed! and time was wasting and where was Cif?

That question was answered when a skiff came sculling quietly along very close to the dock, propelled by Mother Grum sitting in the stern and wagging a single oar from side to side like a fish's tail. When Cif stood up in the boat's midst her head was level with the dock. She caught hold of the hand the Mouser reached down and came up in two long steps.

'Few words,' she said. 'Mother Grum will scull you to *Sprite*,' and she passed the Mouser a purse.

'Silver only,' she said with a wrinkle of her nose as he made to glance into it.

He handed it to Pshawri. 'Two pieces to each man at nightfall, if I'm not returned,' he directed. 'Keep them hard at work. 'Twere well *Flotsam* were seaworthy by noon tomorrow at latest. Go.'

Pshawri saluted and made off.

The Mouser turned to the others. 'Down into the skiff with you.'

They obeyed, Ourph impassive-faced, Mikkidu with an apprehensive sidewise look at their grim boatwoman. Cif touched the Mouser's arm. He turned back.

She looked him evenly in the eye. 'The Maelstrom is dangerous,' she said. 'Here's what perhaps can quell it, if it should trap you. If needs must, hurl it into the pool's exact midst. Guard it well and keep it secret.'

Surprised at the weight of the small cubical object she pressed into his hand, he glanced down at it surreptitiously. 'Gold?' he breathed, a little wonderingly. It was in the form of a skeleton cube, twelve short thick gold-gleaming edges conjoined squarely.

'Yes,' she replied flatly. 'Lives are more valuable.'

'And there's some superstition—?'

'Yes,' she cut him short.

He nodded, pouched it carefully, and without other word descended lightly into the skiff. Mother Grum worked her oar back and forth, sending them toward the one small fishing craft remaining in the harbor.

Cif watched after them as their skiff emerged into full sunlight. After a while she felt the same sunlight on her head and knew it was striking golden highlights from her dark hair. The Mouser never looked around. She did not really want him to. The skiff reached *Sprite* and the three men climbed nimbly aboard.

She could have sworn there'd been no one near, but next she heard the sound of a throat being cleared behind her. She waited a few moments, then turned around.

'Master Groniger,' she greeted.

'Mistress Cif,' he responded in equally mild tones. He did not look like a man who had been sneaking about.

'You send the strangers on a mission?' he remarked after a bit.

She shook her head slowly. 'I rent them a ship, the lady Afreyt's and mine. Perhaps they go fishing.' She shrugged. 'Like any Isler, I turn a dollar when I can and fishing's not the only road to profit. Not captaining your craft today, master?'

He shook his head in turn. 'A harbor chief first has the responsibilities of his office, mistress. The other stranger's not been seen yet today. Nor his men either . . .'

'So?' she asked when he'd paused a while.

'. . . though there's a great racket of work below deck in his sailing galley.'

She nodded and turned to watch *Sprite* making for the harbor mouth under sail and the skiff sculling off with its lone shaggy-haired, squat figure.

'A meeting of the council has been called for tonight,' Groniger said as if in afterthought. She nodded without turning around. He added in explanation, casually, 'An audit has been asked for, Lady Treasurer, of all gold coin and Rimic treasures in your keeping – the golden arrow of truth, the gold circles of unity, the gold cube of square-dealing . . .'

She nodded again, then lifted her hand to her mouth. He heard the sigh of a yawn. The sun was bright on her hair.

By midafternoon Fafhrd's band was high in the Death-lands, here a boulder-studded expanse of barren, dark rock between low glacial walls a bowshot off to the left, closer than that on the right – a sort of broad pass. The westering sun beat down hotly, but the breeze was chill. The blue sky seemed close.

First went the youngest of his berserks, unarmed, as point. (An unarmed man really scans for the foe and does not engage them.) Twoscore yards behind him went Mannimark as cover-point and behind *him* the main party led by Fafhrd with Mara beside him, Skor still bringing up the rear.

A large white hare broke cover ahead and raced away past them the way they had come, taking fantastic bounds, seemingly terrified. Fafhrd waved in the men ahead and arranged two-thirds of his force in an ambush where the stony cover was good, putting Skor in charge of them with orders to hold that position and engage any enemy on sight with heavy arrow fire but on no account to charge. Then he rapidly led the rest by a circuitous and shielded route up onto the nearest glacier. Skullick, Mara, and three others were with them. Thus far the girl had lived up to Afreyt's claims for her, making no trouble.

As he cautiously led them out onto the ice, the silence of the heights was broken by the faint twang of bowstrings and by sharp cries from the direction of the ambush and ahead.

From his point of vantage Fafhrd could see his ambush and, almost a bowshot ahead of it in the pass, a party of some forty men, Mingols by their fur smocks and hats and curvy bows. The men of his ambush and some dozen of the Mingols were exchanging high-arching arrow fire. One of the Mingols was down and their leaders seemed in dispute. Faf quickly strung his bow, ordering the four men with him to do the same, and they sent off a volley of arrows from his flanking position. Another Mingol was hit – one of the disputants. A half dozen returned their fire, but Fafhrd's position had the advantage of height. The rest took cover. One danced up and down, as if in rage, but was dragged behind rocks by companions. After a bit the whole Mingol party, so far as Fafhrd could tell, began to move off the way they'd come, bearing their wounded with them.

'And now charge and destroy 'em?' Skullick ventured, grinning fiendishly. Mara looked eagerly.

'And show 'em we're but a dozen? I forgive you your youth,' Fafhrd retored, halting Skor's fire with a downward wave of his arm. 'No, we'll escort 'em watchfully back to their ship, or Cold Harbor, or whatever. Best foe is one in flight,' and he sent a runner to Skor to convey his plan, meanwhile thinking how the fur-clad Steppe-men seemed less furiously hell-bent on rapine than he'd anticipated. He must watch for Mingol ruses. He wondered what old god Odin (who'd said 'destroy') would think of his decision. Perhaps Mara's eyes, fixed upon him with what looked very much like disappointment, provided an answer.

The Mouser sat on the decked prow of *Sprite*, his back to the mast, his feet resting on the root of the bowsprit, as they re-approached Rime Isle, running down on the island from the northeast. Some distance ahead should lie the spot where the maelstrom would form and now, with the tide ebbing, getting toward the time – if he'd calculated aright and could trust information got earlier from Cif and Ourph. Behind him in the stern the old Mingol managed tiller and triangular fore-and-aft mainsail handily while Mikkidu, closer, watched the single narrow jib.

The Mouser unstrapped the flap of the small deep pouch at his belt and gazed down at the compact dully gold-gleaming 'whirlpool-queller' (to give a name to the object Cif had given him) nested inside. Again it occurred to him how magnificently spendthrift (but also how bone-stupid) it was to make such a necessarily expendable object of gold. Well, you couldn't dictate prudence to superstition . . . Or perhaps you could.

'Mikkidu!' he called sharply.

'Yes, sir?' came the answer – immediate, dutiful and a shade apprehensive.

'You noted the long coil of thin line hanging inside the hatch? The sort of slender yet stout stuff you'd use to lower loot to an accomplice outside a high window or trust your own weight to in a pinch? The sort some stranglers use?'

'Yes, sir!'

'Good. Fetch it for me.'

It proved to be as he'd described it and at least a hundred yards long, he judged. A sardonic smile quirked his lips as he knotted one end of it securely to the whirlpool-queller and the other end to a ring bolt in the deck, checked that the rest of the coil lay running free, and returned the queller to his pouch.

They'd been half a day sailing here. First a swift run to the east with wind abeam as soon as they'd got out of Salthaven harbor, leaving the Rimic fishing fleet very busy to the south-west, where the sea seemed to boil with fish, until they were well past the white salt headland. Then a long slow beat north into the wind, taking them gradually away from the Isle's dark craggy east coast, which, replacing the glittering salt, trended toward the west. Finally, now, a swift return, running before the wind, to that same coast where a shallow bay guarded by twin crags lured the unwary mariner. The sail sang and the small waves, advancing in ranked array, slapped the creaming prow. The sunlight was bright everywhere.

The Mouser stood up, closely scanning the sea immediately ahead for submerged rocks and signs of tides at work. The speed of *Sprite* seemed to increase beyond that given it by the wind, as though a current had ripped it. He noted an eddying ahead, sudden curves in the wave-topping lines of foam. Now was the time! – if there was to be. He called to Ourph to be ready to go about.

Despite all these anticipations he was taken by surprise when (it seemed it must be) an unseen giant hand gripped *Sprite* from below, turned it instantly sideways and jerked it ahead in a curve, tilting it sharply inward. He saw Mikkidu standing in the air over the water a yard from the deck. As he involuntarily moved to join the dumbfounded thief, his left hand automatically seized the mast while his right, stretching out mightily, grabbed Mikkidu by the collar. The Mouser's muscles cracked but took the strain. He deposited Mikkidu on the deck, putting a foot on him to keep him there, then crouched into the wind that was rattling the sails, and managed to look around.

Where ranked waves had been moments before, *Sprite* at prodigious speed was circling a deepening saucer of spinning black water almost two hundred yards across. Dimly past the wildly flapping mainsail the Mouser glimpsed Ourph clinging with both hands to the tiller. Looking again at the whirlpool he saw that *Sprite* was appreciably closer to its deepening center, whence jagged rocks now protruded like a monster's blackened and broken fangs. Without pause he dug in his pouch for the queller and, trying to allow for wind and *Sprite*'s speed, he hurled it at the watery pit's center. For a space it seemed to hang glinting golden-yellow in the sunlight, then fell true.

This time it was as if a hundred giant invisible hands had smote the whirlpool flat. *Sprite* seemed to hit a wall. There was a sudden welter of cross-chopping waves that generated so much foam that it piled up on the deck and one would have sworn the water was filled with soap.

The Mouser reassured himself that Ourph and Mikkidu were there and in an upright position so that, given time, they might recover. Next he ascertained that the sky and sea appeared to be in their proper places. Then he checked on the tiller and sails. His eye falling away from the bedraggled jib lit on the ringbolt in the prow. He reeled in the line attached to it (not very hopefully – surely it would have snagged or snapped in the chaos they'd just endured) but for a wonder it came out with the queller still tightly knotted to the end of it, more golden-bright than ever from its tumbling it had got in the rocks. As he pouched it and laced tight the soggy flap, he felt remarkably self-satisfied.

By now the waves and wind had resumed something like their normal flow and Ourph and Mikkidu were stirring. The Mouser set them back at their duties (refusing to discuss at all the whirlpool's appearance and vanishment) and he cockily had them sail *Sprite* close inshore, where he noted a beach of jagged rocks with considerable gray timber amongst them, bones of dead ships.

Time for the Rime-men to pick up another load, he thought breezily. Have to tell Groniger. Or perhaps best wait for the next wrecks – Mingol ones! – which should provide a prodigious harvest.

Smiling, the Mouser set course for Salthaven, an easy sail now with the favoring wind. Under his breath he hummed, 'Mingols to their deaths must go, down to weedy hell below.' Aye, and their ships to rock-fanged doom.

Somewhere between cloud layers north of Rime Isle there floated miraculously the sphere of black ice that was Khahkht's home and most-times prison. Snow falling steadily between the layers gave the black sphere a white cap. The falling snow also accumulated on and so whitely outlined the mighty wings, back, neck, and crest of the invisible being poised beside the sphere. This being must have been clutching the sphere in some fashion, for whenever it shook its head and shoulders to dislodge the snow, the sphere jogged in the thin air.

Three-quarters of the way down the sphere, a trapdoor had been flung open and from it Khahkht had thrust Its head, shoulders, and one arm, like a peculiarly nasty god looking sidewise down and out of the floor of heaven.

The two beings conversed together.

Khahkht: *Fretful monster! Why do you trouble my celestial*

privacy, rappings on my sphere? Soon I'll be sorry that I gave you wings.

Faroomfar: *I'd as soon shift back to a flying invisible ray-fish. It had advantages.*

Khahkht: *For two black dogs, I'd—!*

Faroomfar: *Contain your ugly self, granddad. I've good reason to knock you up. The Mingols seem to lessen in their frenzy. Gonov of the Sunwise descending on Rime Isle has ordered his ships double-reef for a mere gale. While the Widder-raiders coming down across the Isle have turned back from a force less than a third their size. Have your incantments weakened?*

Khahkht: *Content you. I have been seeking to assess the two new gods who aid Rime Isle: how powerful, whence they come, their final purpose, and whether they may be suborned. My tentative conclusion: They're a treacherous pair, none too strong – rogue gods from a minor universe. We'd best ignore 'em.*

The snow had re-gathered on the flier, a fine dust of it revealing even somewhat of his thin, cruel, patrician features. He shook it off.

Faroomfar: *So, what to do?*

Khahkht: *I'll refire the Mingols where (and if) they flinch back, never you fear. Do you, meanwhile, evade your wicked sisters if you're able and work what devilish mischief you can on Fafhrd (it's he that's cowed the Widder-raiders, right?) and his band. Aim at the girl. To work!*

And he drew back into his black, snow-capped sphere and slammed the trapdoor, like a reverse jack-in-the-box. The falling snow was disturbed in a broad downward sweep as Faroomfar spread wings and began his descent from the heights.

Most commendably, Mother Grum was waiting in the skiff at the anchorage when Ourph and Mikkidu brought *Sprite* breezing in neatly to make fast to the buoy and furl the sail under the Mouser's watchful, approving eye. He was still in a marvelously good mood of self-satisfaction and had even unbent to make a few benign remarks to Mikkidu (which puzzled the latter mightily) and discourse sagely by whimsical fits and starts with the wise, if somewhat taciturn, old Mingol.

Now sharing the skiff's mid thwart with Ourph, while Mikkidu huddled in the prow, the Mouser airily asked the hag as she sculled them in, 'How went the day, Mother? Any word for me from your mistress?' When she answered him only with a grunt that might mean anything or nothing, he merely remarked with mild sententiousness, 'Bless your loyal old bones,' and let his attention wander idly about the harbor.

Night had fallen. The last of the fishing fleet had just come in, low in the water with another record-breaking catch. His attention fixed on the nearest pier, where a ship on the other side was unloading by torchlight and four Rime-men, going in single file, were bearing ashore what were undoubtedly the prizes of their monster (and monstrous) haul.

Yesterday the Rimelanders had impressed him as very solid and sober folk, but now more and more he was finding something oafish and loutish about them, especially these four as they went galumphing along, smirking and gaping and with eyes starting out of their heads beneath their considerable burdens.

First went a bent-over, bearded fellow, bearing upon his back by its finny tail a great silver tunny as long-bodied as he and even thicker.

Next a rangy chap carrying by neck and tail, wound round and over his shoulders, the largest eel the Mouser had ever seen. Its bearer gave the impression that he was wrestling with it as he hobbled – it writhed ponderously, still alive. *Lucky it's not twined about his neck*, the Mouser thought.

The man after the eel-carrier had, by a wicked handhook through its shell, a giant green crab on his back, its ten legs working persistently in the air, its great claws opening and closing. And it was hard to tell which of the two's eyes goggled out the farthest, the shellfish's or the man's.

Finally a fisherman bearing overshoulder by its bound-together tentacles an octopus still turning rainbow colours in its death-spasms, its great sunken eyes filming above its monstrous beak.

Monsters bearing monsters, the Mouser epitomized with a happy chuckle. *Lord, what grotesques we mortals be!*

And now the dock should be coming up. The Mouser turned round in his seat to look that way and saw ... not Cif, he decided regretfully after a moment ... but at any rate (and a little to his initial surprise) Hilsa and Rill at the dock's edge, the latter bearing a torch that flamed most merrily, both of them smiling warm welcomes and looking truly most brave in their fresh paint and whore's finery, Hilsa in her red stockings, Rill in a bright yellow pair, both in short gaudy smocks cut low at the neck. Really, they looked younger this way, or at least a little less shopworn, he thought as he leaped up and joined them on the dock. How nice of Loki to have sent his priestesses ... well, not priestesses exactly, say temple maidens rather ... no, not maidens exactly either, but professional ladies, nurses and playmates of the god ... to welcome home the god's faithful servant.

But no sooner had he bowed to them in turn than they put aside their smiles and Hilsa said to him urgently in a low voice, 'There's ill news, captain. Lady Cif's sent us to tell you that she and the Lady Afreyt have been impeached by the other council members. She's accused of using coined gold she had the keeping of and other Rimic treasures to fee you and the tall captain and your men. She expects you with your famed cleverness, she told me, to concoct some tale to counter all this.'

The Mouser's smile hardly faltered. He was struck rather with how gayly Rill's torch flickered and flared as Hilsa's doleful words poured over him. When Rimic treasures were mentioned he touched his pouch where the queller reposed on its snipped-off length of cord. He had no doubt that it was one of them, yet somehow he was not troubled.

'Is that all?' he asked when Hilsa had done. 'I thought at least you'd tell me the trolls had come, against whom the god has warned us. Lead on, my dears, to the council hall! Ourph and Mikkidu, attend us! Take courage, Mother Grum—' (he called down to the skiff) '—doubt not your mistress' safety.'

And linking arms with Hilsa and Rill he set out briskly,

telling himself that in reverses of fortune such as this, the all-important thing was to behave with vast self-confidence, flame like Rill's torch with it! That was the secret. What matter that he hadn't the faintest idea of what tale he would tell the council? Only maintain the appearance of self-confidence and at the moment when needed, inspiration would come!

What with the late arrival of the fishing fleet the narrow streets were quite crowded as they footed it along. Perhaps it was market night as well, and maybe the council meeting had something to do with it. At any rate there were a lot of 'foreigners' out and Rime Islers too, and for a wonder the latter looked stranger and more drolly grotesque than the former. Here came trudging those four fishers again with their monstrous burdens! A fat boy gaped at them. The Mouser patted his head in passing. Oh, what a show was life!

Hilsa and Rill, infected by the Mouser's lightheartedness, put on their smiles again. He must be a grand sight, he thought, strolling along with two fine whores as if he owned the town.

The blue front of the council hall appeared, its door framed by some gone galleon's massive stern and flanked by two glum louts with quarterstaves. The Mouser felt Hilsa and Rill hesitate, but crying in a loud voice, 'All honor to the council!' he swept them inside with him, Ourph and Mikkidu ducking in after.

The room inside was larger and somewhat more lofty than the one at the Salt Herring, but was gray-timbered like it, built of wrecks. And it had no fireplace, but was inadequately warmed by two smoking braziers and lit by torches that burned blue and sad (perhaps there were bronze nails in them), not merrily golden-yellow like Rill's. The main article of furniture was a long heavy table, at one end of which Cif and Afreyt sat, looking their haughtiest. Drawn away from them toward the other end were seated ten large sober Isle-men of middle years, Groniger in their midst, with such doleful, gloomily indignant, outraged looks on their faces that the Mouser burst out laughing. Other Islers crowded the walls, some women among them. All turned on the newcomers faces of mingled puzzlement and disapproval.

Groniger reared up and thundered at him, 'You dare to laugh at the gathered authority of Rime Isle? You, who come bursting in accompanied by women of the streets and your own trespassing crewmen?'

The Mouser managed to control his laughter and listen with the most open, honest expression imaginable, injured innocence incarnate.

Groniger went on, shaking his finger at the other, 'Well, there he stands, councilors, a chief receiver of the misappropriated gold, perchance even of the gold cube of honest dealing. The man who came to us out of the south with tales of magic storms and day turned night and vanished hostile vessels and a purported Mingol invasion – he who has, as you perceive, Mingols amongst his crew – the man who paid for his dockage in Rime Isle gold!'

Cif stood up at that, her eyes blazing, and said, 'Let him speak, at least, and answer this outrageous charge, since you won't take my word.'

A councilman rose beside Groniger. 'Why should we listen to a stranger's lies?'

Groniger said, 'I thank you, Dwone.'

Afreyt got to her feet. 'No, let him speak. Will you hear nothing but your own voices?'

Another councilman got up.

Groniger said, 'Yes, Zwaakin?'

That one said, 'No harm to hear what he has to say. He may convict himself out of his own mouth.'

Cif glared at Zwaakin and said loudly, 'Tell them, Mouser!'

At that moment the Mouser, glancing at Rill's torch (which seemed to wink at him) felt a godlike power invading and possessing him to the tips of his fingers and toes – nay, to the end of his every hair. Without warning – in fact, without knowing he was going to do it at all – he ran forward across the room and sprang atop the table where its sides were clear toward Cif's end.

He looked around compellingly at all (a sea of cold and hostile faces, mostly), gave them a searching stare, and then –

well, as the godlike force possessed every part of him utterly, his mind was perforce driven completely out of himself, the scene swiftly darkened, he heard himself *beginning* to say something in a mighty voice, but then he (his mind) fell irretrievably into an inner darkness deeper and blacker than any sleep or swound.

Then (for the Mouser) no time at all passed ... or an eternity.

His return to awareness (or rebirth, rather – it seemed that massive a transition) began with whirling yellow lights and grinning, open-mouthed, exalted faces mottling the inner darkness, and the sense of a great noise on the edge of the audible and of a resonant voice speaking words of power, and then without other warning the whole bright and deafening scene materialized with a rush and a roar and he was standing insolently tall on the massive council table, with what felt like a wild (or even demented) smile on his lips, while his left fist rested jauntily on his hip and his right was whirling around his head the golden queller (or cube of square dealing, he reminded himself) on its cord. And all around him every last Rimelander – councilmen, guards, common fishers, women (and Cif, Afreyt, Rill, Hilsa, Mikkidu, needless to say) – was staring at him with rapturous adoration (as if he were a god or legendary hero at least) and standing on their feet (some jumping up and down) and cheering him to the echo! Fists pounded the table, quarterstaves thudded the stony floor resoundingly. While torchmen whirled their sad flambeaux until they flamed as yellow-bright as Rill's.

Now in the name of all the gods at once, the Mouser asked himself, continuing however to grin, *whatever* did I tell or promise them to put them all in such a state? In the fiend's name, *what*?

Groniger swiftly mounted the other end of the table, boosted by those beside him, waved for silence, and as soon as he'd got a little of that commodity assured the Mouser in a great feelingful voice, advancing to make himself heard, 'We'll do it – oh, we'll do it! I myself will lead out the Rimic contingent, half our armed citizenry, across the Deathlands to Fafhrd's aid against the Widdershins, while Dwone and Zwaaken will man the armed fishing fleet with the other half and follow you in *Flotsam* against the Sunwise Mingols. Victory!'

And with that the hall resounded with cries of 'Death to the Mingols!' 'Victory!' and other cheers the Mouser couldn't quite make out. As the noise passed its peak, Groniger shouted, 'Wine! Let's pledge our allegiance!' while Zwaaken cried to the Mouser, 'Summon your crewmen to celebrate with us – they've the freedom of Rime Isle now and forever!' (Mikkidu was soon dispatched.)

The Mouser looked helplessly at Cif – though still maintaining his grin (by now he must look quite glassy-eyed, he thought) – but she only stretched her hand toward him, crying, flush-cheeked, 'I'll sail with you!' while Afreyt beside her proclaimed, 'I'll go ahead across the Deathlands to join Fafhrd, bringing god Odin with me!'

Groniger heard that and called to her, 'I and my men will give you whatever help with that you need, honored councillady,' which told the Mouser that besides all else he'd got the atheistical fishermen believing in gods – Odin and Loki, at any rate. *What* had he told them?

He let Cif and Afreyt draw him down, but before he would begin to question them, Cif had thrown her arms around him, hugged him tight, and was kissing him full on the lips. This was wonderful, something he'd been dreaming of for three months and more (even though he'd pictured it happening in somewhat more private circumstances) and when she at last drew back, starry-eyed, it was another sort of question he was of a mind to ask her, but at that moment tall Afreyt grabbed him and soon was kissing him as soundly.

This was undeniably pleasant, but it took away from Cif's kiss, made it less personal, more a sign of congratulations and expression of overflowing enthusiasm than a mark of special affection. His Cif-dream faded down. And when Afreyt was done with him, he was at once surrounded by a press of wellwishers, some of whom wanted to embrace him also. From the corner of his eye he noted Hilsa and Rill bussing all and sundry – really, all these kisses had no meaning at all, including Cif's of course, he'd been a fool to think differently – and at one point he could have sworn he saw Groniger dancing a jig. Only old Ourph, for some reason, did not join in the merriment. Once he caught the old Mingol looking at him sadly.

And so the celebration began that lasted half the night and involved much drinking and eating and impromptu cheering and dancing and parading round and about and in and out. And the longer it went on, the more grotesque the cavorting and footstamping marches got, and all of it to the rhythm of the vindictive little rhyme that still went on resounding deep in the Mouser's mind, the tune to which everything was beginning to dance: 'Storm clouds thicken round Rime Isle. Nature brews her blackest bile. Monsters quicken, nightmares foal, niss and nicor, drow and troll.' Those lines in particular seemed to the Mouser to describe what was happening just now – a birth of monsters. (But where were the trolls?) And so on (the rhyme) until its doomful and monstrously compelling end: 'Mingols to their deaths must go, down to weedy hell below, never draw an easy breath, suffer an unending death, everlasting pain and strife, everlasting death in life. Mingol madness ever burn! Never peace again return!'

And through it all the Mouser maintained his perhaps glassy-eyed smile and jaunty, insolent air of supreme self-confidence, he answered one repeated question with, 'No, I'm no orator – never had any training – though I've always liked to talk,' but inwardly he seethed with curiosity. As soon as he got a chance, he asked Cif, 'Whatever did I say to bring them around, to change their minds so utterly?'

'Why, you should know,' she told him.

'But tell me in your own words,' he said.

She deliberated. 'You appealed entirely to their feelings, to their emotions,' she said at last, simply. 'It was wonderful.'

'Yes, but what exactly did I say? What were my words?'

'Oh, I can't tell you *that*,' she protested. 'It was so all of a piece that no one thing stood out – I've quite forgotten the details. Content you, it was perfect.'

Later on he ventured to inquire of Groniger, 'At what point did my arguments begin to persuade you?'

'How can you ask that?' the grizzled Rimelander rejoined, a frown of honest puzzlement furrowing his brow. 'It was all so supremely logical, clearly and coldly reasoned. Like two and two makes four. How can one point to one part of arithmetic as being more compelling than another?'

'True, true,' the Mouser echoed reluctantly, and ventured to add, 'I suppose it was the same sort of rigorous logic that persuaded you to accept the gods Odin and Loki?'

'Precisely,' Groniger confirmed.

The Mouser nodded, though he shrugged in spirit. Oh, he knew what had happened all right, he even checked it out a little later with Rill.

'Where did you light your torch?' he asked.

'At the god's fire, of course,' she answered. 'At the god's fire in the Flame Den.' And then she kissed him. (She wasn't too bad at that either, even though there was nothing to the whole kissing business.)

Yes, he knew that the god Loki had come out of the flames and possessed him for a while (as Fafhrd had perhaps once been possessed by the god Issek back in Lankhmar) and spoken through his lips the sort of arguments that are so convincing when voiced by a god or delivered in time of war or comparable crisis – and so empty when proclaimed by a mere mortal on any ordinary occasion.

And really there was no time for speculation about the mystery of what he'd said, now that there was so much to be done, so many life-and-death decisions to be made, so many eventful trains of action to be guided to their conclusions – once these folk had got through celebrating and taken a little rest.

Still, it would be nice to know just a little of what he'd actually said, he thought wistfully. Some of it might even have been clever. Why in heaven's name, for instance, and to illustrate what, had he taken the queller out of his pouch and whirled it around his head?

He had to admit it was rather pleasant being possessed by a god (or would be if one could remember any of it) but it did leave one feeling empty, that is, except for the ever-present

Mingols-to-their-deaths jingle – that he'd never get shut of, it seemed.

Next morning Fafhrd's band got their first sight of Cold Harbor, the sea, and the entire Mingol advance force all at once. The sun and west wind had dissipated the coastal fog and blew it from the glacier, on the edge of which they were now all making their way. It was a much smaller and vastly more primitive settlement than Salthaven. To the north rose the dark crater-summit of Mount Hellglow, so lofty and near that its eastern foothills still cast their shadows on the ice. A wisp of smoke rose from it, trailing off east. At the snowline a shadow on the dark rock seemed to mark the mouth of a cavern leading into the mountain's heart. Its lower slopes were thickly crusted with snow, leading back to the glacier which, narrow at this point, stretched ahead of them north to the glittering gray sea, surprisingly near. From the glacier's not-very-lofty foot, rolling grassy turf with occasional clumps of small northern cedars deformed by the wind stretched off to the southwest and its own now-distant snowy heights, wisps of white fog blowing eastways and vanishing across the rolling sunlit land between.

Glimpses of a few devastated and deserted hill farms late yesterday and early this morning, while they'd been trailing and chivvying the retreating Mingol marauders, had prepared them for what they saw now. Those farmhouses and byres had been of turf or sod solely, with grass and flowers growing on their narrow roofs, smokeholes instead of chimneys. Mara, dry-eyed, pointed out the one she'd dwelt in. Cold Harbor was simply a dozen such dwellings atop a rather steep hill or large mound backed against the glacier and turf-walled – a sort of retreat for the country-dwellers in times of peril. A short distance beyond it, a sandy beach fronted the harbor itself and on it three Mingol galleys had been drawn ashore, identified by the fantastic horse cages that were the above-deck portion of their prows.

Ranged round the mound of Cold Harbor at a fairly respectful distance were some fourscore Mingols, their leaders seemingly in conference with those of the twoscore who'd gone raiding ahead and but now returned. One of these latter was pointing back toward the Deathlands and then up at the glacier, as if describing the force that had pursued them. Beyond them the three Steppe stallions free from their cages were cropping turf. A peaceful scene, yet even as Fafhrd watched, keeping his band mostly hid (he hoped) by a fold in the ice (he did not trust too far Mingol aversion to ice) a spear came arching out of the tranquil-seeming mound and (it was a prodigious cast) struck down a Mingol. There were angry cries and a dozen Mingols returned the fire. Fafhrd judged that the besiegers, now reinforced, would surely try soon a determined assault. Without hesitation he gave orders.

'Skullick, here's action for you. Take your best bowman, oil, and a firepot. Race ahead for your life to where the glacier is nearest their beached ships and drop fire arrows in them, or attempt to. Run!

'Mara, follow them as far as the mound and when you see the ship's smoke, but not before, run down and join your friends if the way is clear. Careful! — Afreyt will have my head if aught befalls you. Tell them the truth about our numbers. Tell them to hold out and to feint a sortie if they see good chance.

'Mannimark! Keep one man of your squad and maintain watch here. Warn us of Mingol advances.

'Skor and the rest, follow me. We'll descend in their rear and briefly counterfeit a pursuing army. Come!'

And he was off at a run with eight berserks lumbering after, arrow-quivers banging against their backs. He'd already picked the stand of stunted cedars from the cover of which he planned to make his demonstration. As he ran, he sought to run in his mind with Skullick and his mate, and with Mara, trying to make the timing right.

He arrived at the cedars and saw Mannimark signaling that the Mingol assault had begun. 'Now howl like wolves,' he told his hard-breathing men, 'and really scream, each of you enough for two. Then we'll pour arrows toward 'em, longest range and fast as you can. Then, when I give command, back on the glacier again! as fast as we came down.'

When all this was done (and without much marking of consequences – there was not time) and he had rejoined Mannimark, followed by his panting band, he saw with delight a thin column of black smoke ascending from the beached galley nearest the glaciers. Mingols began to run in that direction from the slopes of the beleaguered mound, abandoning their assault. Midway he saw the small figure of Mara running down the glacier to Cold Harbor, her red cloak standing out behind her. A woman with a spear had appeared on the earth wall nearest the child, waving her on encouragingly. Then of a sudden Mara appeared to take a fantastically long stride, part of her form was obscured, as if there were a blur in Fafhrd's vision there, and then she seemed to – no, did! – rise in the air, higher and higher, as though clutched by an invisible eagle, or other sightless predatory flier. He kept his eyes on the red cloak, which suddenly grew brighter as the invisible flier mounted from shadow into sunlight with his captive. He heard a muttered exclamation of sympathy and wonder close beside him, spared a sidewise glance, and knew that Skor also had seen the prodigy.

'Keep her in sight, man,' he breathed. 'Don't lose the red cloak for one moment. Mark where she goes through the trackless air.'

The gaze of the two men went upward, then west, then steadily east toward the dark mountain. From time to time Fafhrd looked down to assure himself that there were no untoward developments requiring his attention of the situations at the ships and at Cold Harbor. Each time he feared his eyes would never catch sight of the flying cloak again, but each time they did. The red patch grew smaller, tinier. They almost lost it as it dipped into the shadow again. Finally Skor straightened up.

'Where did it go?' Fafhrd asked.

'To the mouth of the cave at the snowline,' Skor replied. 'The girl was drawn there through the air by what magic I know not. I lost it there.'

Fafhrd nodded. 'Magic of a most special sort,' he said rapidly. 'She was carried there, I must believe, by an invisible flier, ghoul-related, an old enemy of mine, Prince Faroomfar of lofty Stardock. Only I among us have the knowledge to deal with him.'

He felt, in a way, that he was seeing Skor for the first time: a man an inch taller than himself and some five years younger, but with receding hairline and a rather scanty straggling russet beard. His nose had been broken at some time. He looked a thoughtful villain.

Fafhrd said, 'In the Cold Waste near Illek-Ving I hired you. At No-Ombrulsk I named you my chief lieutenant and you swore with the rest to obey me for *Sea Hawk*'s voyage and return.' He locked eyes with the man. 'Now it comes to the test, for you must take command while I seek Mara. Continue to harry the Mingols but avoid a full engagement. Those of Cold Harbor are our friends, but do not join with them in their fort unless no other course is open. Remember we serve the lady Afreyt. Understood?'

Skor frowned, keeping his eyes locked with Fafhrd's, then nodded once.

'Good!' Fafhrd said, not sure at all that it was so, but knowing he was doing what he had to. The smoke from the burning ship was less – the Mingols seemed to have saved her. Skullick and his fellow came running back with their bows, grinning.

'Mannimark!' Fafhrd called. 'Give me two torches. Skullick! – the tinder-pouch.' He unbuckled the belt holding his long-sword Graywand. He retained his ax.

'Men!' he addressed them. 'I must be absent for a space. Command goes to Skor by this token.' He buckled Graywand to that one's side. 'Obey him faithfully. Keep yourselves whole. See that I'm given no cause to rebuke you when I return.'

And without more ado he made off across the glacier toward Mount Hellglow.

The Mouser forced himself to rise soon as he woke and to take a cold bath before his single cup of hot gahveh (he was in that sort of mood). He set his entire crew to work, Mingols and thieves alike, completing *Flotsam*'s repairs, warning them that she must be ready to sail by the morrow's morn at least, in line with Loki god's promise: 'In three days the Mingols come.' He took considerable pleasure in noting that several of them seemed to be suffering from worse hangovers than his own. 'Work them hard, Pshawri,' he commanded. 'No mercy to slug-a-beds and shirkers!'

By then it was time to join with Cif in seeing off Afreyt's and Groniger's overland expedition. He found the Rimelanders offensively bright-eyed, noisy, and energetic, and the way that Groniger bustled about, marshalling them, was a caution.

Cif and Afreyt were clear-eyed and smiling also in their brave russets and blues, but that was easier to take. He and Cif walked a ways with the overland marchers. He noted with some amusement and approval that Afreyt had four of Groniger's men carrying a curtained litter, though she did not occupy it as yet. So she was making the man pay for yesternight's false (or at least, tactless) accusation, and would cross the Deathlands in luxurious ease. That was more in his own style.

He was in an odd state of mind, almost feeling himself a spectator rather than a participant in great events. The incident of the stirring speech he had made last night (or rather the oration that the god Loki had delivered through his lips while he was blacked out) and didn't remember (and couldn't discover) a word of still rankled. He felt the sort of unimportant servant, or errand boy, who's never allowed to know the contents of the sealed messages he's given to deliver.

In this role of observer and critic he was struck by how grotesque was the weaponry of the high-stepping and ebullient Rimelanders. There were the quarterstaves, of course, and heavy single-bladed spears, but also slim fishing spears and great pitchforks and wickedly hooked and notched pikes, and long flails with curious heavy swiples and swingles a-dangle from their ends. A couple even carried long narrow-bladed and sharp-looking spades. He remarked on it to Cif and she asked him how he armed his own thief-band. Afreyt had gone on a little ahead. They were nearing Gallows Hill.

'Why, with slings,' he told Cif. 'They're as good as bows and a lot less trouble to carry. Like this one,' and he showed her the leather sling hanging from his belt. 'See that old gibbet ahead? Now mark.'

He selected a lead ball from his pouch, centered it in the strap and, sighting quickly but carefully, whirled it twice round his head and loosed. The *thunk* as it struck square on was unexpectedly loud and resounding. Some Rimelanders applauded.

Afreyt came hurrying back to tell him not to do that again – it might offend god Odin. Can't do anything right this morning, the Mouser told himself sourly.

But the incident had given him a thought. He said to Cif, 'Say, maybe I was demonstrating the sling in my speech last night when I whirled the cube of square dealing a round on its cord. Do you recall? Sometimes I get drunk on my own words and don't remember too well.'

She shook her head. 'Perhaps you were,' she said. 'Or perhaps you were dramatizing the Great Maelstrom which will swallow the Sun Mingols. Oh, that wondrous speech!'

Meanwhile they had come abreast of Gallows Hill and Afreyt had halted the march. He strolled over with Cif to find out why and for farewells – this was about as far as they'd planned to come.

To his surprise he discovered that Afreyt had set the two men with spades and several others to digging up the gallows, to unrooting it entire, and also had had its bearers set down the litter in front of the little grove of gorse on the north side of the hill, and part its curtains. While he watched puzzledly, he saw the girls May and Gale emerge from the grove, walking slowly and carefully and going through the motions of assisting someone – only there was no one there.

Except for the men trying to rock the gallows loose, everyone had grown silent, watchfully attentive.

In low undertones Cif told the Mouser the girls' names and what was going on.

'You mean to say that's Odin god they're helping and they're able to see him?' he whispered back. 'I remember now, Afreyt said she was taking him along, but – Can *you* see him at all?'

'Not very distinctly in this sunlight,' she admitted. 'But I have done so, by twilight. Afreyt says Fafhrd saw Odin most clearly in the dusk, evening before last. It's given only to Afreyt and the girls to see him clearly.'

The strange slow pantomime was soon concluded. Afreyt cut a few spiny branches of gorse and put them in the litter ('So he'll feel at home,' Cif explained to the Mouser) and started to draw the curtains, but, 'He wants *me* inside with him,' Gale announced in her shrill childish voice. Afreyt nodded, the little girl climbed in with a shrug of resignation, the curtains were drawn at last, and the general hush broke.

Lord, what idiocy! the Mouser thought. We two-footed fantasies will believe anything. And yet it occurred to him uneasily that he was a fine one to talk, who'd heard a god speak out of a fire and had his own body usurped by one. Inconsiderate creatures, gods were.

With a rush and a shout the gallows came down and its base up out of the earth, spraying dirt around, and a half dozen stalwart Rimelanders lifted it onto their shoulders and prepared to carry it so, marching single file after the litter.

'Well, they *could* use it as a battering ram, I suppose,' the Mouser muttered. Cif gave him a look.

Final farewells were said then and last messages for Fafhrd given and mutual assurances of courage until victory and death to the invader, and then the expedition went marching off in great swinging strides, rhythmically. The Mouser, standing with Cif as he watched them go toward the Deathlands, got the impression they were humming under their breaths, 'Mingols to their deaths must go,' and so on, and stepping to its tune. He wondered if he'd begun to say those verses aloud, so that they'd picked it up from him. He shook his head.

But then he and Cif turned back alone, and he saw it was a bright day, pleasantly cool, with the breeze ruffling the heather and wildflowers waving on their delicate stems, and his spirits began to rise. Cif wore her russets in the shape of a short gown, rather than her customary trousers, and her dark golden-glinting hair was loose, and her movements were unforced and impulsive. She still had reserve, but it was not that of a councilman, and the Mouser remembered how thrilling last night's kiss had been, before he'd decided it didn't mean anything. Two fat lemmings popped out just ahead of them and stood on their hind legs, inspecting them, before ducking behind a bush. In stopping so as not to overrun them, Cif stumbled and he caught her and after a moment drew her to him. She yielded for a moment before she drew away, smiling at him troubledly.

'Gray Mouser,' she said softly, 'I am attracted to you, but I have told you how you resemble the god Loki – and last night when you swayed the Isle with your great oratory that resemblance was even more marked. I have also told you of my reluctance to take the god home with me (making me hire Hilsa and Rill, two familiar devils, to take care of him). Now I find, doubtless because of the resemblance, a kindred hesitation with respect to you, so that perhaps it is best we remain captain and councilwoman until the defense of Rime Isle is accomplished and I can sort you out from the god.'

The Mouser took a long breath and said slowly that he supposed that was best, thinking meanwhile that gods surely interfered with one's private life. He was mightily tempted to ask her whether she expected *him* to turn to Hilsa and Rill (devils or no) to be comforted, but doubted she would be inclined to allow him a god's liberties to that degree (granted he desired such), no matter how great the resemblance between them.

In this impasse, he was rather relieved to see beyond Cif's shoulder that which allowed him to say, 'Speaking of the she-demons, who are these that are coming from Salthaven?'

Cif turned at that, and there true enough were Rill and Hilsa hurrying toward them through the heather, with Mother Grum plodding along behind, dark figure to their colorful ones. And although it was bright day three hours and more, Rill carried a lit torch. It was hard to see the flame in the sunlight, but they could mark by the way its shimmer made the heather wave beyond. And as the two harlots drew closer, it was evident that their faces were brimming with excitement and a story to tell, which was poured forth on their arrival and on the Mouser asking dryly: 'Why are you trying to light up the day, Rill?'

'The god spoke to us but now, most clearly from the Flame Den fire,' she began, 'saying "Darkfire, Darkfire, take me to Darkfire. Follow the flame—:" ' Hilsa broke in, ' "—go as it bends," the god said cracklingly, "turn as it wends, all in my name." '

Rill took up again, 'So I lit a fresh torch from the Flame Den blaze for him to travel in, and we carefully marked the flame and followed as it leaned, and it has led us to you!'

'And look,' Hilsa broke in as Mother Grum came up, 'now the flame would have us go to the mountain. It points toward her!' And she waved with her other hand north toward the icefall and the silent black scoriac peak beyond with its smoke-plume blowing west.

Cif and the Mouser dutifully looked at the torch's ghostly flame, narrowing their eyes. After a bit, 'The flame *does* lean over,' the Mouser said, 'but I think that's just because it's burning unevenly. Something in the grain of the wood or its oils and resins—'

'No, indubitably it motions us toward Darkfire,' Cif cried excitedly. 'Lead on, Rill,' and the women all turned sharply north, making for the glacier.

'But ladies, we have hardly time for a trip up-mountain,' the Mouser called after protestingly, 'what with preparations to be made for the Isle's defense and tomorrow's sailing against the Mingols.'

'The god has commanded,' Cif told him overshoulder. 'He knows best.'

Mother Grum said in her growly voice, 'I doubt not he intends us to make a closer journey than mountaintop. Round-about is nearer than straight, I ween.'

And with that mystifying remark the women went on, and the Mouser shrugged and perforce followed after, thinking what fools these women were to be scurrying after a burning bush or branch as if it were the very god, even if the flame *did* bend most puzzlingly. (And he *had* heard fire speak, night before last.) Well, at any rate, he wasn't really needed for today's repairs on *Flotsam*; Phsawri could boss the crew as well as he, or at least well enough. Best keep an eye on Cif while this odd fit was on her and see she – or her three strangely sorted god-servants – came to no harm.

Such a sweet, strong, sensible, ravishing woman, Cif, when not godstruck. Lord, what troublesome, demanding and captious employers gods were, never a-quiet. (It was safe to think such thoughts, he told himself, gods couldn't read your thoughts – everyone had *that* privacy – though they could overhear your slightest word spoken in undertone – and doubtless make deductions from your starts and grimaces.)

Up from the depths of his skull came the wearisome compulsive chant, 'Mingols to their deaths must go,' and he was almost grateful to the malicious little jingle for occupying his mind troubled by the vagaries of gods and women.

The air grew chilly and soon they were at the icefall and in front of it a dead scrubby tree and a mounded upthrust of dark purplish rock, almost black, and in its midst a still blacker opening wide and tall as a door.

Cif said, 'This was not here last year,' and Mother Grum growled, 'The glacier, receding, has uncovered it,' and Rill cried, 'The flame leans toward the cave!' and Cif said, 'Go we down,' and Hilsa quavered, 'It's dark,' and Mother Grum rumbled, 'Have no fear. Dark is sometimes best light, and down best way go up.'

The Mouser wasted no time on words, but broke three branches from the dead tree (Loki-torch might not last forever) and shouldering them, followed swiftly after the women into the rock.

Fafhrd doggedly climbed the last, seemingly endless slope of icy stone below Mount Hellglow's snowline. Orange light from the sun near setting beat on his back without warmth, and bathed the mountainside and the dark peak above with its wispy smoke blowing east. The rock was tough as diamond with frequent hand-holds – made for climbing – but he was weary and beginning to condemn himself for having abandoned his men in peril (it amounted to that) to come on a wild romantical goose-chase. Wind blew from the west, crosswise to his climb.

This was what came of taking a girl on a dangerous expedition and listening to women – or one woman, rather. Afreyt had been so sure of herself, so queenly-commanding – that he'd gone along with her against his better judgment. Why, he was chasing after Mara now mostly for fear of what Afreyt would think of him if aught befell the girl. Oh, he knew all right how he'd justified himself this morning in giving himself this job rather than sending a couple of his men. He'd jumped to the conclusion it was Prince Faroomfar had kidnapped Mara and he'd had the hope (in view of what Afreyt and Cif had told about being rescued from Khahkht's wizardry by flying mountain-princesses) that Princess Hirriwi, his beloved of one glorious night long gone, would come swimming along sightlessly on her invisible fish-of-air to offer him her aid against her hated brother.

That was another trouble with women, they were never there when you wanted or really needed them. They helped each other, all right, but they expected men to do all sorts of impossible feats of derring-do to prove themselves worthy of the great gift of their love (and what was that when you got down to it? – a fleeting clench-and-wriggle in the dark, illuminated only by the mute, incomprehensible perfection of a dainty breast, that left you bewildered and sad).

The way grew steeper, the light redder, and his muscles smarted. The way it was going, darkness would catch him on the rock-face, and then for two hours at least the mountain would hide the rising moon.

Was it solely on Afreyt's account that he was seeking Mara? Wasn't it also because she had the same name as his first young sweetheart whom he'd abandoned with his unborn child when he'd left Cold Corner as a youth to go off with yet another woman, whom he'd in turn abandoned – or led unwittingly to her death, really the same thing? Wasn't he seeking to appease that earlier Mara by rescuing this child one? That was yet another trouble with women, or at least the women you loved or had loved once – they kept on making you feel guilty, even beyond their deaths. Whether you loved them or not, you were invisibly chained to every woman who'd ever kindled you.

And was even *that* the deepest truth about himself going after the girl Mara? – he asked himself, forcing his analysis into the next devious cranny, even as he forced his numbing hands to seek out the next holds on the still steepening face in the dirty red light. Didn't he really quicken at thought of her, just as god Odin did in his senile lubricity? Wasn't he and no other chasing after Faroomfar because he thought of the prince as a lecherous rival for this delicate tidbit of girl flesh?

For that matter, wasn't Afreyt's girlishness – her slenderness despite her height, her small and promising breasts, her tales of childhood make-believe maraudings with Cif, her violet-eyed romancing, her madcap bravado – that had attracted him even in far-off Lankhmar? That and her Rime Isle silver had chained him, and set him on the whole unsuitable course of becoming a responsible captain of men – he who had been all his days a lone wolf – with lone-leopard comrade Mouser. Now he'd reverted back to it, abandoning his men. (Gods grant Skor keep his head and that some at least of his disciplines and preachments of prudence had taken effect!) But oh, this lifelong servitude to girls – whimsical, fleeting, tripping little demons! White, slim-necked, sharp-toothed, restlessly bobbing weasels with the soulful eyes of lemurs!

His blindly reaching hand closed on emptiness and he realized that in his furious self-upbraiding he'd reached the apex of the slope without knowing it. With belated caution he lifted his head until his eyes looked just over the edge. The sun's last dark red beams showed him a shale-scattered ledge some ten feet wide and then the mountain going up again precipitous and snowless. Opposite him in that new face was a great recess or cavern-mouth as wide as the ledge and twice that height. It was very dark inside that great door but he could make out the bright red of Mara's cloak, its hood raised, and within the hood, shadowed by it, her small face, very pale-cheeked, very dark-eyed – really, a smudge in darkness – staring toward him.

He scrambled up, peering around suspiciously, then moved toward her, softly calling her name. She did not reply with word or sign though continuing to stare. There was a warm, faintly sulfurous breeze blowing out of the mountain and it ruffled her cloak. Fafhrd's steps quickened and with a swift-growing anticipation of unknown horror whirled the cloak aside to reveal a small grinning skull set atop a narrow-shouldered wooden cross about four feet high.

Fafhrd moved backwards to the ledge, breathing heavily. The sun had set and the gray sky seemed wider and more palely bright without its rays. The silence was deep. He looked along the ledge in both directions, fruitlessly. Then he stared into the cave again and his jaw tightened. He took flint and iron, opened the tinder-pouch, and kindled a torch. Then holding it high in his left hand and his unbelted ax gently a-swing in his right, he walked forward into the cave and toward the mountain's heart, past the eerie diminutive scarecrow, his foot avoiding its stripped-away red cloak, along the strangely smooth-walled passageway wide and tall enough for a giant, or a winged man.

The Mouser hardly knew how long he'd been closely following the four godstruck females through the strangely tunnel-like cave that was leading them deeper and deeper under the glacier toward the heart of the volcanic mountain Darkfire. Long enough, at any rate, for him to have split and slivered the larger ends of the three dead branches he was carrying, so they would kindle readily. And certainly long enough to become very weary of the Mingols death-chant, or Mingol jingle, that was now not only resounding in his mind but being spoken aloud by the four rapt women as if it were a marching, or rather scurrying song, just as Groniger's men had seemed to do. Of course in this case he didn't have to ask himself where they'd got it, for they'd all originally heard it with him night before last in the Flame Den, when Loki god had seemed to speak from the fire, but that didn't make it any easier to endure or one whit less boresome.

At first he'd tried to reason with Cif as she hurried along with the others like a mad maenad, arguing the unwisdom of venturing so recklessly into an uncharted cavern, but she'd only pointed at Rill's torch and said, 'See how it strains ahead. The god commands us,' and gone back to her chanting.

Well, there was no denying that the flame was bending forward most unnaturally when it should have been streaming back with their rapid advance – and also lasting longer than any torch should. So the Mouser had had to go back to memorizing as well as he could their route through the rock which, chill at first, as one would expect from the ice above, was now perceptibly warmer, while the heating air carried a faint brimstone stench.

But at all events, he told himself, he didn't have to *like* this sense of being the tool and sport of mysterious forces vastly more powerful than himself, forces that didn't even deign to tell him the words they spoke through him (that business of the speech he'd given but not heard one word of bothered him more and more). Above all he didn't have to celebrate this bondage to the inscrutable, as the women were doing, by mindlessly repeating words of death and doom.

Also he didn't like the feeling of being in bondage to women and absorbed more and more into their affairs, such as he'd felt ever since accepting Cif's commission three months ago in Lankhmar, and which had put him in bondage, in turn, to Pshawri and Mikkidu and all his men, and to his ambitions and self-esteem.

Above all, he didn't like being in bondage to the idea of himself being a monstrous clever fellow who could walk widdershins round all the gods and godlets, from whom everyone expected godlike performance. Why couldn't he admit to Cif at least that he'd not heard a word of his supposedly great speech? And if he could do that walk-widdershins bit, why didn't he?

The cavernous tunnel they'd been following so long

debouched into what seemed a far vaster space steaming with vapors, and then they were suddenly brought up short against a great wall that seemed to extend indefinitely upward and to either side.

The women broke off their doom-song and Rill cried, 'Whither now, Loki?' and Hilsa echoed her tremulously. Mother Grum rumbled, 'Tell us, wall,' and Cif intoned strongly, 'Speak, O god.'

And while the women were saying these things, the Mouser stole forward rapidly and laid his hand on the wall. It was so hot he almost snatched back his hand, but did not, and through his palm and outspread fingers he felt a steady strong pulsation, a rhythm in the rock, exactly as if it were itself sounding the women's song.

And then as if in answer to the women's entreaty, the Loki torch, which had burnt down to little more than a stub, flared up into a great seven-branched flame, almost intolerably bright – it was a wonder Rill could hold it – showing the frighteningly vast extent of the rock face. Even as it flared, the rock seemed to heave under the Mouser's hand monstrously with each pulsation of its song and the floor began to rock with it. Then the great rock face bulged, and the heat became monstrous too, and the brimstone stench intensified so they were all set a-gagging and a-coughing even as their imaginations envisioned instant earthquake and cave-brimming floods of red-hot lava exploding from the mountain's heart.

It says much for the Mouser's prudence that in that short period of panic and terrified wonder it occurred to him to thrust one of his frayed branches into the blinding flame. And it was well he did so, for the great god-flame now died down as swiftly as it had flared up, leaving only the feeble illumination of the burning branch of ordinary dead wood afire in his hands. Rill dropped the dead stub of her burnt-out torch with a cry of pain, as if only now feeling how it had burned her, while Hilsa whimpered and all the women groped about dazedly.

And as if command had questionless passed to the Mouser with the torch, he now began to shepherd them back the way they had come, away from the strangling fumes, through the now-bewilderingly shadowy passageways that only he had conned and that still resounded with the dreadful rock music aping their own, a symphony of doom-song monstrously reverberated by solid stone — away toward the blessed outer light and air and sky, and fields and blessed seas.

Nor was that the full measure of the Mouser's far-sighted prudence (so far-sighted that he sometimes couldn't tell what was its aim), for in the moment of greatest panic, when the stub of Loki-torch had fallen from Rill's hand, he had thought to snatch it up from the rocky floor and thrust it, hardly more than a hot black cinder, deep into his pouch. It burnt his fingers a little, he discovered afterwards, but luckily it was not so hot that his pouch caught fire.

Afreyt sat on a lichened rock outside the litter on the broad summit-pass of the Deathlands (near where Fafhrd had first encountered the Mingols, though she didn't know that) with her gray cloak huddled about her, resting. Now and again a wind from the east, whose chilliness seemed that of the violet sky, ruffled the litter's closed curtains. Its bearers had joined the other men at one of the small fires to the fore and rear, built with carried wood to heat chowder during this evening pause in their march. The gallows had been set down by Afreyt's direction and its base and beam-end wedged in rock, so that it rested like a fallen-over 'L', its angle lifting above the litter like a crooked roof, or like a rooftree with one king-post.

There was still enough sunset light in the west for her to wonder if that was smoke she saw moving east above the narrow crater of Mount Hellglow, while in the cold east there was sufficient night for her to see, she was almost sure, a faint glow rising from that of Mount Darkfire. The eastwind blew again and she hunched her shoulders and drew the hood of her cloak more closely against her cheeks.

The curtains of the litter parted for a moment and May slipped out and came and stood in front of Afreyt.

'What's that you've got around your neck?' she asked the girl.

'It's a noose,' the latter explained eagerly, but with a certain solemnity. 'I braided it, Odin showed me how to make the knot. We're all going to belong to the Order of the Noose, which is something Odin and I invented this afternoon while Gale was taking a nap.'

Afreyt hesitatingly reached her hand to the girl's slender throat and inspected the loop of heavy braid with uneasy fascination. There, surely enough, was the cruel hangman's knot drawn rather close, and tucked into it a nosegay of small mountain flowers, somewhat wilted, gathered this morning on the lower slopes.

'I made one for Gale,' the girl said. 'She didn't want to wear it at first because I'd helped invent it. She was jealous.'

Afreyt shook her head reprovingly, though her mind wasn't on that.

'Here,' May continued, lifting her hand which had been hanging close to her side under the cloak. 'I've made one for you, a little bigger. See, it's got flowers too. Put back your hood. You wear it under your hair, of course.'

For a long moment Afreyt looked into the girl's unblinking eyes. Then she drew back her hood, bent down her head, and helped lift her hair through. Using both hands, May drew the knot together at the base of Afreyt's throat. 'There,' she said, 'that's the way you wear it, snug but not tight.'

While this was happening, Groniger had come up, carrying three bowls and a small covered pail of chowder. When the nooses had been explained to him, 'A capital conceit!' he said with a great grin, his eyebrows lifting. 'That'll show the Mingols something, let them know what they're in for. It's a grand chant the Little Captain gave us, isn't it?'

Afreyt nodded, looking sideways a moment at Groniger. 'Yes,' she said, 'his wonderful words.'

Groniger glanced back at her in similar fashion. 'Yes, his wonderful words.'

May said, 'I wish I'd heard him.'

Groniger handed them the bowls and swiftly poured the thick, steaming soup.

May said, 'I'll take Gale hers.'

Groniger said gruffly to Afreyt, 'Sup it while it's hot. Then get some rest. We go on at moonrise, agreed?' and when Afreyt nodded, strode off rather bumptiously, cheerily rumble-humming the chant to which they'd marched all day, the Mouser's – or Loki's, rather.

Afreyt narrowed her brows. Normally Groniger was such a sober man, dull-spirited she'd once thought, but now he was almost like a buffoon. Was 'monstrously comical' too strong an expression? She shook her head slowly. All the Rime-men were getting like that, loutish and grotesque and somehow bigger. Perhaps it was her weariness made her see things askew and magnified, she told herself.

May came back and they got out their spoons and fell to. 'Gale wanted to eat hers inside,' the girl volunteered after a bit. 'I think she and Odin are cooking up something.' She shrugged and went back to her spooning. After another while: 'I'm going to make nooses for Mara and Captain Fafhrd.' Finally she scraped her bowl, set it aside, and said, 'Cousin Afreyt, do you think Groniger's a troll?'

'What's that?' Afreyt asked.

'A word Odin uses. He says Groniger's a troll.'

Gale came excitedly out of the litter with her empty bowl, but remembering to draw the curtains behind her.

'Odin and I have invented a marching song for us!' she announced, stacking her bowl in May's. 'He says the other god's song is all right, but he should have one of his own. Listen, I'll chant it for you. It's shorter and faster than the other.' She screwed up her face. 'It's like a drum,' she explained earnestly. Then, stamping with a foot: 'March, march, over the Deathlands. Go, go, over the Doomlands. Doom! – kill the Mingols. Doom! – die the heroes. Doom! Doom! Glorious doom!' Her voice had grown quite loud by the time she was done.

'Glorious doom?' Afreyt repeated.

'Yes. Come on, May, chant it with me.'

'I don't know that I want to.'

'Oh, come on. I'm wearing your noose, aren't I? Odin says we should all chant it.'

As the two girls repeated the chant in their shrill voices with mounting enthusiasm, Groniger and another Rime-man came up.

'That's good,' he said, collecting the bowls. 'Glorious doom is good.'

'I like that one,' the other man agreed. 'Doóm! – kill the Mingols!' he repeated appreciatively.

They went off chanting it in low voices.

The night darkened. The wind blew. The girls grew quiet.

May said, 'It's cold. The god'll be getting chilly. Gale, we'd better go inside. Will you be all right, cousin Afreyt?'

'I'll be all right.'

A while after the curtains closed behind them, May stuck her head out.

'The god invites you to come inside with us,' she called to Afreyt.

Afreyt caught her breath. Then she said as evenly as she could, 'Thank the god, but tell him I will remain here . . . on guard.'

'Very well,' May said and the curtains closed again.

Afreyt clenched her hands under her cloak. She hadn't admitted to anyone, even Cif, that for some time now, Odin had been fading. She could hardly see even a wispy outline any more. She could still hear his voice, but it had begun to grow faint, lost in wind-moaning. The god had been very real at first on that spring day when she and Cif had found him, and found that there were two gods. He'd seemed so near death then, and she'd labored so hard to save him. She'd been filled with such adoration, as if he were some ancient hero-saint, or her own dear, dead father. And when he had caressed her fumblingly and muttered in disappointment (it sounded), 'You're older than I thought,' and drifted off to sleep, her adoration had been contaminated by horror and rejection. She'd got the idea of bringing in the girls (Did that make her a monster? Well, perhaps) and after that she'd managed very well, keeping it all at a distance.

And then there'd been the excitement of the journey to Lankhmar and the perils of Khahkht's ice-magic and the Mingols and the renewed excitement of the arrival of the Mouser and Fafhrd and the realization that Fafhrd did indeed resemble a younger Odin – was *that* what had made god Odin fade and grow whisper-voiced? She didn't know, but she knew it helped make everything torturesome and confusing – and she couldn't have borne to enter the litter tonight. (Yes, she was a monster.)

She felt a sharp pain in her neck and realized that in her agitation she'd been tugging at the pendant end of the noose beneath her cloak. She loosened it and forced herself to sit quietly. It was full dark now. There *were* faint flames flickering from Darkfire and Hellglow too. She heard snatches of talk from the campfires and bits of the new chant and laughter as the story of that went round. It was very cold, but she did not move. The east grew silvery-pale, the milky effulgence domed up, and at last the white moon edged into view.

The camp stirred then and after a while the bearers came up and unwedged Odin's gallows and lifted it up and the litter too, and Afreyt arose, unkinking her stiff joints and stamping her numbed feet, and they all marched off west across the moon-silvered rock, shouldering their grotesque weapons and the two larger burdens. Some of them limped a bit (after all, they were sailors, their feet unused to marching) but they all went on briskly to the new Odin-chant, hunching their backs against the east wind, which now blew strong and steadily.

Fafhrd had just kindled his second torch from the ember-end of the first and his surroundings had grown warmer, when the lofty passageway he was following debouched into a cavern so vast that the light he bore seemed lost in it. The sound of the cast-away torch-stub hitting rock awakened distant faint echoes and he came to a stop, peering up and around. Then he began to see multitudinous points of light as stars, where flakes of mica in the fire-born stone reflected his torch, and in the middle distance an irregular pillar of mica-flecked rock and on its top a small pale bundle that drew his eye. Then from above he heard the beat of great wings, a pause, then another beat – as though a great vulture were circling in the cavernous dark.

He called, 'Mara!' toward the pillar and the echoes came back and amongst them, shrill and faint, his own name called and the echoes of that. Then he realized that the wing-beat had ceased and that one of the high mica-stars was getting rapidly brighter, as though it were swiftly traveling straight down toward him, and he heard a rush in the air as of a great hawk stooping.

He jerked his whole body aside from the bright sword darting at him and simultaneously struck with his ax just behind it. The torch was torn from his grasp, what seemed like a leather sail struck him to his knees, and then there was a great wing-beat, very close, and another, and then the shrill bellow of a man in agony that despite its extremity held a note of outrage.

As he scrambled to his feet, he saw his torch flaring wide on the rocky floor and transfixing it the bright sword that had struck it from his grasp. Wing-beat and bellowing were going off from him now. He set his boot on the torch handle, preparatory to withdrawing the sword from it, but as he went to take hold of the latter, his fingers encountered a scaly hand, slenderer than his own, gripping it tightly, and (his groping fingers ascertained) warmly wet at the wrist, where it had been chopped off. Both hand and blood alike were invisible, so that although his fingers touched and felt, his eyes saw only the sword's hilt, the silver cross-guard, the pear-shaped silver pommel, and the black leather grip wrapped with braided silver wire.

He heard his name spoken falteringly close behind him and turning saw Mara standing there in her white smock looking woebegone and confused, as if she'd just been lifted from the pillar's top and set down there. As he spoke her name in answer, a voice came out of the air beside Mara and a little above her, speaking in the chilling and confounding tones of a familiar and beloved voice turned hateful in nightmare.

The sightless mountain princess Hirriwi said, 'Woe to you, barbarian, for having come north again without first paying your respects at Stardock. Woe to you for coming at another woman's call, although we favor her cause. Woe for deserting your men to chase this girl-chit, whom we would have (and have) saved without you. Woe for meddling with demons and gods. And woe upon woe for lifting your hand to maim a prince of Stardock, to whom we are joined, though he is our dearest enemy, by bonds stronger than love and hate. A head for a head and a hand for a hand, think on that. Quintuple woe!'

During this recital, Mara had moved to Fafhrd, where he knelt upright, his face working as he stared at and hearkened to emptiness. He had put his arm about her shoulders and together they stared at the speaking gloom.

Hirriwi continued, her voice less ritually passionate, but every whit as cold, 'Keyaira heals and comforts our brother, and I go to join them. At dawn we will return you, journeying upon our fish of air, to your people, where you will know your weird. Until then, rest in the warmth of Hellfire, which is not yet a danger to you.'

With that she broke off and there was the sound of her going away. The torch flickered low, almost consumed, and great weariness took hold of Fafhrd and Mara and they lay down side by side and sleep was drawn up over them from their toes to their eyes. Fafhrd, at last thought, wondered why it should move him so strangely that Mara clutched his left hand, bent up beside his shoulder, in both of hers.

Next day Salthaven was a-bustle so early and so wildly — so fantastically — with preparations for the great sailing that it was hard to tell where the inspirations of nightmare and worry-dream ended and those of (hopefully) wide-eyed day began. Even the 'foreigners' were infected, as if they too had been hearing the Mingols-to-the-deaths chant in their dreams, so that the Mouser had been impelled against his better judgment to man Fafhrd's *Sea Hawk* with the most eager of them under Bomar their 'mayor' and the Ilthmart tavern-owner. He made

Pshawri their captain with half the thieves to support his authority and two of the Mingols, Trenchi and Gavs, to help him con the ship.

'Remember you are boss,' he told Pshawri. 'Make them like it or lump it – and keep to windward of me.'

Pshawri, his new-healed forehead wound still pink, nodded fiercely and went to take up his command. Above the salt cliff the eastern sky was ominously red with sunrise, while glooms of night still lingered in the west. The east wind blew strongly.

From *Flotsam*'s stern the Mouser surveyed the busy harbor and his fleet of fishing boats turned warships. Truly, they were a weird sight, their decks which had so recently been piled with fish now bristling with pikes and various impromptu weapons such as he'd seen Groniger's men shoulder yesterday. Some of them had lashed huge ceremonial spears (bronze-pointed timbers, really) to their bowsprits – for use as rams, he supposed, the Fates be kind to 'em! While others had bent on red and black sails, to indicate bloody and baleful intentions, he guessed – the soberest fisherman was a potential pirate, that was sure. Three were half wreathed in fishnets – protection against arrow fire? The two largest craft were commanded by Dwone and Zwaakin, his sub-admirals, if that could be credited. He shook his head.

If only he had time to get his thoughts straight! But ever since he'd awakened events (and his own unpredictable impulses) had been rushing, nay, stampeding him. Yesterday, he'd managed to lead Cif and the other three women safely out of the quaking and stinking cave-tunnels (he glanced toward Darkfire – it was still venting into the red sky a thick column of black smoke, which the east wind blew west) only to discover that they'd spent an unconscionable time underground and it was already evening. After seeing to Rill's hand, badly burned by the Loki-torch, they'd had to hurry back to Salthaven for conferences with all and sundry – hardly time to compare notes with Cif on the whole cavern experience . . .

And now he had to break off to help Mikkidu instruct the six Rimeland replacements for the thieves they'd lost to *Sea Hawk* – how to man the sweeps and so forth.

And *that* was no sooner done (matter of a few low-voiced instructions to Mikkidu, chiefly) than here came Cif climbing aboard, followed by Rill, Hilsa, and Mother Grum – all of them save for the last in sailorly trousers and jackets with knives at their belts. Rill's right arm was in a sling.

'Here we are, yours to command, captain,' Cif said brightly.

'Dear ... councilwoman,' the Mouser answered, his heart sinking, '*Flotsam* can't sail into possible battle with women aboard, especially—' He let a meaningful look serve for '—whores and witches.'

'Then we'll man *Sprite* and follow you after,' she told him, not at all downcast. 'Or rather range ahead to be the first to sight the Sunwise Mingols – you know *Sprite*'s a fast sailer. Yes, perhaps that's best, a women's fighting-ship for soldieresses.'

The Mouser submitted to the inevitable with what grace he could muster. Rill and Hilsa beamed. Cif touched his arm commiseratingly.

'I'm glad you agreed,' she said. 'I'd already loaned *Sprite* to three other women.' But then her face grew serious as she lowered her voice to say, 'There is a matter that troubles me you should know. We were going to bring god Loki aboard in a firepot, as yesterday he traveled in Rill's torch—'

'Can't have fire aboard a ship going into battle,' the Mouser responded automatically. 'Besides, look how Rill got burned.'

'But this morning, for the first time in over a year, we found the fire in the Flame Den unaccountably gone out,' Cif finished. 'We sifted the ashes. There was not a spark.'

'Well,' said the Mouser thoughtfully, 'perhaps yesterday at the great rock face after he flamed so high the god temporarily shifted his dwelling to the mountain's fiery heart. See how she smokes!' And he pointed toward Darkfire, where the black column going off westward was thicker.

'Yes, but we don't have him at hand that way,' Cif objected troubledly.

'Well, at any rate he's still on the island,' the Mouser told her. 'And in a sense, I'm sure, on *Flotsam* too,' he added, remembering (it made his fire-stung fingers smart anew) the black torch-end he still had in his pouch. That was another thing, he told himself, that wanted thinking about . . .

But just then Dwone came sailing close by to report the Rime fleet ready for action and hardly to be held back. The Mouser had perforce to get *Flotsam* underway, hoisting what sail she could carry for the beat against the wind, and setting his thieves and their green replacements to sweeping while Ourph beat time, so that she'd be able to keep ahead of the handier fishing craft.

There were cheers from the shore and the other ships and for a short while the Mouser was able to bask in self-satisfaction at *Flotsam* moving out so bravely at the head of the fleet, and his crew so well disciplined, and (he could see) Pshawri handling *Sea Hawk* nicely enough, and Cif standing beside him glowing-eyed – and himself a veritable admiral, no less, by Mog!

But then the thoughts which he hadn't had time to straighten all day began to cark him again. Above all else he realized that there was something altogether foolhardy, in fact utterly ridiculous, about them all setting sail so confidently with only one hairbrained plan of action, on nothing more than the crackling word of a fire, the whisper of burning twigs. Still he had a compelling feeling in his bones that they were doing the right thing and nothing could harm them, and he would peradventure find the Mingol fleet and that another wonderful inspiration would come to him at the last minute . . .

At that moment his eye lit on Mikkidu sweeping with considerable style in the bowmost steerside position and he came to a decision.

'Ourph, take the tiller and take her out,' he directed. 'Call time to the sweeps.

'My dear, I must leave you for a brief space,' he told Cif. Then taking the last Mingol with him, he went forward and said in a gruff voice to Mikkidu, 'Come with me to my cabin. A conference. Gib will replace you here,' and then hurried below with his now apprehensive-eyed lieutenant past the wondering glances of the women.

Facing Mikkidu across the table in the low-ceilinged cabin

(*one* good thing about having a short captain and still shorter crew, it occurred to him) he eyed his subordinate mercilessly and said, 'Lieutenant, I made a speech to the Rime Islers in their council hall night before last that had them cheering me at the end. You were there. *What did I say?*'

Mikkidu writhed. 'Oh, captain,' he protested, blushing, 'how can you expect—'

'Now none of that stuff about it being so wonderful you can't remember – or other weaseling out,' the Mouser cut him short. 'Pretend the ship's in a tempest and her safety depends on you giving me a square answer. Gods, haven't I taught you yet that no man of mine ever got hurt from me by telling me the truth?'

Mikkidu digested that with a great gulp and then surrendered. 'Oh captain,' he said, 'I did a terrible thing. That night when I was following you from the docks to the council hall and you were with the two ladies, I bought a drink from a street vendor and gulped it down while you weren't looking. It didn't taste strong at all, I swear it, but it must have had a tremendous delayed kick, for when you jumped on the table and started to talk, I blacked out – my word upon it! When I came to you were saying something about Groniger and Afreyt leading out half the Rimelanders to reinforce Captain Fafhrd and the rest of us sailing out to entice the Sun Mingols into a great whirlpool, and everybody was cheering like mad – and so of course I cheered too, just as if I'd heard everything that they had.'

'You can swear to the truth of that?' the Mouser asked in a terrible voice.

Mikkidu nodded miserably.

The Mouser came swiftly around the table and embraced him and kissed him on his quivering cheek. 'There's a good lieutenant,' he said most warmly, clapping him on the back. 'Now go, good Mikkidu, and invite the lady Cif attend me here. Then make yourself useful on deck in any way your shrewdness may suggest. Don't stand now in a daze. Get at it, man.'

By the time Cif arrived (not long) he had decided on his approach to her.

'Dear Cif,' he said without preamble, coming to her, 'I have a confession to make to you,' and then he told her humbly but clearly and succinctly the truth about his 'wonderful words' – that he simply hadn't heard one of them. When he was done he added, 'So you can see not even my vanity is involved – whatever it was, it was Loki's speech, not mine – so do you now tell me truth about it, sparing me nothing.'

She looked at him with a wondering smile and said, 'Well, I was puzzled as to what you could have said to Mikkidu to make him so head-in-the-clouds happy – and am not sure I understand that even now. But, yes, my experience was, I now confess, identical with his – and not even the taking of an unknown drink to excuse it. My mind went blank, time passed me by, and I heard not a word you said, except those last directions about Afreyt's expedition and the whirlpool. But everyone was cheering and so I pretended to have heard, not wanting to injure your feelings or feel myself a fool. Oh, I was a sheep! Once I was minded to confess my lapse to Afreyt, and now I wish I had, for she had a strange look on her then – But I didn't. You think, as I do now, that she also—?'

The Mouser nodded decisively. 'I think that not one soul of them heard a word to remember of the main body of my – or, rather, Loki's talk, but later they all pretended to have done so, just like so many sheep indeed – and I the black goat leading them on. So only Loki knows what Loki said and we sail out upon an unknown course against the Mingols, taking all on trust.'

'What to do now?' she asked wonderingly.

Looking into her eyes with a tentative smile and a slight shrug that was at once acquiescent and comical, he said, 'Why, we go on, for it is your course and I am committed to it.'

Flotsam gave a long lurch then, with a wave striking along her side, and it nudged Cif against him, and their arms went round each other, and their lips met thrillingly – but not for long, for he must hurry on deck, and she too, to discover (or rather confirm) what had befallen.

Flotsam progressed out of Salthaven harbor and the salt cliff's lee to the Outer Sea where the east wind smote them more urgently and the swells and the sunlight struck their canvas and deck. The Mouser took the tiller from sad-faced Ourph and that old one and Gib and Mikkidu set sail for the first eastward tack. And one by one *Sea Hawk* and the weirdly accoutered fishing boats repeated their maneuver, following *Flotsam* out.

That selfsame east wind which blew west across the southern half of Rime Isle, and against which *Flotsam* labored, farther out at sea was hurrying on the horse-ships of the Sunwise Mingols. The grim galleys, each with its bellying square sail, made a great drove of ships, and now and again a stallion screamed in its bow-cage as they plunged ahead through the waves, which cascaded spray through the black, crazily-angled bars. All eyes strained west-ahead, and it would have been hard to say which eyes glared the more madly, those of the furclad, grinningly whitetoothed men, or those of long-faced, grimacingly white-toothed beasts.

On the poop of the flagship this frenzy looked in a more philosophical direction, where Gonov discoursed with his witch-doctor and attendant sages propounding such questions as, 'Is it sufficient to burn a city to the ground, or must it also be trampled to rubble?' and contemplating such answers as, 'Most meritorious is to pound it to sand, aye, to fine loam, without burning at all.'

While the strong westwind that blew east across the northern half of the island (with a belt of squalls and fierce eddies between the two winds) was hurrying on from the west across trackless ocean the like fleet of the Widdershins Mingols, where Edumir had proposed this query to his philosophers: 'Is death by suicide in the first charge, hurling oneself upon the foeman's virgin spear, to be preferred to death by self-administered poison in the last charge?'

He hearkened to their closely-reasoned answers and to the counter-question: 'Since death is so much to be desired, surpassing the delights of love and mushroom wine, how did our all-noble and revered ancestors ever survive to procreate us?' and at last observed, his white-rimmed eyes gazing east yearningly, 'That is all theory. On Rime Isle we will once more put these recondite matters to the test of practice.'

While high above all winds Khahkht in his icy sphere ceaselessly studied the map lining it, whereon he moved counters for ships and men, horses and women – aye, even gods – bending his bristly face close, so that no unlawful piece might escape his fierce scrutiny.

By early morning sunlight and against the nipping wind, Afreyt hurried on alone through the heather dotted by stunted cedars past the last silent hill farm, with its sagging gray-green turf roofs, before Cold Harbor. She was footsore and weary (even Odin's noose around her neck seemed a heavy weight) for they'd marched all night with only two short rest-stops and midway they'd been buffeted by changing winds reaching tornadic strength as they'd passed through the transition belt between the southeastern, Salthaven half of Rime Isle, which the east wind presently ruled, and the northwestern, Cold Harbor half, where the equally strong west wind now held sway. Yet she forced herself to scan carefully ahead for friend or foe, for she had constituted herself vanguard for Groniger and his grotesquely burdened trampers. A while ago in the twilight before dawn she'd gone from litter-side up to the head of the column and pointed out to Groniger the need of having a guard ahead now that they were nearing their journey's end and should be wary of ambushes. He had seemed unconcerned and heedless, unable to grasp the danger, almost as if he (and all the other Rime men, for that matter) were intent only on marching on and on, glaze-eyed, growling Gale's doom-chant, like so many monstrous automatons, until they met the Mingols, or Fafhrd's force. Failing those, she believed, they would stride into the chilly western ocean with never a halt or waver, as did the lemming hordes in their climacteric. But neither had Groniger voiced any objection to her spying on ahead – nor even concern for her safety. Where *was* the man's one-time clear-headedness and prudence?

Afreyt was not unversed in island woodcraft and she now spotted Skor peering toward Cold Harbor from the grove of dwarf cedars whence Fafhrd had launched yestermorning's brief arrow-fusillade. She called Skor's name, and he whipped around nocking an arrow to his bow, then came up swiftly when he saw her familiar blues.

'Lady Afreyt, what do you here? You look weary,' he greeted her succinctly. He looked weary himself and hollow-eyed, his cheeks and forehead smudged with soot above his straggly russet beard, perhaps against the glare of glacial ice.

She quickly told him about the Rimeland reinforcements approaching behind her.

His weariness seemed to lift from him as she spoke. 'That's brave news,' he said when she had done. 'We joined our lines (I'm now making the rounds of them) with those of the Cold Harbor defenders before sunset yesterday and have the Mingol fore-raiders penned on the beach – and all by bluff! The mere sight of the forces you describe, strategically deployed, will cause 'em to take ship and sail away, I think – and we not lift a finger.'

'Your pardon, lieutenant,' she rejoined, her own weariness lifting at his optimism, 'but I have heard you and your fellows named berserkers – and have always thought it was the way of such to charge the enemy at the first chance, charge wolf-howling and bounding, mother-naked?'

'To tell the truth, that was once my own understanding of it,' he replied, thoughtfully rubbing his broken nose with the back of his hand, 'but the captain's changed my mind for me. He's a great one for sleights and deceits, the captain is! Makes the foe imagine things, sets their own minds to work against 'em, never fights when there's an easier way – and some of his wisdom has rubbed off on us.'

'Why are you wearing Fafhrd's sword?' she asked, seeing it suddenly.

'Oh, he went off yestermorning to Hellglow after the girl, leaving me in command, and he's not yet returned,' Skor answered readily, though a crease of concern appeared between his brows, and he went on briefly to tell Afreyt about Mara's strange abduction.

'I wonder at him leaving you all so long to shift without him, merely for that,' Afreyt commented, frowning.

'Truth to tell, I wondered at it myself, yestermorning,' Skor admitted. 'But as events came on us, I asked myself what the captain would do in each case, and did that, and it's worked out – so far.' He hooked a middle-finger over a fore-one.

There came a faint tramping and the whispers of a hoarse chant and turning they saw the front of the Rime column coming downhill.

'Well, they look fearsome enough,' Skor said, after a moment. 'Strange, too,' he added, as the litter and gallows hove into view. The girls in their red cloaks were walking beside the former.

'Yes, they are that,' Afreyt said.

'How are they armed?' he asked her. 'I mean, besides the pikes and spears and quarterstaves and such?'

She told him those were their only weapons, as far as she knew.

'They'd not stand up to Mingols, then, not if they had to cover any distance to attack,' he judged. 'Still, if we showed 'em under the right conditions, and put a few bowmen amongst 'em . . .'

'The problem, I think, will be to keep them from charging,' Afreyt told him. 'Or, at any rate, to get them to stop marching.'

'Oh, so it's that way,' he said, raising an eyebrow.

'Cousin Afreyt! Cousin Afreyt!' May and Gale were crying shrilly while they waved at her. But then the girls were pointing overhead and calling, 'Look! Look!' and next they were running downhill alongside the column, still waving and calling and pointing at the sky.

Afreyt and Skor looked up and saw, at least a hundred yards above them, the figures of a man and a small girl (Mara by her red cloak) stretched out flat on their faces and clinging to each other and to something invisible that was swiftly swooping toward Cold Harbor. They came around in a great curve, getting lower all the time, and headed straight for Skor and Afreyt. She saw it was Fafhrd and Mara, all right, and she realized that she and Cif must have looked just so when they were being rescued from Khahkht's blizzard by the invisible mountain princesses. She clutched Skor, saying rapidly and somewhat breathlessly, 'They're all right. They're hanging onto a fish-of-the-air, which is like a thick flying carpet that's alive, but invisible. It's guided by an invisible woman.'

'It would be,' he retorted obscurely. Then they were buffeted by a great gust of air as Fafhrd and Mara sped past close overhead and still flat out – both of them grinning excitedly, Afreyt was able to note as she cringed down, at least Fafhrd's lips were drawn back from his teeth. They came to rest midway between her and Groniger at the head of the column, which had slowed to gawk, about a foot above the heather, which was pressed down in a large oval patch, as if Fafhrd and Mara were lying prone on an invisible mattress wide and thick enough for a king's bed.

Then the air travelers had scrambled to their feet and jumped down after an unsteady step or two. Skor and Afreyt were closing in on them from one side and May and Gale from the other, while the Rimelanders stared openmouthed. Mara was shrieking to the other girls, 'I was abducted by a very nasty demon, but Fafhrd rescued me! He chopped off its hand!' And Fafhrd had thrown his arms around Afreyt (she realized she'd invited it) and he was saying, 'Afreyt, thank Kos you're here. What's that you've got around your neck?' Next, without letting Afreyt go, to Skor, 'How are the men? What's your position?' All the while the staring Rimelanders marched on slowly and almost painfully, like sleepers peering at another wonder out of a nightmare which has entrapped them.

And then all others grew suddenly silent and Fafhrd's arms dropped away from Afreyt as a voice that she had last heard in a cave on Darkfire called out like an articulate silver trumpet, 'Farewell, girl. Farewell, barbarian. Next time, think of the courtesies due between orders and of your limitations. My debt's discharged, while yours has but begun.'

And with that a wind blew out from where Fafhrd and Mara had landed (from *under* the invisible mattress, one must think), bending the heather and blowing the girls' red coats out straight from them (Afreyt felt it and got a whiff of animal stench neither fish nor fowl nor four-legged) and then it was as if something large and living were taking off into the air and swiftly away, while a silvery laughter receded.

Fafhrd threw up his hand in farewell, then brought it down in a sweeping gesture that seemed to mean, 'Let's say goodbye to all that!' His expression, which had grown bleakly troubled during Hirriwi's speaking, became grimly determined as he saw the Rime column marching slowly into them. 'Master Groniger!' he said sharply. 'Captain Fafhrd?' that one replied thickly, as one half-rousing from a dream. 'Halt your men!' Fafhrd commanded, and then turned to Skor, who made report, telling his leader in somewhat more detail matter told earlier to Afreyt, while the column slowly ground to a halt, piling up around Groniger in a disorderly array.

Meanwhile Afreyt had knelt beside Mara, assured herself that the girl wasn't outwardly injured, and was listening bemused as Mara proudly but deprecatingly told the other girls about her abduction and rescue. 'He made a scarecrow out of my cloak and the skull of the last little girl he'd eaten alive, and he kept touching me, just like Odin does, but Fafhrd cut off his hand and Princess Hirriwi got my cloak back this morning. It was neat riding through the sky. I didn't get dizzy once.'

Gale said, 'Odin and I made up a marching song. It's about killing Mingols. Everyone's chanting it.' May said, 'I made nooses with flowers in them. They're a mark of honor from Odin. We're all wearing them. I made one for you and a big one for Fafhrd. Say, I've got to give Fafhrd his noose. It's time he was wearing it, with a big battle coming.'

Fafhrd listened patiently, for he'd wanted to know what that ugly thing around Afreyt's neck was. But when Mara had asked him to bend down his head, and he looked up spying the curtained litter, and recognized the uprooted gallows beyond it, he felt a shivery revulsion and said angrily, 'No, I won't wear it. I won't mount his eight-legged horse. Get those things off your necks, all of you!'

But then he saw the hurt, distrustful look in the girls' eyes as Mara protested, 'But it's to make you strong in battle. It's an honor from Odin.' And then the look of concern in Afreyt's eyes as she gestured toward the litter, its curtains fluttering in the wind (he sensed the grim holiness that seemed to emanate from it), and the look of expectation in the eyes of Groniger and the other Rimers, made him change his mind. He said, making his voice eager, 'I'll tell you what I'll do, I'll wear it around my wrist, to strengthen it,' and he thrust his left hand through the noose and after a moment May tightened it.

'My left arm,' he explained, lying somewhat, 'has always been markedly weaker than my right in battle. This noose will help strengthen it. I'll take yours too,' he said to Afreyt with a meaningful look.

She loosened it from around her neck with feelings of relief which partly changed to apprehension as she saw it tightened around Fafhrd's wrist beside the first noose.

'And yours, and yours, and yours,' he said to the three girls. 'That way I'll be wearing a noose for each of you. Come on, you wouldn't want my left arm weak in battle, would you?'

'There!' he said when it was done, gripping the five pendant cords in his left hand and whirling them. 'We'll whip the Mingols off Rime Isle, we will!'

The girls, who had seemed a little unhappy about losing their nooses, laughed delighted, and the Rimers raised an unexpected cheer.

Then they marched on, Skor scouting ahead after remembering to give Fafhrd back his sword, and Fafhrd trying to put some order into the Rimers and keep them quiet — although the wind helpfully blew the drum-noise of their chant from the beach. The girls and Afreyt dropped back with the litter, though not as far as Fafhrd wished. The company picked up a couple of Fafhrd's men, who reported the Mingols massing on the beach around their ships. And then they mounted a slight rise where the lines extended south from the fortress-hump of Cold Harbor, Fafhrd and his men holding back the now overeager Rimers. A mounting cry of woe came from the beach beyond and they all beheld a wonderfully satisfying sight: the three Sea Mingol galleys launching into the wind, forward oars out and working frantically while small figures gave a last heave to the sterns and scrambled aboard.

Then came an arresting cry from Cold Harbor and they began to see out in the watery west a host of sails coming up over the horizon: the Widder-Mingol fleet. And with the sight of it they became aware also of a faint distant rumbling, as of the hoofbeat of innumerable war-horses charging across the steppes. But the Rimelanders recognized it as the voice of Hellfire, threatening eruption where it smoked blackly to the north. While to the south churned high-domed clouds, betokening a change of wind and weather.

The Gray Mouser fully realized that he was in one of the tightest spots he'd ever been in during the course of a danger-dappled career – with this difference, that this time the spot was shared by three hundred friendly folk (even dear, thinking of Cif beside him), along with any number of enemies (the Sun-Sea-Mingol fleet, that was, in close pursuit). He'd raised *them* (the Mingols) with the greatest of ease and was now luring them so successfully to their destruction that *Flotsam* was last, not first, of the Rime Island fleet, which was spread out disorderly before him, *Sea Hawk* nearest, and within arrow range of the pursuing Mingols, who came in endless foaming shrieking whinnying numbers, their galleys sailing faster with the wind than he. Moments ago one of the horse-ships had driven herself under with excess of sail, and foundered, and not a sister ship had paused to give her aid. Dead ahead some four leagues distant was the Rimic coast with the two crags and inviting bay (and blackly smoking Darkfire beyond) that marked the position of the Great Maelstrom. North, the clouds churned, promising change of weather. The problem, as always, was how to get the Mingols into the Maelstrom, while avoiding it himself (and his friends with him), but he had never *appreciated* the problem quite so well as now. The hoped-for solution was that the whirlpool would turn on just *after* the Rimers and *Sea Hawk* and he had sailed across it, and so catch at least the van of the close-crowding Mingol fleet. And the way they were all bunched now, that required perfect, indeed God-like timing, but he'd worked his hardest at it and after all the gods were supposed to be on his side, weren't they? – at least two of them.

The horse-galleys of the Mingols were so close that Mikkidu and his thieves had their slings ready, loaded with leaden ball, though under orders not to cast unless the Mingols started arrow fire. Across the waves a stallion screamed from its cage.

Thought of the Maelstrom made the Mouser look in his pouch for the golden queller. He found it, all right, but somehow the charred stub of the Loki-torch had got wedged inside it. It was really no more than a black cinder. No wonder Rill had burned herself so badly, he thought, glancing at her bandaged hand – when Cif had stayed on deck, the harlots, and Mother Grum, had insisted on the same privilege and it seemed to cheer the men.

The Mouser started to unwedge the black god-brand, but then the odd thought occurred to him that Loki, being a god (and in some sense this cinder was Loki), deserved a golden house, or carapace, so on a whim he wrapped the length of stout cord attached to it tightly round and round the weighty golden cube and knotted it, so that the two objects – queller and god-brand – were inextricably conjoined.

Cif nudged him. Her gold-flecked green eyes were dancing, as if to say, 'Isn't this exciting!'

He nodded a somewhat temperate agreement. Oh, it was exciting, all right, but it was also damnably uncertain – everything had to work out just so – why, he could still only guess at the directions god Loki had given them in the speech he had forgotten and none else had heard . . .

He looked around the deck, surveying faces. It was strange, but everyone's eyes seemed to flash with the same eager juvend excitement as was in Cif's . . . it was even in Gavs'. Trenchi's, and Gib's (the Mingols) . . . even in Mother Grum's, bright as black beads . . .

In all eyes, that is, except the wrinkle-netted ones of old Ourph helping Gavs with the tiller. They seemed to express a sad and patient resignation, as though contemplating tranquilly from some distance a great and universal woe. On an impulse the Mouser took him from his task and drew him to the lee rail.

'Old man,' he said, 'you were at the council hall the night before last when I spoke to them all and they cheered me. I take it that, like the rest, you heard not one word of what I said, or at best only a few – the directives for Groniger's party and our sailing today?'

For the space of perhaps two breaths the old Mingol stared at him curiously, then he slowly shook his bald dome, saying, 'No, captain, I heard every last word you spoke (my eyes begin to fail me a little, but my ears not) and they greatly saddened me (your words) for they expressed the same philosophy as seizes upon my steppe-folk at their climacterics (and often otherwhen), the malign philosophy that caused me to part company with them in early years and make my life among the heathen.'

'What do you mean?' the Mouser demanded. 'A favor – be brief as possible.'

'Why, you spoke – most winningly indeed (even I was tempted) – of the glories of death and of what a grand thing it was to go down joyfully to destruction carrying your enemies with you (and as many as possible of your friends also), how this was the law of life and its crowning beauty and grandeur, its supreme satisfaction. And as you told them all that they soon must die and how, they all cheered you as heartily as would have my own Mingols in their climacteric and with the selfsame gleam in their eyes. I well know that gleam. And, as I say, it greatly saddened me (to find you so fervent a death-lover) but since you are my captain, I accepted it.'

The Mouser turned his head and looked straight into the astonished eyes of Cif, who had followed close behind him and heard every word old Ourph had spoken, and looking into each other's eyes they saw the same identical understanding.

At that very instant the Mouser felt *Flotsam* beneath his feet slammed to a stop, spun sideways to her course, and sent off circling at prodigious speed just as had happened to *Sprite* day before yesterday, but with a greater force proportionate to her larger size. The heaven reeled, the sea went black. He and Cif were brought up against the taffrail along with a clutter of thieves, whores, witches (well, one witch), and Mingol sailors. He bid Cif cling to it for dearest life, then found his footing on the tilted deck, and raced past the rattling whipping mainsail (and past young Mikkidu embracing the mainmast with eyes tight shut in ultimate terror or perhaps in rapture) to where his own vision was unimpeded.

Flotsam, Sea Hawk, and the whole Rime fleet were circling at dizzying velocity more than halfway down the sides of a whirlpool at least two leagues wide, whose wide-spinning upper reaches held what looked like the entire Mingol fleet, the galleys near the edge tiny as toys against the churning sky, while at the maelstrom's still-distant center the fanged rocks protruding through the white welter there were like a field of death.

Next below *Flotsam* in the vast wheel of doom spun Dwone's fishing smack, so close he could see faces. The Rimers clutching their weird weapons and each other looked monstrously happy, like drunken and lopsided giants bound for a ball. Of course, he told himself, these were the monsters whose quickening Loki had envisioned, these were the trolls or whatever. And that reminded him of what, by Ourph's irrefutable testimony, Loki intended for them all and peradventure for Fafhrd and Afreyt also, and all the universe of seas and stars.

He snatched the golden queller from his pouch and seeing the black cinder at its heart thought, 'Good! – rid of two evils at one stroke.' Aye, but he must pitch it to the whirlpool's midst, and how to get it there, so far away? There was some simple solution, he was sure, it was on the tip of his unseen thoughts, but there were really so many distractions at the moment ...

Cif nudged him in the waist – one more distraction. As he might have expected, she had followed him close against his strictest bidding and now with a wicked grin was pointing at ... of course, his sling!

He centered the precious missile in the strap and motioning Cif to the mast to give him room, tried out his footing on the tilted deck, taking short dancing steps, and measuring out distance, speed, windage, and various imponderables with eyes and brain. And as he did those things, whirling the queller-brand about his head, dancing out as it were the prelude to what must be his life's longest and supremest cast, there danced up from his mind's darkest deep words that must have been brewing there for days, words that matched Loki's final four evil couplets in every particular, even the rhymes (almost), but that totally reversed their meaning. And as the words came bobbing to the surface of his awareness he spoke them out, softly he thought, though in a very clear voice – until he saw that Cif was listening to him with unmistakable delight at each turn of phrase, and Mikkidu had his shut eyes open and was hearing, and the monstrous Rimers on Dwone's smack had all their sobering faces turned his way. He somehow had the conviction that in the midst of that monstrous tumult of the elements his words were nevertheless being heard to the whirlpool's league-distant rim – aye, and beyond that, he knew not how far. And this is what he spoke: 'Mingols to their deaths must go? Oh, not so, not so, not so! Mingols, draw an easy breath. Leave to wanton after death. Let there be an end to strife – even Mingols relish life. Mingol madness cease to burn. Gods to proper worlds return.'

And with that he spun dancingly across the deck, as though he were hurling the discus, the queller-brand at the end of his sling a gold-glinting circlet above his head, and loosed. The queller-brand sped up gleaming toward the whirlpool's midst until it was too small for sight.

And then ... the vasty whirlpool was struck flat. Black water foamed white. Sea and sky churned as one. And through that hell of the winds' howling and the waves' crash there came a rumbling earth-shaking thunder and the red flash of huge distant flames as Darkfire erupted, compounding pandemonium, adding the strokes of earth and fire to those of water and air, completing the uproar and riot of the four elements. All ships were chips in chaos, glimpsed dimly if at all, to which men clung like ants. Squalls blew from every compass-point, it seemed, warring together. Foam covered decks, mounded to mast tops.

But before that had transpired quite in *Flotsam*'s case, the

Mouser and some others too, gripping rail or mast, eyes stinging with salt sea, had seen, mounting for a few brief moments to the sky, from the whirlpool's very midst as it was smitten flat, what looked like the end of a black rainbow (or a skinny and curving black waterspout impossibly tall, some said afterwards) that left a hole behind it in the dark clouds, through which *something* maddening and powerful had vanished forever from their minds, their beings, and from all Nehwon.

And then the Mouser and his crew and the women with them were all fighting to save themselves and *Flotsam* in the midst of an ocean that was all cross chop and in the teeth of a gale that had reversed direction completely and now blew from the west, carrying the thick black smoke from Darkfire out toward them. Around them other ships fought the same fight in a great roiling confusion covering several square leagues that gradually sorted itself out. The Rime fishing boats and smacks (somewhat larger) with their handier rigs (and *Flotsam* and *Sea Hawk* too) were able to tack southwest against the wind and set slow courses for Salthaven. The Mingol galleys with their square sails could only run before it (the heavy seas preventing the use of oars) away from the sobering chaos of the dreadful isle whose black smoke pursued them and their dreary drenched stallions. Some of the horse-ships may have sunk, for *Flotsam* fished two Mingols out of the waves, but these were unclear as to whether they had been swept overboard or their ships lost, and far too miserable to seem like foes. Ourph, smiling serenely, later brought them hot chowder, while the west wind cleared the sky. (Regarding the winds, at the moment of decision the west wind had spilled south, blowing out all along the east coast of Rime Isle, and the east wind had spilled north, driving away from the whole west coast of the island, while the belt of storm between had rotated clockwise somewhat, causing wild, veering whirlwinds in the Deathlands.)

At the same instant as the Mouser slung the queller-brand, Fafhrd was standing on the seaward turf-wall of Cold Harbor, confronting the Widder-Mingol fleet as it neared the beach and brandishing his sword. This was no mere barbarian gesture of defiance, but part of a carefully thought-out demonstration done in the hope of awing the Sea-Mingols, even though Fafhrd admitted (to himself only) that the hope was a forlorn one. Earlier, when the three Mingol advance-raiders had departed the beach, they had made no move to join with or await their fleet, although they surely must have sighted its sails, but had instead rowed steadily away south as long as eye followed. This had made Fafhrd wonder whether they had not taken some fright on the isle which they had not wanted to face again, even with the backing of their main force. In this connection he had particularly remembered the cries of woe and dread that had come from the Mingols as Groniger's Rime Islers had topped the rise and hove into their view. Afreyt had confided to him how during the long march overland those same countrymen of hers had come to seem monstrous to her and somehow bigger, and he had had to admit that they made the same strange impression on him. And if they seemed bigger (and monstrous) to him and her, how much bigger might they not appear to Mingols?

And so they had taken thought together, Fafhrd and Afreyt, and had made suggestions and given commands (supplemented by bullyings and blandishments as needed) and as a result Groniger's relief-force was posted at intervals of twenty paces in a long line that began far up on the glacier and continued along the ramparts of Cold Harbor and along the rise and stretched off for almost a league south of the settlement, each Isler brandishing his pike or other weapon. While betwixt and between them all along were stationed the defenders of Cold Harbor (their countrymen, though lacking their aura of monstrousness) and Fafhrd's berserks, to swell their sheer numbers and also to keep the Salthaven Islers at their posts, from which they still had a dreamy, automatonlike tendency to go marching off. Midmost on the broad ramparts of Cold Harbor, widely flanked by Groniger and another pike-waver, rested Odin's litter with the gallows propped over it as in the Deathlands, while around it were stationed Fafhrd, Afreyt, and the three girls, the last waving their red cloaks on long rakes like flags. (Anything for effect, Fafhrd had said, and the girls were eager to play their part in the demonstration.) Afreyt had a borrowed spear while Fafhrd alternately shook his sword and the cords of the five nooses drawn around his left hand – shook them at the massed Mingol ships nearing the harbor. Groniger and the other Islers were shouting Gale's (or Odin's) doom-chant: 'Doom! Kill the Mingols! Doom! Die the heroes.'

And then (just as, on the other side of Rime Isle, the Mouser hurled his queller-brand, as has been said) the whirlwinds betokening the reversal of gales moved across them northward, whipping the red flags, and the heavens were darkened and there came the thunder of Hellfire erupting in sympathy with Darkfire. The sea was troubled and soon pocked to the north by the ejecta of Hellglow, great rocks that fell into the waves like the shouted 'Doom! Doom!' of the chant in a great cannonading. And the Widder-Mingol fleet was retreating out to sea under the urging of the wind that now blew off the shore – away, away from that dreadful burning coast that appeared to be guarded by a wall of giants taller than trees and by all the powers of the four elements. And Hellfire's smoke stretched out above them like a pall.

But before that had all transpired (in fact, at the same instant as, a hundred leagues east, a black rainbow or waterspout shot up to the sky from the whirlpool's center) Odin's litter began to rock and toss on the ramparts, and the heavy gallows to twitch and strain upward like a straw or like a compass needle responding to an unknown upward magnetism. Afreyt screamed as she saw Fafhrd's left hand turn black before her eyes. And Fafhrd bellowed with sudden agony as he felt the nooses May had braided (and decorated with flowers) tighten relentlessly about his wrist as so many steel wires, contracting deeper and deeper between arm bones and wrist bones, cutting skin and flesh, parting gristle and tendons and all tenderer stuff, while that hand was restlessly dragged upward. And then the curtains of the litter all shot up vertically and the gallows stood up on its beam end and vibrated. Suddenly something black and gleaming shot up to the sky, holing the clouds, and Fafhrd's black severed hand and all the nooses went with it.

Then the curtains fell back and the gallows crashed from the wall and Fafhrd stared stupidly at the blood pouring from the stump that ended his left arm. Mastering her horror, Afreyt clamped her fingers on the spouting arteries and bid May, who was nearest at hand, take knife and slash up the skirt of her white smock for bandages. The girl acted quickly, and with these folded in wads and also used as ties, Afreyt bound up Fafhrd's great wound in its own blood and staunched the flow of that while he watched blank-faced. When it was done, he muttered, ' "A head for a head and a hand for a hand," she said,' and Afreyt retorted sharply, 'Better a hand than a head — or five.'

In Its cramping sphere Khahkht of the Black Ice smote the sharply curving walls in Its fury and tried to scratch Rime Isle off the map. It ground together the pieces representing Fafhrd and the Mouser and the rest between Its opposed horny black palms and scrabbled frantically for the pieces standing for the two intrusive gods – but those two pieces were gone. While in far Stardock, maimed Prince Faroomfar slept more easily, knowing himself avenged.

A full two months after the events before-narrated, Afreyt had a modest fish-dinner in her low-eaved, violet-tinted house on the north edge of Salthaven, to which were invited Groniger, Skor, Pshawri, Rill, old Ourph, and of course Cif, the Gray Mouser, and Fafhrd – the largest number her table would accommodate without undue crowding. The occasion was the Mouser's sailing on the morrow in *Sea Hawk* with Skor, the Mingols, Mikkidu, and three others of his original crew on a trading venture to No-Ombrulsk with goods selected (purchased and otherwise accumulated) chiefly by Cif and himself. He and Fafhrd were solely in need of money to pay for dockage on their vessels, crew-wages, and many another expenses, while the two ladies were no better off, owing yet-to-be-finally-determined sums to the council – of which, however, they were still members, as yet. Fafhrd had to travel no distance at all to get to the feast, for he was guesting with Afreyt while he convalesced from his maiming – just as the Mouser was staying at Cif's place on no particular excuse at all. There had been raised eyebrows at these arrangements from the rather straight-laced Islers, which the four principals had handled by firmly overlooking them.

During the course of the dinner, which consisted of oyster chowder, salmon baked with Island leeks and herbs, corn cakes made of costly Lankhmar grain, and light wine of Ilthmar, conversation had ranged around the recent volcanic eruptions and attendant and merely coincidental events, and their consequences, particularly the general shortage of money. Salthaven had suffered some damage from the earthquake and more from the resultant fire. The council hall had survived but the Salt Herring tavern had been burned to the ground with its Flame Den. ('Loki was a conspicuously destructive god,' the Mouser observed, 'especially where his métier, fire, was involved.' 'It was an unsavory haunt,' Groniger opined.) In Cold Harbor, three turf roofs had collapsed, unoccupied of course because everyone had been taking part in the defensive demonstration at the time. The Salthaven Islers had begun their homeward journey next day, the litter being used to carry Fafhrd. 'So some mortal got some use of it besides the girls,' Afreyt remarked. 'It was a haunted-seeming conveyance,' Fafhrd allowed, 'but I was feverish.'

But it was the short store of cash, and the contrivances adopted to increase that, which they chiefly talked about. Skor had found work for himself and the other berserks for a while helping the Islers harvest drift-timber from the Beach of Bleached Bones, but there had not been the anticipated glut of Mingol wrecks. Fafhrd talked of manning *Flotsam* with some of his men and bringing back from Ool Plerns a cargo of natural wood. ('When you're entirely recovered, yes,' Afreyt said.) The Mouser's men had gone to work as fishermen bossed by Pshawri, and had been able to feed both crews and sometimes have a small surplus left to sell. Strangely, or perhaps not so, the monster catches made during the great run had all spoiled, despite their salting-down, and gone stinking bad, worse than dead jellyfish, and had had to be burned. (Cif said, 'I told you Khahkht magicked that run – and so they were phantom fish in some sense, tainted by his touch, no matter how solid-seeming.') She and Afreyt had sold *Sprite* to Rill and Hilsa for a tidy sum; the two professionals' adventure on *Flotsam*, amazingly, had given them a taste for the sea-life and they were now making a living as fisherwomen, though not above turning a trick at their old trade in off hours. Hilsa was out night-fishing this very evening with Mother Grum. Even the foe had fallen on hard times. Two of the three fore-raiding Sea-Mingol galleys that had rowed off south had put into Salthaven three weeks later in great distress, having been battered about by storms and then becalmed, after having fled off ill-provisioned. The crew of one had been reduced to eating their sacred bow-stallion, while that of the other had so far lost their fanatic pride along with their madness that they had sold theirs to 'Mayor' Bomar, who wanted to be the first Rime Isle man (or 'foreigner') to own a horse, but succeeded only in breaking his neck on his first attempt to ride it. (Pshawri commented, 'He was – *absit omen* – a somewhat overweening man. He tried to take away from me command of *Sea Hawk*.')

Groniger claimed that Rime Isle, meaning the council chiefly, was as badly off as anyone. The bluff harbor master, seemingly more hard-headed and skeptical than ever for his one experience of enchantment and the supernatural, made a point of taking a very hard line with Afreyt and Cif and a very dim view of the latter's irregular disbursements from the Rime treasury in the isle's defense. (Actually he was their best friend on the council, but he had his crustiness to maintain.) 'And then there's the Gold Cube of Square Dealing,' he reminded her accusingly, 'gone forever!' She smiled. Afreyt served them hot gahveh, an innovation in Rimeland, for they'd decided to make an early evening of it what with tomorrow's sailing.

'I wouldn't be too sure of that,' Skor said. 'Working around the Beach of Bleached Bones you get the feeling that everything washes ashore there, eventually.'

'Or we could dive for it,' Pshawri proposed.

'What?—and get Loki-cinder back with it?' the Mouser asked, chuckling. He looked toward Groniger. 'Then you'd still be a cloudy-headed god's-man, you old atheist!'

'That's as may be,' the Isler retorted. 'Afreyt said I was a troll-giant for a space, too. But here I am.'

'I doubt you'd find it, dove you never so deep,' Fafhrd averred softly, his gaze on the leather stall covering his still bandaged stump. 'I think Loki-cinder vanished out of Nehwon-world entire, and many another curious thing with it – the queller (after it had done its work) that had become his home (Gods love gold) and Odin-ghost and some of his appurtenances.'

Rill, beside him, touched the stall with her burnt hand which had been almost as long as his stump in healing. It had created a certain sympathy between them.

'You'll wear a hook on it?' she asked.

He nodded. 'Or a socket for various tools, utensils, and instruments. There are possibilities.'

Old Ourph said, sipping his steaming gahveh, 'It was strange how closely the two gods were linked, so that when one departed, the other went.'

'When Cif and I first found them, we thought they were one,' Afreyt told him.

'We saved their lives,' Cif asserted. 'We were very good hosts, on the whole, to both of them.' She caught Rill's eye, who smiled.

'When you save a suicide, you take upon yourself responsibilities,' Afreyt said, her eyes drifting toward Fafhrd's stump. 'If on his next attempt, he takes others with him, it's your doing.'

'You're gloomy tonight, Lady Afreyt,' the Mouser suggested, 'and reason too curiously. When you set out in that mood there's no end to the places you can go, eh, Fafhrd? We set out to be captains, and seem in process of becoming merchants. What next? Bankers? – or pirates?'

'As much as you like of either,' Cif told him meaningly, 'as long as you remember the council holds Pshawri and your men here, hostage for you.'

'As mine will be for me, when I seek that timber,' Fafhrd said. 'The pines at Ool Plerns are very green and tall.'

THE WORLD'S GREATEST SCIENCE FICTION
AUTHORS NOW AVAILABLE IN PANTHER BOOKS

E E 'Doc' Smith

'Classic Lensman Series'

Masters of the Vortex	75p	☐
Children of the Lens	65p	☐
Second Stage Lensman	75p	☐
Grey Lensman	85p	☐
Galactic Patrol	75p	☐
First Lensman	85p	☐
Triplanetary	65p	☐
'Lensman' Gift Set	£4.25	☐

'Skylark Series'

The Skylark of Space	75p	☐
Skylark Three	75p	☐
The Skylark of Valeron	75p	☐
Skylark Duquesne	75p	☐
'Skylark' Gift Set	£2.40	☐

'Family D'Alembert Series' (*with Stephen Goldin*)

The Imperial Stars	60p	☐
Stranglers' Moon	50p	☐

All these books are available at your local bookshop or newsagent, or can be ordered direct from the publisher. Just tick the titles you want and fill in the form below.

Name...

Address..

....

Write to Mayflower Cash Sales, PO Box 11, Falmouth, Cornwall TR10 9EN.
Please enclose remittance to the value of the cover price plus:
UK: 22p for the first book plus 10p per copy for each additional book ordered to a maximum charge of 82p.
BFPO and EIRE: 22p for the first book plus 10p per copy for the next 6 books, thereafter 3p per book.
OVERSEAS: 30p for the first book and 10p for each additional book.

Granada Publishing reserve the right to show new retail prices on covers, which may differ from those previously advertised in the text or elsewhere.